NUROC,
THE GIANT KILLER

Nuroc rushed across the open courtyard to the base of the tower. He was about to enter the unguarded doorway when a giant, larger than any he had seen before, strode out to meet him, brandishing a length of chain, with a spike-covered ball of iron at its end.

Nuroc ducked as the giant lashed out with the chain. The lethal ball *whooshed* within inches of Nuroc's skull before biting into the wooden pole supporting the hand-railing. The pole splintered under the impact.

As the giant lowered his aim, Nuroc jumped upwards, clearing the whistling swath and grabbing onto the sloped roof that extended out over the doorway. He kicked forward with all his might, striking the giant in the chest with a force that sent him reeling off balance. Before the giant could recover, Nuroc let go of the roof and landed with a crouch before springing forward. The giant's eyes widened as he saw the condor-dagger pierce his chest. Howling in agony, he swiped at Nuroc with his free hand and sent the youth flying into the frame of the doorway, knocking him senseless.

The wound did not seem to hinder the giant aside from the pain, until he reached down and pulled the dagger free. The life went out of his eyes in an instant.

Nuroc stirred and shook his head, panting for breath as he pushed the giant clear of the ceremonial dagger. He rose to his feet and cautiously entered the tower, eyes searching the darkened shadows for sign of any others who might foil his attempt to save his lover. . . .

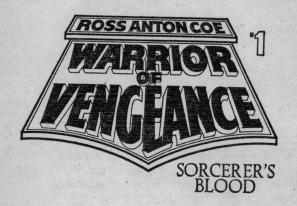

ROSS ANTON COE

WARRIOR OF VENGEANCE

#1

SORCERER'S BLOOD

PINNACLE BOOKS   NEW YORK

WARRIOR OF VENGEANCE #1:
SORCERER'S BLOOD

Copyright © 1982 by Ron Renauld

An original Pinnacle Books edition, published for the first time anywhere.

First printing, April 1982

ISBN: 0-523-41709-8

Cover illustration by Romas

Printed in the United States of America

PINNACLE BOOKS, INC.
1430 Broadway
New York, New York 10018

For mes Goobs.

L.M.B.
with thanks to Robert E. Howard
and Jack Bis

SORCERER'S
BLOOD

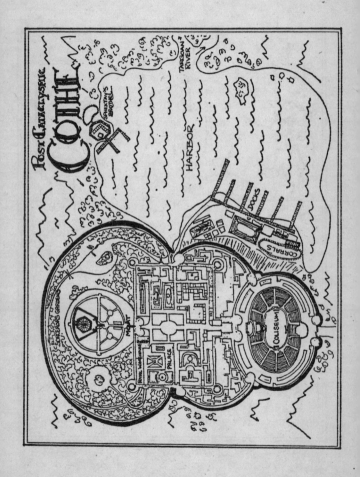

Prologue

It was in the distant, shrouded past, a time long lost save for the frail shred of legends handed down through the ages, that a map of the continent men now call Dorban was first outlined on scrolls of yellowed parchment with quills dipped in the blood of rebellious slaves.

As the legend is told, it was Noj-Syb, first of the sorcerer-kings to claim the vast expanse of the continent as his sole domain, who dispatched surveyors and cartographers by both land and sea to record the shape of his kingdom. It was a major undertaking, involving no less than twenty separate expeditions, each comprised of either a full fleet or battalion under command of a different chartist. Several of these chosen souls, swooned by the power entrusted them, broke from the king and set up their own rule in reaches far from the capital of Cothe. Wars broke out as Noj-Syb sent forces to snuff out these small pockets of insurrection and execute their perpetrators. Other cartographers succumbed to deaths brought on by the whims of pestilence and foul weather. Still, after many years, nine of the twenty surveyors at last returned to Cothe and set about the arduous task of comparing their thousands of crude sketches and measurements depicting the lay of the land and the contour of the coastline. The expertise of the men was evident, for, despite the expected discrepancies over finer details, they all arrived at completed drawings, which depicted the continent as taking the shape of a condor's head, set in profile, with two

1

peninsulas to the southwest opened like beaks around the azure waters of the Targoan Sea.

The significance of this discovery was dramatic. Among the many deities worshiped throughout the land by both ruler and ruled, the most revered was Dorjbayn, the condor-god. In the sparkling heavens where the gods were said to dwell, the constellation Dorjbayn stood out from the others, alone and brilliant, its stars more vibrant than polished gems. Dorjbayn, with the night's twin moons as its eyes, was the source of power for the highest of chants spoken by Noj-Syb and the other sorcerers who would come to reside and reign in the towering obelisk that rose from the royal gardens of Cothe.

The land and the constellation shared the same form, and so it was decreed by Noj-Syb that his kingdom would also share the name of its celestial protector. Other kings would come to rule the land, bathe it in the blood of conflict, apportion large estates to greedy generals and wealthy merchants, give it a plethora of new languages. But throughout the creeping march of time, the land retained the name placed upon it by its first king. The spelling changed in time to suit the tongue of the day, but the meaning remained constant. So, too, did the worship of the condor-god, and the rule of the land by sorcerers who could summon forth powers from the heavens.

Then came the night when an underling to the sorcerer-king Talmon-Khash placed his greed for power above the cautions of his training.

Dorban would never be the same....

part one

BLACK MOON OVER DORBAN

One

Nuroc stole silently through the tall, rippling grass, grateful for the shifting of the slight evening breeze. It carried his scent away from his prey now, making his task less difficult. He didn't have much time. The twin moons were already beginning to merge, and the dim light they cast was fading by the moment.

He was twelve, slight of build but possessed with a wiry agility and supple strength. Son of the king's servants, Nuroc was the youngest of the shepherds charged with tending the royal sheep and guarding them against the intrusion of poachers and predators. He was now in pursuit of the latter, a solitary kildwolf he had spotted slinking into the meadows moments before. There had to be significance in the beast's timely arrival, Nuroc felt. It was an omen. Whether for good or evil, he could not be sure, but he placed his hopes in the former.

Lowering himself to his stomach, Nuroc crawled slowly across a carpet of bending grasses to the top of a knoll, where he smiled with satisfaction. Down the shallow slope, less than ten feet away, the kildwolf stood shoulder deep in the high grass. It was a fully matured wolf, matching Nuroc in weight and sporting a gray fur with darkened splotches. The tip of its long tongue hung out over the lower row of sharp, yellowing teeth as the wolf stared at the royal flock. Several hundred sheep, bred carefully over a dozen generations to provide the finest wool and mutton for kings and nobility, grazed on the flattened meadows that stretched for miles inland before bowing to the. foothills of the lower Kanghats. The mountains' jagged peaks rose like hulking shadows on the dark horizon. It was a powerful yet tranquil sight, inspiring verse from the other shepherds, who plucked lyres as they sang at their posts elsewhere on the emerald sward. Nuroc could hear their pleasant harmonies carried on the wind, but he could not see them save for their distant campfires and the silhouettes of their tethered mounts. Being the youngest of the lot, Nuroc was stationed at the most remote stretch of the royal pasture, near the cliffs that emptied into the Targoan Sea. His watch over the herd was always the first to begin and the last to end, what with the long jaunt he had to make to and from the main camp. He did not mind the arrangement, however, because his removed station left him with time to himself, time to scheme grand futures and dream of the day when he would forsake the staff of the shepherd and take up the weapons of a warrior. When he came of age, he would join the royal guard and rise through the ranks until he was a leader of men, not the brunt of smirking jokes whispered by the other shepherds.

Shifting positions where he lay, Nuroc took from the corded belt about his waist a leather sling. In a small pouch also tied to the belt, he carried several small stones, rounded by weather and well suited for the sling. As he was reaching into the pouch, the stones gently clattered against one another. The sound was barely audible, and yet the kildwolf suddenly perked its ears and whirled about to face Nuroc.

The boy froze, pressing himself lower in the grass, but he could see the old wolf's lambent eyes trained on his own. A tense growl sounded from deep inside the beast's throat, and behind the pointing ears there rose stiff hairs along the wolf's shoulders. Lethal fangs were bared as the growl grew louder.

Moving as little as he could, Nuroc gently fit one of the stones into his sling and drew back his arm. When the kildwolf leaned back on its haunches and tensed for attack, Nuroc let the stone fly. It cut through the air and struck the wolf firmly in the chest. At so close

6

a range, the missile did not have the speed behind it to prove fatal, but Nuroc's aim was sufficient to knock the beast off-balance before it could spring forward. In the few seconds gained by this ploy, Nuroc sprang to his feet and pulled forth his hunting knife from a leather sheath. When the enraged wolf snarled and lunged at him, the young shepherd dropped to his knees and held the weapon out with both hands. The predator's leap brought it flying onto the pointed blade, and as both man and beast tumbled to the ground, Nuroc could feel the dampness of the wolf's blood.

The wolf was far from slain, however. It writhed madly on top of Nuroc, who had let go of the dagger to secure a hold on the beast's neck to keep the slavering jaws from biting into him. Nuroc could feel the hot, fetid breath of his attacker, and he groaned with pain as flailing paws left bleeding cuts on his exposed arms and legs. Still he held on, pulling the beast closer and pushing in on the dagger with his chest. Nuroc felt fear pushing the blood through his system at a furious pace, giving him needed strength against the untamed frenzy of the kildwolf. The snapping jaws clicked in the air before his face, then caught on the shoulder of his tunic and ripped out a strip of cloth, grazing his flesh.

"Die!" Nuroc gasped defiantly at the kildwolf, his voice trembling. But in the eyes of the beast there was only fierce life and loathing. Foam played at the corners of its mouth and bubbled between its teeth as it continued to strain against the boy's grip. Nuroc began to feel himself weakening. This was nothing like the jestful wrestling matches he engaged in with his father, where he could cry out when he had had enough and wished to rest. Now he fought for his life.

In desperation, Nuroc summoned forth the last of his reserved strength and rolled to one side, shifting his weight so that he moved on top of the wolf. The animal let out a howl of anguish, and blood spilled out through the flecks of foam dabbling its jaw. For a few seconds, it jerked about with a violence that wrested it clear of Nuroc's grip, then went suddenly still. The

7

knife had finally pushed through to the heart and brought on a blood-drenched death.

Nuroc crawled away from the limp form, wary that a last flicker of life might still linger in the wolf. He was wet with sweat and blood from the beast and his own wounds. He could see the clawmarks and trailing blood, but there was no pain yet. He felt only a strange sense of enervation, as if in the wake of his spent energies he had been drained of all strength. He watched the kildwolf until he was satified that it would not attack him, then he slumped down into the lush grass atop the knoll. He stared out at the meadows, where the flock was bleating frantically as it fled from the scene of the skirmish. Figures darted about the distant campfires, and Nuroc smiled through his consuming fatigue, wondering what the other shepherds would have to say if they saw him now. No more would they taunt him, calling him Dreamchild and the lamb among lambs. It was with that smile of pride and triumph that Nuroc collapsed with exhaustion and passed out in the grass.

He had been unconscious for only a few minutes when he came to, but the speed with which his sleeping thoughts had traveled was so swift that it seemed as if hours had passed. In a panic, he jolted upright, feeling at once the pain of countless wounds that had come alive after the initial shock of his battle with the kildwolf.

As he began to inspect the wounds, Nuroc became suddenly aware of the dull drumming sound that had awakened him. He thought he had been dreaming the sound, but now realized that it was real enough. Confused, he stared over the top of the grassline at the pasture, but could see no sign of abnormal activity. The scattered sheep were silent and grazing, and the other shepherds were back before their blazing fires at the other posts.

The sound drew nearer, and Nuroc began to feel the

slightest vibration of the ground beneath his knees. He bent over and pressed an ear to the soil. The sound came even clearer to him, and there could be no mistaking the steady clop of hooves. But from where? Nuroc once again scanned the land around him and saw only the bending grasses.

He felt his head, wondering if he might have received some unfelt blow that had wreaked havoc with his senses. There were streaks of blood, most of it already caking to his flesh and hair, but it was from the wolf and not any wound he had suffered.

As he continued to puzzle over the strangeness of the sourceless sound, there came from the base of the knoll a sudden grating. Startled, Nuroc forgot about his wounds and quickly leaned over, pulling his knife free from the carcass of the slain kildwolf. He tightened his grip on the handle as he slowly crept forward to where he could see down the hill.

A large slab of rock had slipped away from its place amidst a cluster of larger boulders. Nuroc had played about those rocks countless times, never suspecting that one of them was so precariously situated that it would fall free. Intrigued, he started down the slope toward the formation, then stopped and gazed in wonder.

Where the flat rock had once lain there was now exposed the wide mouth of a cave, black with shadow. Nuroc quickly realized that it was from this dark orifice that he now heard the sound of approaching hooves. Instinctively, he crouched down behind the cover of the nearest brush.

Seconds later, there burst forth from the opening a robed horseman, driving his steed with fierce slaps to the quadruped's hindquarters. Another rider followed behind, then still another. Over the next few seconds, more than twenty horses charged from the heart of the knoll and cut a narrow swath through the green sward as their riders reined them in tight formation. Nuroc watched on, uncomprehending. The robes of the horsemen, snapping in the wind, identified them as sorcerers,

9

and Nuroc further recognized a few of them as acolytes to Talmon-Khash from the sorcerer's temples in Cothe, several miles to the north. How was it they sprang forth from the earth this far away? he wondered. Other questions rose and were left unanswered as the youth watched the sorcerers ride west toward the nearest stretch of foothills. Soon they were gone from sight.

Nuroc stayed near the brush until the sound of hoofbeats faded to silence, then stepped forward and cautiously made his way to the mouth of the cave. Bending over, he saw that a runner of carved stone stretched across the opening, grooved in the center with the same width as the slab of stone that had fallen away.

"A secret doorway," he murmured with fascination. Pausing outside the opening, he strained his eyes to see what lay within the reaches of the opening. But the darkness was all-consuming, and he could not see beyond the stone runner.

While he deliberated entering the cave and groping his way in darkness, he heard the distant peal of a single trumpet.

"Dorban!" Nuroc said with a start. "The black moons!"

In the frenzy of activity he had completely forgotten. Fast as his heart was already beating, it pulsed even swifter as Nuroc stepped away from the opening and looked up to the sky. The twin moons were on the verge of eclipse, mere slivers of curved light drawing close together. Soon they would line up and appear as one, then vanish from sight for several lingering moments before their march across the night skies would make them shine anew with the first glow of waxing.

Nuroc had only minutes in which to act. He ran to the top of the knoll and gasped for breath as he looked for the nearest sheep. None were close to him. There was no time for him to race across the meadow in hopes of reaching them. Fear and hopelessness began

10

to assail him when he turned and suddenly smiled at the sight of the slain kildwolf.

"Of course," he whispered joyously. "This will do even better!"

Bending over the beast, Nuroc clenched his teeth and secured a firm grip around the bleeding torso. He sagged under the inert weight of the wolf, then shifted the load so that it rested primarily on his shoulders. With difficulty, he started down the knoll. Blood seeped through the matted fur and trickled down the front of his tunic. Nuroc kept his eyes and ears keenly attuned to the surrounding countryside. Kildwolves stalked the wild in packs, and he was worried that the scent of blood might reach the comrades of the beast he had killed. He was fortunate to have escaped with his life against one wolf. He had seen too many bare-boned carcasses of stray sheep to think he might stand a chance against the butchering assault of half a dozen of the predators.

Fortunately, Nuroc's way was easier on the flatlands, and he was able to clear the distance from the knoll to the cliffs without encountering intruders, although a pair of owls had begun circling in the air above him. Along the way, he wondered further at the strange sight of the riding sorcerers. He had never seen nor heard of their kind ever leaving the confines of the sorcerers's gardens in Cothe. His parents, too, had never ventured far from the obelisk where Talmon-Khash, the present king, practiced his necromantic arts while he ruled over the land. He would have to speak to them about what he had seen.

As Nuroc trudged closer to the edge of the cliffs, the mighty Targoan slowly revealed itself to him and he began to hear the steady crash of waves far down upon the reefs. The sea was alive tonight, churning up wide banners of white froth atop the crest of each wave as far as the eye could see. The dim light cast by the slivered moons sparkled between the waves in a thousand glimmers. Breakers thundered and the wind blew in sharp gusts, flapping the long blonde locks of the youth's hair about his face like angry tendrils spotted with blood.

When he came to the edge of the cliff, Nuroc set the wolf on top of a flat rock similar in size to the one that had blocked the entrance to the mysterious tunnel. He had decided long ago that the rock would make an ideal altar for his sacrifice to Dorban, and had a small heap of kindling already prepared, bound tight against the wind by a length of vine and set in a natural wedge between the limbs of a squat and lonely tree that grew near the precipice.

Nuroc set the kindling in a shallow recess on the surface of the rock, then placed the slain wolf on top. He next took several pieces of thick driftwood retrieved from the shores below weeks before, and set them around the edges of the kindling, propping the wolf up where necessary. It had the makings of a fine pyre, and Nuroc was pleased at the thought that, while the other shepherds were sacrificing mere lambs to Dorban, he would be offering up a kildwolf that he had personally slain. There could be no doubting as to which gesture would please the condor-god more.

Nuroc stepped around the altar, turning his back to the sea in hopes of blocking the wind as he withdrew a shard of flint and the dulled tip of an old lance from his pouch. The wind still worked past him, however, and each time he struck the two pieces together, sparks leapt and died before they could ignite the brown grass amidst the kindling. He huddled in closer and continued to work the stones, faster and faster, until at last a faint flame sent up a curl of smoke that spread through the grass.

Nuroc remained between the wind and the fire, fanning the blaze with waves of his hand as it grew. Smoke swirled up into his face and stung his eyes. He blinked and squinted through tears, concentrating on the fire. Once the flames ignited the twigs, the altar became bright and he could feel a surge of heat. The smoke turned color as the wolf's fur singed, and the

12

smell of burning flesh wafted up from the sacrifice, forcing the young shepherd to step back.

Aware that the wind around him was dying, Nuroc turned and glanced out at the sea. He was scant yards from the edge of the precipice and could see where only the gentlest of waves rolled lazily over the thin ribbon of beach far below. Beds of upwrested kelp lay in the sand, branches swaying with the play of the tides. Where the white fists of breakers had, moments before, pummeled the reefs, the sea now lapped calmly at the coral.

Nuroc felt both awe and a prickling of fear. He had never witnessed so quick a change from tempest to tranquility. The stillness in the air was grim, filled with foreboding. He circled back around the altar and knelt before the fiery sacrifice, staring through the smoke and flames at the sky.

Out on the black mantle of night, the stars waned like the last flickers of candles burned down to the end of their wicks. To the north, the twin eyes of Dorban were barely visible blades of light, drawing together like swords prepared to meet in the first blow of battle. Once the light vanished and darkness reigned over the sky, it was said that the condor-god would take leave of its celestial roost and fly down to the land that bore its name, where it would stare into the souls of all mankind. If one were wise, one made sacrifice to Dorban during the black moons and uttered chants imploring the condor-god to find him worthy of a life among the dominion of stars once he ceased to dwell in human form. Those judged unworthy, the sorcerers taught, died forever once they died as man or woman.

Nuroc did not consider himself unworthy. He lived according to the teachings of the sorcerers and obeyed the wishes of his parents. Still, one could never be too careful, so he was prepared for the black moons, which graced the skies but once in every five years. He began to move his lips in prayer as he saw the last of the visible moons merge. The words he mouthed were from a long-dead language, said to be that spoken by the gods

13

themselves in the days when they lived among men. He had memorized the chant over the past weeks, emblazoning it on his mind so that it would tumble forth without effort. He was thankful now for the time he had spent on the difficult task, enduring the jibes of his fellow shepherds, because he was now in the grip of some nameless terror and, had he not memorized the chant, he felt he would be misjudged by Dorban, even damned.

He had not yet finished the chant when he was distracted by a flash of light at the point where the twin moons met. It was as if the moons were like the stones he had struck to ignite the flame under his offering. His jaw hung slack in wonder at the sight. Then, in the time it would take to open a fist and spread out one's fingers, the flash between the moons erupted outward with an intensity that blotted out the entire sky with a dazzling brightness.

Screaming with horror, Nuroc fell away from the altar, clutching at his eyes. Blinded, he staggered to his feet and fled in panic from the altar, stumbling over rolling terrain before reaching the flat stretch of meadow. It was fear that drove him on without regard for the threat of falling or fleeing into the midst of the other kildwolves. He managed to stay on his feet only because there were no obstructions to fall over. His course veered and pitched, although he thought he was running straight. All the while he blinked constantly and continued to rub at his eyes.

He was almost to the knoll when a fringe of darkness played at the edge of his vision and slowly grew, replacing the brightness which had blinded him. The mad pacing of his heart slowed, and he stopped his running to focus his eyes on the meadows. Like a parted curtain, the blindness lifted and he could see again.

His relief was short-lived, however, because he noticed that the winds had picked up again, blowing with the rage of a hurricane. A hearty gust almost knocked him off his feet. As he crouched down low to lessen the impact, he felt a new trembling under the soles of his sandals and heard a growing rumble that far surpassed that made by the horsemen he had seen earlier.

He looked to the cave, but the sound was coming from all around him. As he stood up, he realized the earth was shaking.

"Madness!" he cried out. "Dorban, have mercy!" He strode uncertainly to the top of the knoll, then looked up to the sky once more, half-expecting to see the great condor-god outlined against the night, flapping its wings to make the wind blow so harshly that the earth trembled. After all, the legends told of such happenings during the black moons. His own grandfather claimed to have once witnessed the gods tossing stars to one another across the heavens during an eclipse, and others told of more fantastic occurrences. But, as the shepherd searched the skies for the miraculous, he saw little more than a black void.

As the earth continued to heave and sway beneath him, he heard the faraway cries of the sheep and shepherds and figured the disruption must be reaching far inland. He looked out toward the coast, and stared speechless. The sum of his previous encounters could not match the cold shiver of terror Nuroc felt grab his spine at the sight before him.

Out on the sea, as far back as the wide channel through which the Targoan embraced the great ocean beyond, there rose a single wave, of the like no man had ever seen. Like a cobra rearing to strike, it fanned outward as it grew in size and swept forward. Far away as it was, Nuroc could still hear the raw power of the wave's building force above the rush of the wind and the trembling roar of the land.

Although the cliffs rose to a height two hundred feet above the sea, Nuroc could see, to his horror, that the wave's size and momentum was going to carry it over the cliffs and onto land. Tearing his gaze away from the watery juggernaut, he broke into a run, returning to the cave and rushing inside.

Swallowed by darkness, he groped along the chiseled

15

walls to find his way. His hands fell upon a level made of carved jaunwood and he pulled on it. There was a crashing sound near the mouth of the cave. Glancing back at the faint rim of light that marked where he had entered, Nuroc saw the stone slab rolling back into place, sealing the entry. Seconds later, Nuroc heard the sickening roar of the tidal wave thrashing onto land and surging across the meadow. The walls of the cave shuddered and he was showered with loose stones. The sound that filled the darkened space was deafening, and Nuroc put his hands to his ears as he continued to stumble along in darkness.

As he reached a turn in the cavern and found himself striding down a narrowed tunnel, Nuroc began to feel cold water seeping up about his ankles. Within five steps the level reached his calves and he could feel the sting of salt water on his bare wounds. The floodwaters were leaking through the secret entrance to the tunnel, he realized. Although he was still making his way in total blackness, he picked up speed as best he could. But the water was rising too swiftly and moving in its own current. Finally he lifted his feet from the stone floor and allowed himself to be carried along by the subterranean river.

The tunnel seemed to bore on forever, taking sharp turns. The fierce current battered Nuroc against the rocky walls as he struggled to keep from being sucked under. He had no perception of time, no time to concern himself with anything but survival. His fingers brushed against objects he could only guess were mounted torches, but he could never manage to secure a firm enough hold on them to stop himself from being carried off.

Close to the end of his endurance, he bounded off three walls in quick succession and found himself whisked by the current into a vast chamber dim with a faint light. The current wavered and he had a chance to tread the water and take a better look at what lay above its surface.

The light was coming from a horizontal opening the

size of a doorway, which led down to a stone staircase. Only the top few steps were visible above the water-line. Besides the steps, the faint light also revealed walls of pressed brick lining the chamber and framing the opening.

Nuroc had no idea where he was, but knew that his fate lay in reaching the steps and pulling himself from the water before he succumbed to the current. He began swimming toward the steps. After taking several strokes, however, he realized he was making no progress. Glancing over his shoulder, he saw that he was caught in a whirlpool that was sucking him into its swirling center on the other side of the chamber. He tried again to swim free of its grip, but was only drawn closer to the vortex, which gave off an eerie sound from the force of the spinning waters.

Hoping that the pull might not be as strong below the surface, Nuroc sucked in a deep breath and dove underwater. He opened his eyes, mindless of the salty sting, and peered through the murky depths as he fanned his arms out and pulled himself through the water. He began to make progress and soon perceived the steps. He stroked his way toward them, reaching out once he saw the railing of carved wood running the length of the staircase. Securing a grip on the rail, he grappled himself to the surface and gasped, letting his lungs take in the welcome air.

As soon as he recovered from this latest ordeal, Nuroc climbed over the railing and made his way up the steps.

"By the gods!" he cried out when he had cleared the steps and come through the opening. In his state of total exhaustion, he felt giddy with disbelief and began to laugh. Tears came to his eyes and his laughter turned into manic jabbering, for he found himself in the obe-lisk back at Cothe, safely home, staring into the stunned eyes of his parents and the sorcerer king Tal-mon-Khash.

Stromthroad, his father, rushed forward and grasped the boy as he slumped to the floor. As the toll of his escapades ushered him into the arms of unconsciousness, Nuroc's gaze took in one final vision: Over his father's shoulder, a hundred feet up and out through the uppermost portal of the obelisk, he could see the crescent of a single moon, tilted in the night sky like a twisted smile.

Two

The wrath of the elements was not restricted to the shores of the Targoan. The whole continent was held in the grips of cataclysm throughout the course of the night. Where the charging waves did not take their toll, earthquakes did. Temples crashed down on cowering worshippers, leaving hundreds dead or dying in the rubble. Thatch-roofed homes were flattened on top of families huddled in corners seeking a futile refuge. Rivers foamed over their banks, snapping boats and bodies like dry sticks as floods surged through towns and villages. Beasts scurried to treetops for safety, only to find that no place was safe. Trees were toppled and boulders rolled lethally before the fury of wind and water.

By dawn, the cataclysm had spent its rage. An unsuspecting sun rose, burning off the morning haze to clear the skies. The day was as beautiful as the land was scarred. The survivors crept from the ruins, numb with shock, and slowly began to survey the damage and tend to those less fortunate. Everywhere there was the litter of death and destruction, and some could only fall to the ground and wail hopelessly. Others cursed the gods and brooded wearily over their fate. A staunch few braced themselves with courage and set about doing what they felt must be done. They treated the wounded, buried the dead, and began to reconstruct the homes and towns they had lost. Anyone so unwise as to take advantage of the calamity and try looting salvable goods from abandoned homes or untended merchant stalls found themselves beset by upright citizens and put to a swift and gruesome death as a warning to others. The land was filled with foul moods and dark hearts.

As the days wore on, a rumor took wing throughout the land, passed along in both bitter whispers and loud cries. It was said that, for all the carnage and ruin, there was one place on the continent where no harm had fallen. In Cothe, the embittered were told, the city walls and its buildings still stood, as did the tall stone obelisk in the sorcerers' gardens, where Talmon-Khash practised his occult arts and instructed anointed acolytes in the craft of necromancy. If the truth were to be known, more than one soul was heard to claim, the capital had been miraculously bypassed by floodwaters, which had split into separate courses only a spear's throw from the main gates to the city.

The news of Cothe's fate preyed ill on the minds of the populace. They felt no relief in knowing that the king and his kind had been spared. Rather, the realization festered in the bosoms of those who had suffered so greatly, turning by the days into a fitful rage. They thought on the issue and decided that the ruling sorcerers had been saved, not by good fortune, but by malicious design. After all, the rebellious insisted, had not Talmon-Khash himself expressed anger at the recent murmurings amongst the peasants that their lot was inadequately served by the ruling class? True, he had later put an end to the dissent by allowing the workers to place a spokesman in the royal hall to voice their wants and needs, but it now seemed that the gesture was no more than a ploy, a means of suppressing the disenchanted until he could conjure up a show of power that would bring the workers to their knees.

So, now that Talmon-Khash had played out his

hand, the agitators shouted on, were they to fall into meek submission and return to their former lot or, daresay, an even more lowly fate?

No! cried the masses, spurred on by the rhetoric. *A thousand times no! We have survived the worst they could heap upon us! Now it is time they learned that we, too, have power!*

The cry of revolution carried with a speed to match the rumors which had spawned it. From all points of the battered continent, men, women, and children set out for the capital by whatever means were available. Along the way they gathered more support, and each night there were more fires in the hills surrounding Cothe, as the downtrodden set up camps and waited.

At last came the fog-hung morning when thousands slipped silently down from the hills and converged about the lofty brick walls that surrounded the city. The king's militia lined the battlements and raised their weapons in a show of power meant to dissuade all thoughts of assault.

The people were not so easily fooled, however. The ranks of the militia were fixed in number, whereas the aroused citizenry grew in size by the hour. The war-horns sounded, and the factions battled in earnest. The attackers stormed the walls from all sides with hastily-made ladders. For every three ladders the soldiers prevented from reaching the battlements, one was put in place, providing the rioters with access to the city. By midday, a force had battled its way inside the walls to the main gates and opened the way for the others to enter Cothe.

All around the magnificent coliseum, where the people had once gathered annually to share in the festive watching of games, blood flowed with a sickening abandon as peasants and farmers matched the unwieldy tools of their trade against the polished weapons of the military. Both sides claimed death after death from their adversaries, but it was the unpracticed hordes, fueled by the constant arrival of vengeful reinforcements, who could bear up best against the staggering losses. The militia, soon dwindled to several dozen, at last turned heel and retreated as best they could, beating a path to secret exits or charging their armored steeds through the seething masses to the uncertain freedom, which lay beyond the gates.

As more and more of the arriving citizens poured through the gates and trampled corpses in their mindless anger, a collective madness drove them out of control. Left unchallenged, they greeted the fall of night with bright fires set to stables, merchant booths, and any other structure made of wood. Buildings of stone were entered and ransacked. Pottery urns were shattered with bricks, statues were rocked from their pedestals and sent crashing onto tiled floors. The destruction was widespread and as undiscriminating as the quakes and flooding that had wreaked total havoc elsewhere in the land. Soon the entire city was lit in the glow of arson, with the fires reflected in the glint of countless eyes already burning with hate.

For all their vented rage, the people had yet to face the true objects of their wrath. Soldiers and peasants lay dead in the reddened dirt, and here and there one could see a slain merchant or fat-bellied noble, but nowhere was a victim wearing the robes of a sorcerer. The intended victims had somehow eluded their executioners.

There could be only one answer. Almost in unison, all hate-filled eyes turned to the far edge of the city, where lay both the ancient obelisk and rambling gardens that were the exclusive province of the sorcerers. The mob charged down the city streets, furthering the wake of their carnage, until they came to the second wall that separated the realm of the sorcerers from that of the layman. It was only a matter of time before the thick wood of the arched gate was splintered by a battering ram procured from the headquarters of the military. From that same area, and from the bodies of slain soldiers, the commoners exchanged their plowshares for swords, their hoes for spears and lances.

Into the garden they charged, brandishing hand-held

21

torches to light the way. They marched in a column, following the beaten dirt path leading to the obelisk. Off in the brush, a menagerie of trained beasts fled in fear from the moving phalanx, giving off feeble roars, which were drowned out by the cries of the mob. Shouts and screams echoed in the night, their import lost to the cacophony of varied chants and curses. Only a single name could be discerned, its mention a constant punctuation to the babble.

The name was Talmon-Khash.

The sorcerer-king stood on a platform near the top of the obelisk, looking out through the opened portal at the approaching horde. He seemed oddly composed as he rubbed a thin, ring-studded hand across his silverish beard. There was an enigma to his appearance and bearing. He looked at once both aged and vital, frail and yet bristling with some unseen energy that lurked beneath his yellowing skin. His robe was simple in design, but made of a cloth unsurpassed in texture and endurance. No one knew the source of the material, or even the manner by which it was woven. There were statues in Cothe of kings who had worn the same garb centuries before. Some said that the mighty Noj-Syb himself had been given the robe by the gods in the early years of his rule. It was green in color, the same dark shade as the heart of the forest.

Talmon-Khash was not alone. Beside him stood Nuroc, recovered from his wounds through the application of herbs and ointments. The shepherd stared at the scene below with alarm. For hours he had watched the battle taking place in the city, bristling with a desire to join in the clash of arms on behalf of the king. His parents had forbade him to leave the obelisk, however, and even Talmon-Khash had said his services would be of more use here instead of the battlefield. He was secretly relieved now, for the cries of anguish that had leapt through the night chilled his blood, and the sight of the capital burning like so much kindling

22

gave him pause to consider the realities of warfare. What he saw had little to do with his imagined battling, which was done with grinning confidence and stoic grandeur. Those he slew in his dreams did not scream their agony or succeed in making a few of their blows connect before being dispatched to their ancestors. This carnage below was neither grand nor heroic. It was an orgy of bloodlust and severed limbs, of scorched flesh and gouged eyes, of savage screams and pathetic whimpers.

"Blind vengeance," Talmon-Khash murmured, his eyes still on the crowd. "They think this destruction can cure the pain in their hearts, the pain that only time cures."

"They come for you, Talmon-Khash," Nuroc said, turning to the king. "You must flee, like the others."

Talmon-Khash shook his head, but said nothing. There was a sadness in his gray eyes that seemed to bear an insurmountable grief.

As they stood near the portal, there was motion behind them, near the steps leading to the platform. A sorcerer in the yellow robes of his station stepped across the platform, followed by Nuroc's parents, who wore, like Nuroc, unadorned cotton tunics. Stromthroad, a tall man with the dark eyes of a Cothian, nodded grimly to his son and bowed to the king. Thouris, red hair spilling in billowing curls about her shoulders, knelt before Talmon-Khash. Tears coursed down her cheeks as she clutched at the king's withered hand.

"Inkemisa says you are staying behind while we leave," she sobbed. "You can't face them alone. They blame you for the cataclysm and will put you to death! It wasn't your doing! You yourself told us it was Augage who crashed the moons and loosed the tides after fleeing Cothe, hoping to discredit you and lay claim to the throne. You can't—"

Talmon-Khash placed a finger over Thouris's lips. He spoke calmly, but his voice carried a vigor and command that would rival any man half his age. "The

23

truth is not the issue now, Thouris. I am responsible for the actions of those I have taught. Their betrayal is still my burden."

"But they'll kill you!" Stromthroad blurted out.

Talmon-Khash sighed and turned from the portal. He looked up and around at the vast enclosure of the obelisk. Here, close to the top, the stone ceiling sloped and narrowed toward its inevitable peak, and yet the distance between opposing sides was still more than fifty feet. The light from below waned as it reached upward to this great height, and the finer details of the tower's interior were obscured by shadow. All along the walls, however, ancient runes were faintly visible in the stone, carved by forgotten hands in a forgotten tongue. These myriad hieroglyphics contained the wisdom of the ages, and it was through the translation of the confusing symbols into the proper oaths and chants that a sorcerer advanced in the mastery of his calling.

"This tower is the heart of all wizardry," Talmon-Khash pronounced to the others. "I must act to save it, no matter the risk to myself."

Hearing the pandemonium in the gardens, Nuroc turned worriedly to his parents. They exchanged looks of grave concern. They were as devoted to the king as they were to each other, and could not bear the thought of deserting him.

"I'm staying!" Nuroc announced determinedly. "I'll fight by your side to the end!"

"Yes," Stromthroad added. "We'll stay and help as best we can."

A smile, however sad, came to Talmon-Khash's face. Again he shook his head. "You misjudge the situation. As I told you before, there is a better way that you might serve your king than to toss away your lives like idle change."

Talmon-Khash looked away from the family and nodded at Inkemisa, the other sorcerer. Going over to a table of polished onyx set near the edge of the platform, Inkemisa opened a teakwood box lined with gold trim. Reaching inside, he withdrew a ceremonial dagger. As he carried it back to the others, the blade coruscated brilliantly in the torchlight.

Taking the dagger, Talmon-Khash turned to the portal and directed his gaze to the heavens. Dorban's single moon was half full now, and the rest of the constellation shone clearly in the night. Holding the knife across the flat of his opened palms, the sorcerer-king raised his arms as if offering the blade to the condor-god. His eyes closed and he began to whisper in the unintelligible magetongue.

From where he stood, Nuroc could see the dagger, and he marveled at its wondrous craftsmanship. The blade was flat and razor sharp, as long as a man's forearm, made of a strange translucent metal that seemed to alternately reflect and absorb light. The hilt was equally unique, carved of ebony into the shape of the continent Dorban, with inset gems of unknown origin glowing as the condor's eyes.

As he was completing the final words of his incantation, Talmon-Khash shifted the dagger in his hands, securing a firm grip on the ornate hilt and quickly drawing the blade's edge across his wrist.

"No!" Nuroc cried out, stepping quickly toward the king. Even swifter was Inkemisa, who blocked Nuroc's way and silenced the youth with a stern, forceful gaze. Stromthroad reached out and touched his son from behind, gesturing for him to step back. Nuroc looked to his parents for an explanation, but their eyes were on the king, anxious and yet filled with faith in the wisdom of their master. Nuroc stood beside them and followed their gaze back to Talmon-Khash, who once again held the dagger upward in a gesture of supplication as he recited another chant. To the youth's amazement, he saw that the blade's once-clear luster had taken on a crimson hue.

Talmon-Khash slowly turned to face the others, his face bathed in serenity, showing no sign of pain. Nuroc could see the king's wrist, but there was no trace of the wound he had inflicted upon himself.

25

While Inkemisa bowed to the king and turned to leave the platform, Talmon-Khash spoke quietly to the family before him. "You three have served me most of your lives, and with a loyalty that goes unquestioned. To you alone can I entrust the power to summon me back to this earthly realm once I have invoked the Oath of Dissolvement." He paused a moment, and Nuroc felt a shudder of dread at the import of the king's words. Talmon-Khash curled his thin fingers around the hilt of the sacred dagger and continued, "Now, place your wrists before me, and do not fear."

Without hesitation, Stromthroad and Thouris held their arms out to the king and twisted their hands to expose the underside of their wrists. Nuroc swallowed hard and did the same. Talmon-Khash took the youth's wrist and swiftly cut across the skin. Nuroc winced at the slight tingle of pain, then summoned the courage to look down at his wrist. Where the blade cut and rested, no blood came forth. Instead, the crimson blade began to revert back to its previous translucence. While the king removed the dagger and repeated the ritual with Stromthroad and Thouris, Nuroc continued to look down at his wrist, seeing the incision seal, mend, and heal in a matter of seconds, so that it looked as if the skin had never met the sharp edge of a blade.

"Now you must listen carefully," Talmon-Khash told them when he had finished with his chant. "Once the Oath is consummated, my blood will be my life in your veins and those of your future born. Only you will be able to summon me back to this earthly realm, and only then if you commit to memory the necessary chant. I will tell you the chant, then you must go below and assist Inkemisa in distracting the hordes from interfering before I have a chance to complete what must be done to save the obelisk."

The sorcerer-king gestured for them to walk beside him as he headed across the platform to the winding staircase of stone blocks that Inkemisa had descended. The steps were built into the wall of the obelisk. Talmon-Khash paused long enough to place his hand over a large cut gem mounted at the head of the stairs. After mouthing a few words of the magetongue, he took away his hand and led the others down the steps, conversing with them in earnest whisperings. He repeated the ritual with other mounted jewels as they descended past several more levels of platforms similar to the one they had just vacated. In each instance, the platform ran only a few feet out from the wall, leaving the central area of the obelisk open-spaced. As with the upper level, there were inscribed on each section of the obelisk wall more hieroglyphics relating to chants of the former ages. The higher the level, the more difficult the chants to be deciphered and, consequently, the more potent the power derived from their mastery. Novitiates began their studies at the first platform above the ground floor and proceeded upward only after learning all the first level's inscriptions. Only Talmon-Khash, as the ranking high-sorcerer, was allowed access to the highest level in the obelisk, and he ventured to that summit only rarely, for the chants carved into the inner peak were deemed forbidden because of their unwieldy power. It was one such chant that the rebel sorcerer Augage had translated after broaching the uppermost passage the night of the cataclysm. He had left Cothe with his allied traitors and attempted the chant from atop the distant Kanghats to the south, away from the possible intervention of Talmon-Khash. When the chant had brought upon the churning of waves and quaking of land, it was Talmon-Khash who had been forced to summon forth the sum of his powers to still the cataclysm before it destroyed all of Dorban. Although the people condemned Talmon-Khash as a destroyer, he was in fact their savior.

Halfway down the dozen levels of the tower, they came upon Inkemisa, who stood near the edge of the platform, fitting a crossbow into a special fixture on the railing. Secured, the weapon was capable of swiveling back and forth as well as up and down.

"The others are ready as well," Inkemisa told Talmon-Khash.

"Good," the sorcerer-king said. "There is little time left." Talmon-Khash handed the ceremonial dagger to Stromthroad. "Watch over this well, for it has a value beyond measure. And these, too," he continued, pulling from his fingers several rings and handing one to each of the others. They were all alike, made of old bone carved into the shape of condor talons and tipped with polished stones the color of flame. Nuroc slipped his onto his left hand. He could not pull the ring past his knuckle until Talmon-Khash reached out and brushed his fingertips across the set stones. Nuroc felt the carved talons loosen their grip long enough for him to pull the ring onto his finger, then harden to their previous state.

Nuroc looked up from the ring and stared into the piercing gaze of Talmon-Khash.

"Dorban spared you by a string of miracles during the cataclysm," the king told Nuroc. "There is meaning to the gesture. You have a destiny to fulfill, and the gods will watch over you so long as you remain worthy of their cause. Remember that, always."

"What cause?" Nuroc wondered aloud. "What is my destiny?"

"I can say no more," Talmon-Khash said. "I must return to the upper reaches and begin the final chants."

Stromthroad and Thouris rushed forward and embraced their ruler. Thouris wept anew. Nuroc remained where he was, still absorbing the words of the king. Talmon-Khash kissed his servants gently on the cheeks, then stepped aside for a hushed word with Inkemisa before turning to the staircase and beginning his ascent up the steps. Nuroc watched until Talmon-Khash was gone from view, then joined his parents.

"Now, then," Inkemisa intoned seriously as he came back to the others. "We have much to do before we leave the obelisk. Talmon-Khash must call upon the highest sorcery to perform his incantations, so I cannot draw off the moon with chants of my own to help de-

28

fend the obelisk. We will have to resort to more conventional means and hope for the best . . ."

Set in the center of the lush, verdant sprawl of the sorcerers' gardens, the obelisk had been built upon a small island, around which flowed a moat fed by an offshoot of the Targoan River. The moat was dark and still, spanned by a drawbridge made of hearty jaunwood, a thick tree whose sap turned each layer of outer bark stronger than most metals forged by the city blacksmiths. The bridge had been left down, and the blood-crazed pillagers now crossed to the island, shouting as they formed a widening ring about the obelisk, seeking entry. The sole entrance was an imposing gate as tall and wide as two men and made of the strongest metal to be found in all the Kanghat Mountains. The gate was locked from within, and there were no outside hinges or grasps for the invaders to beat upon in hopes of forcing their way in. Shouts were cried out and stones clattered off the side of the obelisk. The crowd's ire had a life all its own.

This impasse had been anticipated by the cooler minds in the mob, and back in the gardens they drove on a team of broad-shouldered oxen, straining at their hitches as they pulled a massive wheeled catapult that the insurgents had confiscated along with the battering ram. In the cradled arm of the catapult was a boulder weighing several tons. The sheer weight sank the wooden wheels into the soft dirt of the path, slowing its progress toward the obelisk. A large crew of volunteers broke from the column and fell in behind the catapult, heaving their weight against the wheels to keep them from bogging down in the dirt. Whips cracked above the heads of the oxen to urge them on, and in time the great weapon was hauled to the edge of the moat. It was quickly decided that the bridge would not support the weight of the catapult, so the oxen were unhitched and led away, leaving the weapon situated so that its volley would send the boulder flying headlong into the obelisk with a force that would break down the entry gate, if not cave in the entire structure.

Cries went out for those on the island to move clear of the obelisk, lest they be showered by loose stone or crushed by the boulder following its impact. But the hysteria of the mob had escalated beyond control, and the call went unheard by some and unheeded by others. In their restlessness, some began to hurl their torches at the obelisk, sprinkling those around them with burning sparks. Maddened howls cut through the din as the wounded heaved away the fallen torches. Most of the torches sizzled as they were extinguished in the moat, but a few caught fire in the gardens. At the sight of the erupting blazes, more torches were thrown despite the shouted warnings of those who feared the consequences.

There came forth from the burning brush a chorus of hideous bellows, and a pack of enraged Shangoran lions, each one a quarter-ton of four-legged terror, charged through the flora and plunged into the crowd, rending instant death with swipes of their lethal paws. Angry jaws snapped as the beasts sank teeth into whatever flesh lay in their path, breaking bones and crushing skulls in the process. No less than twenty men and women had been slain before the lions themselves were beaten still by the delirious mob. The air was charged with lunacy.

Two men with axes took up positions on either side of the thick, woven rope that was drawn taut against the bend of the catapult. Before they could bring down the edges of their blades against the rope, however, they were distracted by an inhuman shriek coming from the obelisk. They looked up and joined the countless eyes cast toward the slowly opening gates of the tower. The screeching continued, coming from the sound of unused hinges and the scrape of metal across the stone floor of the obelisk.

An unnatural radiance emanated from within the temple of the sorcerers, dazzling the masses into a state of wonder. Never before had anyone of them stared into the secret interior of the looming spire. Any sense

30

of caution over the strange manner of the gate's opening was cast aside, however, once the source of the radiance came into view. With whoops of almost childlike enthusiasm, those already on the island poured into the opening; others scrambled over the unused catapult to gain a footing on the drawbridge and join in this, the ultimate infiltration of their avowed enemy's lair.

The ground floor of the obelisk was a vault of immeasurable wealth. Chests filled with precious stones lay open and glittering in the torchlight. The walls were lined with ornate frescoes, bordered with inlaid gems—diamonds, rubies, topaz, opal, tourmaline—there were even stones with lost names and unimagined splendor. A rack of jewel-encrusted weapons was supported on one wall by statues of winged panthers with ivory fangs and sapphire eyes. Potions and rolled parchments lay among the other implements of spell-casting on an ornate jaunwood bench that had turned to stone with age.

All of these things, for all their entrancing beauty, paled in comparison to the imposing sight of a magnificent condor, chiseled from a single block of brownish stone found nowhere else in the land. It stood more than thirty feet high, and had been shaped with an uncanny eye for detail. It almost seemed, in the flickering light, that the condor-god itself was perched there, vibrant with life, staring down at the rounded altar of creamy alabaster set before it.

Those in the chamber stared uneasily when their eyes fell on the unseeing gaze of the stone idol. Much as they had spurned the worship of Dorban in the wake of the cataclysm, there still existed in each man and woman a primordial sense of devotion to the god that had been their heart of being for so many centuries. Fear, shame, and humility were the first reactions of the gathered, overriding the insanity that had brought them to raid the inner sanctum of worship. But greed proved a stronger motivation than reverence, and the mob soon fell lustfully upon the plunder of the

31

obelisk. Pouches and pockets began to bulge with loot, and fights broke out as others continued to crowd into the chamber and lay claim to a share of the wealth. No one spoke of vengeance any more.

Far above, half-hidden in the shadowy reaches of the tower's apex, Talmon-Khash stood in a trance before the wall of hieroglyphics he had just translated into the magetongue. Sweat clung to his brow and his face was tensed with concentration. He slowly withdrew from the far reaches he had sent his mind to, and his eyes opened. He breathed deeply and sagged visibly from the strain of the ordeal. Already he had performed two preparatory chants, and he would have to regain his strength before going on to the culminating oath that would call into play the powers he had tapped from the previous two.

He paced about the platform, trying to blot from his mind the sounds coming from below. It was his hope that by opening the doors and luring the mob inside he could prevent them from disrupting the obelisk before he finished his chant. He had succeeded in keeping the catapult from loosing its destruction, but he had underestimated his concern for the material riches held within the walls. He could not help but glance down upon the looting, and the sight cut through his concentration and resolve. The gentleness drained from his features. Blood rushed through the pallor of his face, and veins pulsed with the rage that inevitably sought release.

"You! Citizens of Dorban!" he finally shouted, his deep voice bounding thunderously off the walls of the obelisk. Those below were startled by the outburst and looked up from their looting. "You, who hang thieves who so much as desire your belongings, now fall upon the wealth of antiquity like jackals on carrion!"

At the sight of Talmon-Khash, the charged silence swept over the crowd once more. Face to face with their king, many were instantly stripped of their self-righteous wrath and left cowering anew in shame. Others were smitten with a fear greater than that they had felt at the sight of the stone idol. The stone merely represented a god; the man who stared down at them was the most powerful mortal on the face of the earth.

Murmurings soon crept through the silence as those below turned to one another for reassurance. They bolstered one another with a false courage, reminding themselves of their initial intent in storming the obelisk. A second time the lull was broken by pandemonium. Fists and weapons were raised toward the sorcerer and shaken threateningly. A florid-faced woman pointed up at Talmon-Khash with her hand clenched around a strand of stolen pearls. She wailed through her tears, "All the wealth in this room cannot replace the son I lost to the flood you brought upon us!"

Talmon-Khash opened his mouth to refute the charge, but knew at once it was of no use. The fire of vengeance had been rekindled, and it was quickly fed by more cries.

"Death to Talmon-Khash!"

"Death to the bringer of the cataclysm!"

"Slay the vile tyrant where he stands!"

The various cries merged in a boisterous din and Talmon-Khash cursed his human frailty for having brought on the outburst. Now it would be difficult for him to lapse back into a state of trance and recite the Oath of Dissolvement. He moved back, away from the railing, and faced the wall before him. Placing his hands to the sides of his face, he pressed his fingers gently against his temples and ears. He closed his eyes and began to recite a mantra repeatedly so that the resonance of the words soon drowned out the death chants from below. Lapsing again into a trance, he opened his eyes. The pupils had vanished into his eye sockets and only the whites showed as he began to mouth the Oath of Dissolvement.

Down below, much of the mob continued to voice their contempt for the sorcerer-king while others fell back to their looting. A few among the incensed multitude carried bows. Shouting for room, they nocked arrows and prepared to loose volleys up toward the pinnacle. Before fingers could release tensed bow-strings, however, four arrows showered down from above, each one claiming an archer. Gasps went up from those near the slain, and heads turned upward, seeking the source of arrowfire. Several flights up they spotted Nuroc, Inkemisa, Stromthroad, and Thouris standing near the railing, poised over their mounted crossbows, which were already loaded with more quarrels.

"Anyone else who dares fire upon the king will be likewise slain." Inkemisa shouted down at the masses. To prove his threat, the yellow-robed sorcerer sent another shaft burrowing into the chest of an archer who attempted to work his bow.

Nuroc spotted a man drawing back his arm to hurl a spear at his mother. Pivoting the crossbow with practiced ease, Nuroc released the catch and a second later the spearthrower was sagging to the floor, clutching at the arrow in his shoulder.

Several of the archers below stole to the edge of the crowd, reaching the staircase and ascending the steps. The steps were positioned so that they could make their way beyond the range of the crossbows.

The first man to reach the second level charged past the mounted gem at the head of the steps without touching it, much less proffering the essential chant. A snapping sizzle, like the sound of fresh meat set on a heated grill, sounded from the gem as it suddenly brightened and gave off a thin, jagged shaft of light. The crackling shaft sought out the disbelieving archer, smiting him in the chest. Screaming with agony, the man dropped his weapon. His life went out with the scream and he limply tumbled down the stone steps. Those behind him leapt away, seeing a smouldering cavity where the dead man's heart had once been. No one dared to climb the steps further.

From his post behind the crossbow, Nuroc saw fingers pointing upwards to the top of the obelisk and looked up to see Talmon-Khash standing at the edge of the elevated platform, removing a section of the jaun-wood railing so that nothing lay between him and the smoke-filled air. One step would send him falling two hundred feet to the floor of the obelisk. He remained there at the edge, his eyes closed and his lips moving silently.

While the throng divided its attention between star-ing at the king and ripping at the wealth of the obelisk, a tall archer carrying a crafted longbow pushed his way to the bench containing scrolls and potions. He climbed up onto the bench, securing himself at a point where he was clear of the sentinels above. Both Stromthroad and Nuroc spotted him and fired at the bench, but their arrows splintered off the petrified wood he hid be-hind. From his quiver he withdrew a sleek arrow with a forged tip and fit it to his bow. At Nuroc's urging, Inkemisa and Thouris attempted to stop the archer with their bows, but again he was concealed from the flight of their arrows. Grinning savagely, he pulled back his bowstring as far as he could, feeling his muscles strain from the effort. With a groan, he re-leased the arrow and watched it cut through the smoky air toward the sorcerer-king.

But the shaft did not imbed itself in its target. In-stead, once it struck Talmon-Khash, the arrow merely hung in place, trapped in the folds of the ageless robe it had failed to pierce. The sorcerer reached for the ar-row without interrupting the flow of his chant and cast it aside. He wavered on the brink a moment, complet-ing the incantation, then toppled forward.

Screams pierced the obelisk as the people saw Tal-mon-Khash falling toward them, his robe flapping wildly about him. They pushed back into one another in their effort to move clear of the rounded altar, where his fall was taking him. As he drew nearer to the altar, however, Talmon-Khash began to fade in the air, like an apparition losing substance under close scrutiny. More screams pealed in the night, and some gazed in speechless wonder as the sorcerer, rather than splattering against the altar, simply vanished, as if he had dissolved into it.

Those closest to the altar pushed themselves back even farther, dropping their loot as their eyes widened with shock. Others looked to the altar uncertainly. Some fainted, while others fell to their knees and began whimpering, broken by the sight.

Nuroc was baffled. Living among sorcerers all his life, he was used to remarkable feats practiced in the obelisk and out in the gardens, but this was unlike anything he had ever seen. He had helped his parents polish the rounded altar enough times to know its solidity, and Talmon-Khash had been a man of flesh and blood. That the king should disappear within the white stone seemed incredible. And yet, he recalled, only moments before he had seen blood flow into a blade of solid metal, and then flow back out. It was a night of great magic, and there was yet more to happen.

"Quick, Nuroc," Inkemisa called out, distracting Nuroc from his stunned musings. Nuroc looked over and saw the sorcerer standing with his parents before an opened doorway leading to a chamber built into the thick walls of the obelisk. Leaving the crossbow, he followed the platform around to the side where the others awaited him. Together, they hastened into the chamber. Inkemisa closed the door behind them. Thouris carried a torch and in its wavering light Nuroc saw the rungs of a ladder running along the inner cavity. Inkemisa was the first to step onto the rungs. He began lowering himself and Thouris followed.

"I never knew of this," Nuroc told his father.

"Nor I," Stromthroad said. "Without it we would be lost, though."

The older man continued down the ladder. Nuroc paused and saw that the rungs reached upward into darkness as well. Shaking his head in wonder, he followed his father down the stone walled shaft and soon they were beneath the obelisk, where the floodwaters had long dried up, leaving open the various tunnels leading from the gardens.

"We go east," Inkemisa said, starting down the tunnel closest to him. The others quickly fell in beside him, leaving behind a life they could never return to.

Overhead, within the obelisk, the rounded altar began to brighten visibly, giving off a radiant heat. In a matter of seconds, the altar glowed like a small sun, and the condor idol also began to change in color as it absorbed the heat and light and radiated it outward.

Looters shrieked with pain, dropping their plunder and turning their eyes from the blinding light of the altar. Blisters of raw pain formed on fingers that had touched the riches of the obelisk. The panic spread as fast as the blinding light and intense heat.

"The goods are afire!" several cried out.

"A curse has fallen!"

"Flee! Flee or we all die!"

Crazed with fright, the crowd retreated upon itself. Those kneeling fell beneath the rush and were trampled underfoot. There were painful groans among the hysterical wailings as the wounded struggled to their feet and clutched at the clothing of others for help in clearing the obelisk. Many lay dead on the stone floor, their skin already reddened from the intensity of the heat.

Outside, the gardens blazed like an inferno. Dozens more died in the frantic exodus as hundreds charged along the footpaths to the gate and raced back through the city streets, seeking the quickest exit from the dying capital. Once they were clear of the walls, they continued to run without looking back.

Near the drawbridge, flames leapt up onto the abandoned catapult, licking a fiery course along the wood before falling on the taut rope holding the poised boulder. In seconds the rope was burned thin enough to snap, and the gigantic rock was flung full-force across the moat. Its destructive power was no match for the web of wizardry Talmon-Khash had flung about the obelisk, however, and the rock exploded into a shower of stone that splashed harmlessly into the moat without having wreaked the slightest damage to the enchanted spire.

Three

Nuroc pushed up on the camouflaged doorway marking the end of the tunnel, then pulled himself from the hole in the earth. He found himself standing amidst a lush belt of pines that rimmed a section of forest bordering the foothills of the central Kanghats. The scent of pine was a welcome change from the musty, foul odor of the tunnels. He had been below for some time, traversing three miles of subterranean passage with the others. Unlike the sorcerers he had seen fleeing from the other leg of the tunnel the night of the cataclysm, their flight had taken them away from the coast.

After looking around to make certain he was unobserved, Nuroc crouched over the opening and extended a hand to the sorcerer Inkemisa. Stromthroad followed and assisted Thouris to the surface. They were all smeared with dirt and bore scrapes from the walls of the tunnel.

Inkemisa led the group from the pines and past a twin-trunked jaunwood to a clearing. This was an area seldomed traveled by anyone but hunters, and the nearest roadway was a few hundred feet downhill. Torches bobbed along the road in both directions, and excited voices merged into a senseless din, although Nuroc guessed that the majority of conversations had to do with the burning of Cothe.

From where they stood, the refugees had a clear

view of the capital blazing in the west with a crown of fire about the city walls. The city had been built with its outer walls shaped into the outline of a human skull, and from their perspective Cothe seemed like a burning face that stared in silent pain to the heavens above. Smoke curled in great billowing clouds, through which rose the pinnacle of the unmolested obelisk.

"The fools," Inkemisa muttered bitterly. "They've destroyed the city while the true villains have already fled."

"I still don't understand why Augage and the others went west." Nuroc told the sorcerer. "Beyond the royal pastures the land is barren as far as the tip of the western peninsula. No one dwells there but the hill tribes, who would as soon slay a mage as stare into his eye."

"You underestimate Augage's power and cunning, not to mention his determination," Inkemisa replied. "Having failed in his dream to wrest the throne from Talmon-Khash, he will no doubt carve himself a smaller kingdom and build his power gradually. The west coast is most fertile for such a plan. There is no unity among the hill peoples, and Augage will no doubt find a way to tame them, tribe by tribe. All in all, it is the only place he could have fled to. Anywhere else and he would be slain before he could amass sufficient power to establish rule."

Embracing his wife, Stromthroad looked over her shoulder at Inkemisa. "But isn't it true that as long as Augage is gone from the obelisk, he cannot achieve the full potential of his powers? And what of the change in the skies? With only one moon to draw upon, can the chants still be worked as if both eyes of Dorban graced the night?"

"You saw Talmon-Khash prove that only moments ago," Inkemisa said, looking to the other three. "You carry his blood only by way of the highest sorcery, and even then only because you are all unpracticed in the arts of our king. Had he tried to mingle his blood with mine, we both would have died at once. You see, it is

39

one thing to master a chant and another to know and control its consequences. That is where Talmon-Khash was forever Augage's superior. Augage has power but only the barest control over it. He cannot do all that he could if he were in the obelisk and able to study the walls, but he will still be a force to reckon with. I fear we have yet to see the last of his menace. I tell you, there are times when I feel a share of guilt for holding my tongue when I first began to suspect Augage was up to some nefarious scheme. Had I told Talmon-Khash sooner, he might have been able to intercede before—"

The sorcerer went silent as they all heard a rustling in the pines—horses heading toward them. Before the others could react, Nuroc had his knife out and was charging silently across the grassy clearing toward the sound. He felt pride in his swift action and even smiled menacingly as he brushed aside the first few limbs of the pines. Here was his chance to prove himself to his parents, show them that he was a deserving warrior. He would storm the horsemen and slay them before they could voice cries that might be heard from the roadway below, thus preventing the grim fate that would await them if they were discovered.

He slowed his pace and made his way crouching through the branches. Once he spotted the legs and shod hooves of three horses, he broke into a run and leapt forward through the brush, holding his blade before him to strike at the first rider.

There was no rider upon the first horse, however, and Nuroc was thrown off balance in his shock. His momentum carried him over the vacant saddle and tumbling to the ground. He rolled with his fall and sprang back to his feet. Whirling about to continue his assault, Nuroc came close to impaling himself on the pointed tip of a lance that the lone rider held on him. In the saddle was a young woman, dressed in a silken kirtle that draped alluringly over her full-formed figure. Dark hair floated in airy wisps around her head, and her cobalt blue eyes focused on Nuroc with a concentration of mind that came close to mesmerizing him. He froze in mid-motion, then stepped back from the lance, feeling a thin trail of blood seep from where the sharp tip had grazed his chest.

"Nuroc!" the young woman gasped, pulling the lance back. "By the gods, I almost slew you!"

Nuroc scowled, not so much in anger at her as himself. He must have looked like a fool springing out at a riderless horse. For her of all people to witness his mistake. . . .

"Didn't my father tell you I was coming with horses?" she asked, lifting the two sets of reins she was carrying in addition to her own.

"Yes, he told us," Nuroc snapped, reaching out for the reins. At the last second, the woman pulled them away from him.

"You don't have to be angry at me, then, do you?" she said, a sparkle of mirth coming to her dark eyes.

"Give me the reins, Myrania," Nuroc insisted, still holding his hand out.

"Myrania?" came Inkemisa's voice from the clearing. "Nuroc, did you—"

"Yes, it's me, Father," Myrania called out, handing Nuroc the two reins for the other steeds. Nuroc noticed that one of the horses had some of his belongings packed behind the saddle. Looking at the other horses, he realized that his parents' things were there as well, placed hastily in burlap satchels strapped across the horses' hindflanks.

"I hope I did not leave out anything important," Myrania said, noticing the rove of Nuroc's eyes. "Someone set a torch to the servants' quarters while I was packing your things. I left in a hurry."

Nuroc said, "This is more than I thought I would be leaving with. Thank you."

Myrania slid down from her saddle to help lead the horses to the clearing. Despite the gravity of the situation, Nuroc could not help but feast his eyes on the lithe figure of the young woman. She was several years his senior, and for as long as he could remember he

41

had loved her, secretly, for he knew it was forbidden for a sorceress to marry a commoner. She had always looked upon him as a child, he felt, and he was forever wondering about the ways he might impress her. Several nights before he had seen the first sign of a change. When Myrania had listened to him recount his strange experience the night of the cataclysm, he had seen her eyes linger on him, although he had pretended not to notice. And now she was walking beside him through the pines, the lingering scent of her perfume making his heart race with excitement. As they started through the last of the pines, she suddenly stopped and moved in front of him, staring at his chest.

"You're bleeding," she said, reaching out and pulling aside the collar of Nuroc's tunic.

"I hadn't noticed," he stammered, looking down at the slim fingers that stroked his flesh around the wound. He saw his skin prickle at her touch and his face turned red with embarrassment. He tried to avert his gaze, but in looking up he saw Myrania's eyes turned up toward him, filled with emotion.

"I'll miss you, Nuroc," she said.

Nuroc was left speechless. Myrania drew close to him and her maddening scent assailed his nostrils as she grazed his cheek with her lips. When she stepped back, she was smiling, although her eyes told of sadness and regret. "We should go," she said simply, giving tug to the reins and leading her horse through the last of the pines. Nuroc followed, still dazed by the encounter.

Stromthroad and Thouris exchanged greetings with Myrania before she hugged her father.

"Were there any problems?" Inkemisa asked her.

"As I told Nuroc, the plunderers set fire to the servants' quarters while I was packing their things. Fortunately, they did their torching at the front, and I was able to reach the stables before the horses had bolted from their stalls in panic." Myrania looked to Stromthroad and Thouris. "Your horses had been stolen, no doubt by other servants fleeing the city. I hope that our own will prove adequate."

"But you are not going with us?" Thouris asked, suddenly alarmed.

Inkemisa shook his head. "We must return to the obelisk. Once the looters have fled, I must see to it that the gateway and portals are sealed against further entry should memories of tonight grow dim and petty thieves begin to think a fortune awaits anyone willing to retrieve it. Do not worry. We will be all right."

Nuroc and Myrania stole glances at one another, and he cursed the restraint he had used in his dealings with her over the years. Had he only known her true feelings. When his father came toward him, he handed him the reins to one of the horses and climbed into the saddle of the other, a dappled mount with a full black mane that swayed lightly in the breeze.

As Stromthroad helped Thouris onto her mount, Inkemisa continued, "There are hunting paths that run through the pines, parallel to the road below but still far enough away that you may travel unseen and unheard if you are cautious. Should you run into anyone, you must present yourselves with new identities. You face death as servants and shepherd to Talmon-Khash, and so long as you carry his life in your blood, you must survive at any cost."

"But we have never been beyond the land of the king," Thouris moaned fearfully, trembling in the saddle. "How are we to survive?"

As Stromthroad mounted his horse and cantered to his wife's side, Inkemisa took a step forward and told them firmly, "You will survive because you have to. That is the way of the world. You must turn a deaf ear to despair and fear and listen only to those instincts that will aid in your survival. Your wits will develop just as a soldier develops his muscles in the training yard. Live! Embrace life and pass it on to your children." He turned so that Nuroc fell into the range of his scrutinous gaze. "It is your calling, your duty. You three carry within you the future of Dorban. Never let

43

that fact escape your minds. Now, go! If you ride through the night, dawn will find you far from Cothe and those who might recognize you."

With that, Inkemisa turned and took his daughter's hand, leading her back across the clearing toward the entrance to the tunnel. Myrania turned back a moment, matching the longing expression fixed on Nuroc's face. Nuroc watched until they were gone from sight, then guided his horse alongside his father, who was comforting Thouris. Stromthroad's eyes were misty with heavy emotion as well, and Nuroc felt a tug at his heart at the sight of them.

"These will be the last of our tears," Stromthroad said. "Once we turn our horses about and leave from Cothe, we must resolve to be strong and live up to the trust of our king."

Thouris nodded, blinking her eyes dry. Nuroc took a deep breath and willed himself to be strong. They looked down the hill one final time, staring at the fiery skull of Cothe, then reined their horses about and rode back into the pines. Stromthroad led them, followed by Thouris. Nuroc took up the rear, one hand on the reins, the other on the hilt of his knife. A thousand feelings dashed through his mind as he rode, ducking under the pine branches until they reached the hunting paths. He was leaving one life behind and heading uncertainly toward another, with the promise of an important destiny ringing in his ears. He would seek out that destiny and fulfill it, he resolved, then he would return and seek out Myrania. He would claim her for his own, and in light of his achievements no one would dare say he did not deserve her hand.

Once the trail wound its way to a straighter course, the canopy of pines thinned out and they had a glimpse of the sky overhead. The partial moon cast its light on the surrounding stars, and Nuroc could see the outline of Dorban. It seemed to him that the condor-god was staring down at him with its eye half-opened in a look of sorrow and anxiety.

44

"Fear not, Dorban," Nuroc whispered to himself. "I will prove worthy." He repeated the words continually as they rode through the night. By dawn he believed them.

part two

LAST CHANTS

Four

Although Inkemisa's prediction for the fate of Dorban was mere conjecture and not a prophecy based on a chant-inspired vision or consultation with the proffax blossom dreamers of Numeria, all that he foresaw that fateful night at the outskirts of Cothe came to pass in the five years that followed the overthrow of the capital.

Augage fled to the western peninsula with a handful of sorcerers loyal to his cause. Together they tamed the hill tribes and brought them under his rule. A palace and temple were erected to the north, near the rim of the long dead volcano Velley, the eye of the continent. Augage called his kingdom Ghetite, from the magetongue word for "usurper." His subjects labored hard to make the land fertile and self-sufficient, for no one else on the continent would deal with the likes of sorcerers.

Elsewhere, other new kingdoms sprouted from the riot-torn soil as various factions sought to carve their own nations. Along the coast just north of Ghetite, farmers worked the rich earth of Shangora. To the east was Eldoth, of the ranging deserts and merchant barons. Belgore formed the lower jaw of Dorban, clinging to the sea and taking its wealth from her shores.

That left Aerda, the central kingdom, with its borders touching every other country, save for the uninhabited iceland of Drysk to the distant north. With so much of its territory requiring a vigilant eye, it was no mere coincidence that Aerda came under rule of the military. One in three men who lived under the shield

*of Aerda were soldiers, and many of those who did not
bear arms were still involved in the support of the military. Most important were the miners, charged with
culling from the heart of the Kanghat Mountains
enough raw ore to be forged into the weapons of
gleaming metal that far surpassed those made by
neighboring kingdoms in both strength and design. The
most productive of the mines was near the hamlet of
Wheshi, where hundreds of workers toiled at the rich
vein buried in the central Kanghats, extracting ore at a
pace to keep up with the demands of the military. If
Cothe, reconstructed over the years to suit the tastes of
a new ruling class, was considered the head of Aerda,
Wheshi was the heart. . . .*

Tar-soaked torches set in copper sconces bathed the
caves with a yellow glow as the mining crew labored to
fill the last of three wooden carts with chunks of rock
flecked with traces of mineral. The men were drenched
in their own sweat, streaked with the grime of their ex-
ertion. They worked silently, save for the grunts that
pushed through their clenched teeth each time the pick
or hammer was brought slamming hard against the
cavern walls, bidding these rich-veined bowels of the
Kanghats to yield forth more of their treasures.

Most of the miners were middle-aged, strong men
with broad chests and arms rippling with firm biceps
that told of years spent in the mines, swinging the pick
and pushing cart after cart of ore to the surface. Nuroc
worked among them, muscular yet still lean of build.
He made up in height what he lacked in girth. His hair,
beneath the layered grime, was light as straw, and his
gray eyes, as was often the case these days, held a
faraway gaze as he chipped at the scalloped walls of
the cave with listless strokes of the pick. His lips were
curled in an expression of displeasure.

Beside him Stromthroad paused from his work,
wiping the sweat off his brow with a scrap of cloth

from his belt. White streaks had crept into his beard, but there was much life and vitality in his face.

"Put your back to it, Nuroc," he chided good-naturedly, dark eyes glistening as he grinned at the younger man. "We're miners here, not sculptors."

The other miners laughed. One of the younger men, Peutor, stroked his chin with the back of his hand and chortled, "Let the boy be, Stromthroad. Maybe he'll carve us out a stone wench to feast our eyes on."

Peutor's twin brother, Fromm, sneered between heaves of his pick, "You're already wed to a stone wench, Peutor. Why bother with another, eh?" The two brothers were constant adversaries, forever at odds. They worked on either side of the middle cart. Hearing the jibe, Peutor fumed and leaned over, shoving several of the ore-laden nuggets off the top of the cart at his brother. Startled, Fromm was struck on the thigh by one of the rocks before he could move out of the way. Cursing as he flung down his pick, Fromm charged around the cart and caught his fingers around the collar of Peutor's jupon. They glared at one another, face to face, like a mirrored image.

"What did you say, brother?" Fromm snarled threateningly.

Peutor laughed in his brother's face, pushing Fromm to the ground. As the two men grappled in the dirt, cocking arms and trading rough punches with their thick fists, they both grinned like mischievous school-boys, fighting more in play than earnest. The other miners fell in around them, cheering on the fracas.

"Enough!" Stromthroad bellowed, pushing his way through the others. He reached for the collars of both brothers and yanked hard, prying them apart. He caught a few punches from both sides before Peutor and Fromm dropped their arms to their sides and tried to hide their smirks behind looks of chastisement.

"You heard what he said about my wife," Peutor said petulantly. "I had no choice but to defend her honor.

"Never mind that," Stromthroad admonished. "You

51

two would fight over claims about the weather if you ran out of other excuses. And as for the rest of you," he continued, turning his baleful gaze on the men around him. "We still have one more cart to fill before we can crawl from this wretched hole. I, for one, can do without seeing the time spent wrestling like children in the dirt. What about you, men?"

"Take heart, Stromthroad," the eldest of the miners, Yordat, said as the others fell back to their labors. "It is the first day of the Festival. You must expect the men to brace slightly at the bit."

"True," Stromthroad said, facing the older man. "But if they are in so much of a hurry to celebrate, it would seem they would want to see our work finished early, not late."

"Do not expect logic of youth," the older man advised, groaning as he tightened his grip on his hammer and chisel. As Yordat turned back to his work, Stromthroad walked back to Nuroc's side. Nuroc was watching him, the hint of a smile now pressed against his lips.

"Is there something amusing I should know about, son?" Stromthroad asked.

"No, Father. Not at all." Still the grin remained on Nuroc's face.

Stromthroad commenced chipping away more fragments from the cave wall and knocking loose dirt from the ore before tossing it into the partially filled cart. Nuroc matched his father's output, blow for blow, nugget for nugget, until at last the cart was heaped high with the day's haul.

"Praised be the gods of the dirt!" Peutor howled at the sight. "We're done for the day!"

The miners placed their tools in holds built into the sides of the carts as a team of work horses was led into the caves from their grazing outside. There were six of the beasts, thick of build with large hooves and great flowing manes. Two horses were hitched up to each cart, then led by several of the miners up the gentle grade leading to the surface. The other men lagged behind, quaffing their thirsts with cool water bubbling up from an underground spring.

Once they had drunk their share, Stromthroad and Nuroc started up to the surface, walking ahead of the others. Nuroc's grin had faded back to a partial scowl, and his father noticed the change.

"What is gnawing at your mind, Nuroc?" Stromthroad finally asked. "For weeks now you've slacked off at the mines whenever I stop goading you to work hard."

Nuroc was reluctant to answer, but as they drew closer to the mouth of the tunnel he finally blurted out, "This is not the destiny I had in mind for myself. I'm sick of battling cave walls and spending the days in this cursed darkness."

"Is that all?" Stromthroad asked, smiling. "Do you think that the rest of us enjoy the work, perhaps?"

"You like it well enough," Nuroc said, his voice surly.

"I'm glad you know my mind so well, son."

"Don't be angry with me," Nuroc pleaded, changing his tone. "I just want to see what there is beyond the caves and Lake Wheshi and our small village. Five years we have lived here, trapped behind picks and afraid to look at strangers for fear of being recognized. It wearies me." Nuroc kicked at the dirt beneath his feet. A spark came to his eyes as his distant gaze seemed to focus on some imagined wonder. "I hear the stories from those who have been elsewhere and it fills me with envy. I want to go and find some stories of my own, see things that will dazzle my mind! The destiny Talmon-Khash told me of awaits somewhere out there, not here. I know it! I have to seek it out."

Stromthroad sighed as they emerged from the caves and squinted their eyes against the sudden brightness of the late-day sun. The path down which the horse-drawn carts were led bisected the thin strip of grazing pasture, and Stromthroad led his son off through the hardy grass to a fallen log. He bade Nuroc to sit down beside him, and together they watched as the other miners ran past the pastures to the cove that lay beyond. A curved beach embraced Lake Wheshi in its sandy arms, and the men dove pleasurably into the chilled waters, rinsing off the dirt they carried from the mines.

Nuroc's gaze soon strayed back to the hills surrounding the mouth of the cave. There, amidst the scattering of foliage, armed soldiers held their guard at strategic positions behind rocks and thick jaunwoods, weapons tensed and ready. They were in the hire of King Pencroft, who had stationed them in the mountains as a precaution against raids that Shangoran hill tribes had been making on the mines of late. Several groups of the soldiers descended from their watchposts and fell in beside the ore carts, guarding them during the passage to the loading docks a quarter of a mile away. Nuroc watched the precision of the soldiers with a mixture of envy and admiration.

"Nuroc," Stromthroad finally said, plucking up a blade of grass and picking at it with his soiled fingers. "We have been through this argument many times before. I know you wish to enlist in the military, but I cannot allow it so long as Pencroft sits on the throne of Aerda. He knows your face from his years as general under Talmon-Khash. You know of his present hatred for the old order. Only last month he chanced to cross paths with Whistoff, servant to Inkemisa before the cataclysm. You heard what happened. Whistoff had grown a beard and moustache and was standing five rows back during a call to inspection by the king. Still Pencroft spotted him. . . ." Stromthroad paused to toss away the blade of grass and face his son. "Now, can you truly say that you wish to run the risk of having your bleached skull riding a post next to that of Whistoff in the royal courtyard?"

"Yes," Nuroc said determinedly, "I'll take that risk and others if need be, but I tell you, Father, my calling lies beyond the boundaries of Wheshi. Let me seek it out. You and Mother have two more children now carrying the blood of Talmon-Khash, so if I were to

54

die they would still be able to continue his link with the living, along with you and Mother. But, I assure you, I have no plans to die before I have met my fate and seen its hand dealt—"

"Enough," Stromthroad said, rising from the log and starting through the grass toward the cove. "If you will see us through the end of the season, you may go, with my blessing, provided that you pursue a life out of the military and far from the capital. That will still leave you with many options. There is the sea, or the merchant caravans. They are always in need of another hand."

Nuroc bounded to his feet and circled in front of his father. His eyes were filled with shock and wondrous surprise. "I can go?" he said excitedly. "You understand?"

Stromthroad smiled weakly. "I understood all along, Nuroc. Do you think I was born an old man? I know the yearnings of youth. I know the mind of my own son. I was waiting for the day when you would speak to me of your dreams as a man instead of a child. That day has come."

Nuroc flashed a joyous smile as he embraced Stromthroad.

"Thank you, Father," he said. "From now till the end of the season you'll never have to coax me into doing my best, I promise you. I'll be the finest miner in all of Wheshi. You'll see. I'll load up a whole cart on my own and—"

Stromthroad interrupted his son with a laugh and slapped Nuroc on the back, pushing him away. "Spare me the boasting, Son. Be your best and it will be good enough for me. Now, go dunk yourself in the cove with the others. I'll join you once I check on the carts down by the docks."

Nuroc nodded, then turned and ran the distance to the cove. There was a tilted jaunwood that leaned out over the water, and he scrambled up its trunk and lunged out from the first limb, landing with a splash amidst the other miners. Surfacing, he whooped triumphantly and spat seawater at the brothers Peutor and Fromm, who treaded water nearby.

"Why the change of heart, Nuroc?" Peutor asked. "Did your father promote you to stableboy for the horses?"

Fromm laughed and splashed water back at Nuroc.

"You two will be the last to know," Nuroc taunted before turning on his side and swimming out toward the edge of the cove, where large rocks rose from the waters and were surrounded by the breaking foam of lapping waves. The twins followed in pursuit and all three climbed the moss-slick sides of the boulders to a spot where they could oversee the whole lake. The sun beat down with the last of its daily glory, and the youths could feel their skin dry under the welcome rays.

Accompanied by the surrounding sounds and scents, basking on the rocks was an experience without rival, a treat to the senses, a breeding ground for the dreams of young men. For generations, the miners of Wheshi had sought out the inspiration of the cove and its rocky point to give balance to the soul-numbing drudgery of the mines, and so long as the Kanghats held in their heart more of the precious ore craved by farmers and militia alike, there would be sons and grandsons who would come here to rest on the carpet of algae and let their minds wander.

Nuroc's thoughts raced like stallions in countless directions as he pondered his future. To leave Wheshi would be in itself an achievement. North, east, south, west—wherever he steered his horse he would find adventure and excitement. The secret lay in determining which course might lead him to his destiny. All corners of the continent, save for the forbidden turf of Ghetite, beckoned to him. Shangora bade him to climb its steep mountains and ride rampant through its lush meadows. The sands of Eldoth whispered promises of sights such as he'd never before seen—strange beasts that lived off the desert and hapless merchants who strayed too far from trading routes. Belgore offered him the sea and the sail, as well as inland jungles, dense with exotic fauna and eyes that glowed like embers in the darkened shadows. Even his own country lay before him, begging to be explored. Aerda had elements of all the other countries, touching as it did the sea, desert, jungles, and verdant flatlands. He would have to begin narrowing down his choices now. It was already late summer. In a few months snow would descend upon the Kanghats and turn the earth too cold and firm to be efficiently worked. With snow would come his freedom.

"So, then, Nuroc," Fromm pried, pushing at a growth of barnacles with his toes. "Out with this secret that has you smiling like the fox who's snatched the hen."

Nuroc shook his head and flicked wet pebbles out into the pounding surf.

"Perhaps he needs encouragement," Peutor said slyly, looking to his brother. They were sitting on either side of Nuroc. Together they reached out to grab him by the arms. He was prepared for their mischief, however, and he quickly sprang to his feet and stepped clear of their outreached hands. Knees bent, he was about to dive back into the cove when he suddenly stopped. Fromm and Peutor noticed his awkward pose and turned their heads to see what he was looking at.

A ship had rounded the point, its sails filled with the gusty winds blowing across the lake. It was a modest craft, riding low in the waters, with almost its entire deck enclosed by walls and rows of rounded portals. Young boys in their early teens scrambled about the deck and masts like roving monkeys, wearing only ragged loincloths. A dozen women strode the narrow band of walkway surrounding the central structure, their hands on the railing as they watched the shoreline. They were dressed in an array of fine-spun silks and brightly dyed cottons that ruffled about them in the breeze. As their eyes fell upon the youths, who were some thirty yards away, several of the women smiled and waved. Others pursed their lips and blew kisses while running their slender fingers along the drapery that veiled their lush bodies.

"Ho-ho!" Peutor cried out, "A whoreship bound for the docks." Both he and Fromm gained their feet and waved with fervor at the women.

"You, with the light hair!" Peutor called out, cupping his hands about his mouth to amplify his words. "Save yourself for me! Peutor's my name, and I please women like no other!"

The blonde-haired woman aboard the ship laughed with the others around her, then shouted back, "It's coins that please me most, fair Peutor. Come to the docks and we'll see if there's truth to your boasting!"

"For the same price he'll give you," Fromm insisted loudly, "I'll teach you things you've yet to learn from a dozen men!"

"Lies!" Peutor cried out. "Pay him no heed. We may look the same to you now, but once I've shed my tunic you'll favor my sword to his puny dagger!"

As the women aboard the ship turned to one another and burst out with another round of mirth, the twins turned to one another, exchanging blows and stumbling off the curved slope of the rocks into the waters of the cove. Carried by the wind, the whoreship slowly drifted past.

Nuroc had watched on all this time in silence. He had never traded his wages for the likes of those women who descended upon the mining docks each month when the miners were paid, but he had been unable to turn a deaf ear to the ringing tales told between blows of the ax inside the caves by the other workers. The amorous couplings they told of both repelled and intrigued him, for he had yet to partake of the joys of a woman's naked embrace.

Even as he was reflecting upon the reason for his years of restraint from the lure of temptresses, that reason was revealed to him in a sudden glimpse. Staring at the starboard quarter of the retreating vessel, he was stunned by the sight of one of the women. Standing apart from the others, her eyes were on the faint wake

58

trailing from the wooden scull. Her arms were folded before her and Nuroc could detect only a portion of her profile beneath the sumptuous flow of her dark hair. But his heart was stirred and for several seconds he gaped disbelievingly at her, doubting his vision and yet at the same time begging it to be true.

"Myrania!" he finally shouted, although the words came out in a strained squeak. He called out again, but the boat had drifted too far, and the woman aboard gave no indication that she had heard his cry.

Frantic, Nuroc crouched and hurled himself headlong into the waters, surfacing immediately and sweeping his arms in great strokes against the lake's rolling swells.

"Where are you going, Nuroc?" Fromm called out, pushing his brother away from him and treading water. Nuroc swam on, making slight headway against the current.

"Why not walk to the docks like the rest of us?" Peutor called out, laughing. "You don't even have anything to pay with, you fool!"

Once he was clear of the cove, Nuroc started to swim along the swells instead of against them. He made better time, but already the whoreship had pulled far beyond his reach. Even aboard a fast-traveling skiff he would not be able to overtake the craft before it reached the mining docks, visible several hundred yards down the shore. Nuroc let up with his fierce thrashing and watched the boat a moment more before turning back, his mind boiling with a thousand questions that would have to wait for answers.

Five

The mining camp and loading docks were both located along the northern shore of Lake Wheshi, where the waters were deep enough to allow for the passage of wide-hulled carriers that would haul the loaded ore to the Targoan River and then down its bending course to Cothe, where the blacksmiths would forge it into tools and weaponry.

A number of the Aerdan militia were scattered about the sprinkling of small shanties and the warehouse that had been converted into their barracks. Their weapons were visible, but not in hand. The camp was situated in the center of a vast clearing that stretched between sea and mountain, and there could be no assault that came without sufficient warning for them to take up their arms. Also, the raiders had yet to be so brazen as to strike at the camps. Their strategy had always involved stealth and ambush, usually along the narrow paths that wound through the mountains between the camp and the mines.

At one corner of the camp, a group of soldiers sat under the shade of an aged oak, eating fresh fruit they had purchased from a squat, grizzled peddler. The vendor, Solat, now stood before them, attaching a feedbag to the head of his donkey as he lectured the men over his shoulder.

"And there is surely not one among you who truly believes for a moment that these are mere hill tribes raiding your mines, is there?" He paused to let his words take effect. His gritty voice was curious in its inflection. Mastery of many dialects made his a speech borrowed from each. Once he had secured the feedbag, he waddled over to the saddlebags draped over the beast's swayed back. Coins jingled in the pockets of his ragged smock as he reached into one of the bags and withdrew a parchment scroll and unrolled it, revealing a map of the continent. As he continued to speak, his stubby finger swept across the area on the map depicting the area surrounding Wheshi and the border between Aerda and Shangora. "Devil soldiers they be," he continued, "in the pay of the Ghetites. You mine the ore and they steal it to use against you."

There was a murmuring amongst the soldiers as they looked at one another and chuckled lightly. Several spit seeds and pits from their fruit in Solat's direction. He glared at the gesture and leaned closer to the men, raising his voice. "Do you doubt it? Well, you best wisen fast, lads, for the mountains are crawling with these devil soldiers. All the way along your northern borders they hide in the Kanghats, stealing ore, forging weapons, and waiting. Soon, too soon, the black moon will be upon us, and the trumpets of war will sound from Velley to Lamaine. Devil soldiers will flow down from the mountains like lava. Cities will burn. Many will die. To the east, Eldoth will fall even as siege is laid to Cothe. With Eldoth gone to Shangora—yes, none can doubt that Shangora and Ghetite are wed in sorcerous alliance—I tell you that when Shangora sweeps into Eldoth, they will join Ghetite in forming a mighty hand in whose palm rests Aerda and all the southern provinces."

Solat eyed the soldiers, but could see they were still skeptical, if not amused. Undaunted, he rummaged through his pockets and pulled forth a ripe tomato. Setting the map aside, he held the tomato forth in his palm and slowly crushed it, letting the juice drain down his fingers to the ground so that it looked as if his hand were bleeding. "This," he warned, "will be the fate of Aerda if the Ghetites and Shangorans are allowed to make good their plans. They mean to carve an empire of Dorban, with Augage of Ghetite crowned ruler of all!"

However, none but Solat himself were swept up by his words. The soldiers smirked louder, then burst into a chorus of derisive laughter.

"Your talents are ill-spent, peddler," one of them called out. "With your vast knowledge of Dorban's affairs, you could be a general!"

Another soldier interjected, "Nay. A king he could be. Solat, King of Tall Tales."

Soon the others joined in a mocking chant.

"Hail, King Solat!"

"I tell the truth!" Solat shouted at them.

A coin was thrown at his feet. Looking into the crowd, Solat saw that the soldier who had first taunted him held two more silver pieces in his hand.

"That was for the tomato, old man," the soldier laughed. "It's these for a story filled with wenches. Those be the tomatoes meant for squeezing."

The others whooped with pleasure at the joke, further irritating the peddler. He wiped his hand on the smock and ground the coin into the dirt beneath his booted heel. "You'll learn soon enough," he muttered bitterly. "Soon enough."

The confrontation was interrupted by loud exclamations from the docks. Heads turned and the soldiers scrambled to their feet with excitement.

"The whoreship!" one hailed. "And not a day too soon!"

Another winked lasciviously at Solat. "Never mind with stories of wenches, old man. We'll have our fill of the real thing now!"

In a mad rush, soldiers from all parts of the camp converged upon the docks, aiding the whoreship to its mooring as they ogled over the women on the deck and began shouting out their bids. Faces soon peered out through the portals, drawing renewed cries from the men. The door to the ship's main chamber opened, and out strode a diminutive man in robes of satin and a leather skullcap. He had large eyes filled with grim malice as he took in the soldiers. Behind him emerged two giants, each one a head taller than any of the soldiers, wearing only loincloths so that the bulging muscles that lined their glistening torsos further told of their brute strength. If their presence alone was insufficient to bring the soldiers into line, each of the bodyguards held chain leashes affixed to the collars of trained Shangoran lions. The four-legged beasts strode the deck on either side of the small man, their faces calmly taking in the throng on the docks. At the slightest provocation, the lions could be counted on to bring death to whomever the man in satin pointed. The soldiers knew this from previous experience and fell silent as the boat was moored and a plank was extended to the docks by the agile youths, who eyed the soldiers with sly smiles and winking eyes.

"Half the women will come ashore here," the whoremaster called out in a high-pitched voice void of emotion. "The others will go across the lake to town and sell their favors at the tavern."

There was a grumbling of discontent amongst the soldiers at this news. The price of a wench's time ran high enough when a hundred men were bidding over the usual three dozen women. With only half that number to be haggled for, it was certain that the fee for pleasure would be much higher. A week's wage for an hour's dalliance was not an uncommon bid under such circumstances.

Half of the women already on deck were joined by another dozen from within the vessel's quarters. They came in every variety and to suit every taste. Their eyes were hard except when they were trained on a prospective client, and then they turned soft and inviting, offering the fulfillment of every desire. While the whoremaster Sphextay remained on deck, his oversized bodyguards walked their beasts down the plank, clearing a spot on the docks. One by one the eighteen women followed until they filled the clearing. One of the giants pushed the plank back aboard the vessel and untied it from its moorings. Oars appeared through

63

holes in the sides of the ship and unseen slaves rowed the ship away from the docks. The whoremaster stared at the soldiers and called out, "Enjoy them as you wish, but death comes to he who harms one of my lovelies. I shall return in the morning before we set sail to Thutchers. Until then, may your observance of the Festival be pleasurable."

Once the boat was far out into the lake, heading toward the distant shore and the hamlet of Wheshi, one of the lumbering giants motioned to one of the women, a dark-skinned beauty in a gossamer shift that did little to conceal her supple flesh as she stepped up on a small keg.

"Nyathiesse, from Eldoth," the giant said in a deep, baritone voice. "She has danced in royal halls before kings and princes. Great is her agility and grace. If you are not well rested you'd do best to pass on her favors."

Nyathiesse scanned the men before her, her thin lips drawn tight into a coquettish smirk. She turned to and fro, undulating her limbs with a fluidity that brought forth moans of desire from the ranks. Several hands were raised upwards.

"Five lampich!" came the first bid.

The giants looked at one another and laughed.

"Seven!" shouted another.

"Ten!"

"Twelve. A day's wage!"

"Fifteen!"

As the bidding escalated, back at the camp the miners arrived with their daily haul of ore accompanied by the mounted guard that had supervised their passage through the mountains. The miners had dried off from their dip in the cove, and they let out their own cries of jubilation at the sight of the women standing on the docks, next to the galley that would carry their ore to Cothe.

Stromthroad and Nuroc were walking side-by-side at the head of the procession. Seeing the boat,

Stromthroad asked his son, "You're certain it was her?"

"It was difficult to see," Nuroc said, "but I thought so. But I can't believe she would have come to this!" His voice carried a note of despair and anguish. Much as he craved to see Myrania, to know she was among women who serviced the riverports of the Targoan was a prospect that tore at his heart. He begged it not to be so.

Other miners were already rushing past them toward the paymaster's tent, in hopes of securing their pay in time to squander it on one of the courtesans on the docks.

"You'd best check, then," Stromthroad said, nodding toward the docks. "I'll see to your pay for you."

"Thanks," Nuroc said excitedly, breaking into a run across the bare earth of the camp and raising dust in his wake. Because the other miners had to stop by the paymaster's tent for their wages, he easily outraced them to the docks.

Half the women already had been bid off and they stood to one side, awaiting the moment when their fellow courtesans would all be spoken for and the festivities would be transferred to the barracks. There the women would see to their first clients while bids were being taken for the second round, to take place after supper. In all, each of the courtesans would sell their pleasures to five men through the course of the night, then spend the next day traveling to the next riverpost in Thutchers and repeating the ritual. The money to be earned matched that of the wealthiest merchants, but it was seldom the reason the women wandered into the profession. Most were runaways, lured by the whoremaster Sphextay's promise of security and protection from the grimmer fates that awaited loners ill-equipped to defend themselves. It was the thought that Myrania had tumbled to such a state that weighed so heavily on Nuroc as he desperately searched for her amongst those gathered on the docks.

The woman who now stood upon the bartering keg

looked similar to Myrania, but she was dressed differently from the woman Nuroc had seen on the boat. Hers was a garb of pure white, tight-fitting about the outline of her voluptuous torso and ending at midthigh, so that soldiers were bending low in hopes their lurid gazes might land upon a free glimpse of hidden flesh.

Concerned, Nuroc nudged the soldier beside him and asked, "Where is the ship these women came on? Weren't there others besides these?"

The soldier turned and nodded impatiently, "Sphextay's taken half the wenches to town, the scoundrel!" He raised his hand and shouted to the giants, "Fifteen lampich for her!" Beneath his breath he muttered, "You robbing cutthroats. Any other time I could have her at half the price."

"Sixteen!" shouted another soldier.

"Eighteen!" the man beside Nuroc spat angrily, glancing at the handful of coins in his palm. He looked to the other bidder and pleaded, "It's all I have. Have a heart!"

The other soldier looked back at him and smiled maliciously. He turned to the giants and called out, "Twenty lampich I give you for her!" To the man beside Nuroc he added, "Perhaps you can have her the second time for eighteen."

Dejected, Nuroc stepped back from the others and cast a final look at the women. *Not you, Myrania,* he thought to himself. *Don't be among the others, I beg you.*

He walked to the other end of the docks, where men were loading the day's ore into the holds of a large galley, using ramps and shovels to hasten the task. Needing something to take his mind off his worries, he fell in beside the workers, pushing the carts up loading ramps once they were unhitched from the horses. He could recognize some of the chunks of rock he had chiseled from the walls by the pattern of mineral in the stone. How strange, he thought it, that those streaks of color could be transformed into blades with strong,

66

sharp edges that could sever limbs and hack through bucklers of hard wood with the ease of an oar through water. It seemed to him an act that rivaled some of the chants he recalled from his youth in Cothe, when he saw the acolytes under Talmon-Khash practice their newly acquired talents in far corners of the sorcerers' gardens.

Once he had finished helping with the loading, Nuroc stood on the docks and watched the last of the bidding for the courtesans. Some of the miners had joined in, including Peutor, who was making his offers for the wench he'd called out to back at the cove. His brother was bidding against him out of spite, and when a third party outbid the both of them, the twins turned on one another, each accusing the other of raising the bidding to the point where neither could afford the price. They came to blows, fighting in the midst of the soldiers, many of whom were also irritated at having been denied a chance for the first bedding of the courtesans because of the steep price of the bidding. Tempers raced through the crowd and soon the docks were a tempest of fist-flying fury. Curses were shouted and several men were wrestled over the edge and into the deep waters of the port.

The women retreated behind the two giants and their leashed lions. When the fighting escalated to the point that blades were being unsheathed, each giant uttered a single word to his beast and the lions gave forth ferocious growls through bared teeth. As the giants pulled on the chain leashes, the beasts reared slightly and swiped at the air with their deadly paws. The demonstration by the beasts was threatening enough to suppress the riotous throng until ranking officers could reach the scene and lend their own threats to the tableau.

Order restored, the men dispersed from the docks. The winning bidders made straight for the barracks, rubbing their hands together in anxious anticipation. Soldiers grumbled back to their posts and luckless miners trudged down the docks to the longboat that would take them back to Wheshi. Peutor and Fromm, still feuding, rubbed bruises from their various scraps and fell in beside Nuroc.

"We'll take to the tavern tonight, then," Fromm said, "and we'll do our bidding for different women. Perhaps we can sneak them away and trade off rather than paying for second rounds, eh?"

"A fine idea so long as the first pick is mine," Peutor said, inspecting a scrape on his elbow that bled continually. "After all, I'd have had my lover already if you hadn't stepped in and—"

"Let's not start on that again, dear brother," Fromm said snidely as they reached the boat and climbed in. The craft was long and narrow, comprised of little more than continuous rows of oar benches, each one made for two rowers. Half the benches were filled, and Nuroc paused on the docks to make sure Fromm and Peutor took up places far from where he would sit. He'd heard enough of their trying banter for one day, especially with regards to women. He looked back to the shore, where his father was next in line at the paymaster's tent.

There, a row of attentive guards flanked a pot-bellied officer with the foul scent of stale wine lingering on his thick lips as he dipped his fingers into a dust-covered chest. He gave each of the miners four identical coins. Lampich they were, the coins of the realm, stamped silver with the king's profile on one side and the Shield of Aerda on the other.

There was a moment's hesitation as Stromthroad spoke to the paymaster, then pointed to his son. From the docks, Nuroc waved back. The officer sneered and muttered something to Stromthroad, who in turn spoke back firmly. With a stifled belch, the officer gave Stromthroad eight coins and waved him away.

Nuroc was about to turn back to the boat when he noticed, out of the corner of his eye, the fleeting sweep of a shadow across the packed dirt of the campground. Placing a hand over his eyes to block the sun's rays, he looked up.

Framed against the ragged tatters of thin clouds, a magnificent condor circled above the lake, gliding on its outstretched wings. The effortless grace of its flight was impressive, and Nuroc stared in unconcerned awe until he saw the bird suddenly drift from its course and swoop downward, talons stretched out. It was diving straight for him, he realized, and he reflexively dove off the docks seconds before the talons would have torn into him.

He rose to the lake's surface close to the rowboat, and several of the other miners helped him aboard.

"Well done, condor-bait," Fromm jeered from his bench.

"I see it even runs in the family," Peutor added, looking to the shore, where the bird of prey was flapping its wings furiously as it hovered over Stromthroad. The miner had his sword out and was weaving it through the air to ward off the condor.

"I've never seen the likes of this," mumbled the old miner Yordat next to Nuroc. "It's not like the condor to attack men without provocation."

Nuroc watched his father struggling with the beast, feeling an uncertain sense of foreboding in the encounter. Yordat was correct. The condor never preyed on men and was even held sacred by those who still worshipped Dorban. In its earthly form, the bird was also favored by farmers, as it fed primarily on those small beasts of the wild that preyed on crops and livestock.

From the vicinity of the large oak, the peddler Solat urged his donkey forward, at the same time raising one arm and shouting out a series of unintelligible words. With a shriek, the condor snapped its beak another time at Stromthroad and then flew over to Solat, lighting on the peddler's outstretched arm. As Stromthroad watched, the peddler rode toward him, then dismounted from his donkey. The condor remained perched on Solat's covered wrist as the peddler pointed to Stromthroad's hand and began to converse with him in a low voice that Nuroc could not hear from the longboat.

Nuroc looked down at his own hand and fingered the talon ring given to him by Talmon-Khash. Long-dormant memories came back to him in a vivid rush, and he wondered further at the meaning of the condor's strange attack.

Behind him, Fromm shouted from his post at the rudder of the boat, "More haste, Stromthroad! You're in one piece. Dusk comes swiftly and I've lovers waiting for me at the tavern!"

To the west, the fiery tip of the setting sun was fast dipping behind the mountain peaks, sending long streamers of color the length of the horizon. In the eastern skies, Nuroc could barely detect the gibbous slice of the year's fifth moon; the moon fated for the first eclipse since the cataclysm.

Stromthroad waved a hand for the men in the boat to wait, all the while keeping his eyes on Solat as the shabby peddler continued to talk excitedly.

Peutor turned to his fellow miners and said, "Was it not Stromthroad who railed at us for dallying in the mines when he wished to rush home?"

"Aye," Fromm called out with a playful gleam in his eyes. "The same Stromthroad who now keeps us all waiting while he barters with a vagabond peddler with a bird fetish."

Peutor, standing poised near the starboard bow, leaned forward and unmoored the longboat from the docks, calling out, "Last chance to come aboard, Stromthroad!"

Stromthroad turned from Solat and shouted back, "Go on without me! I'll come across with the galley later this evening."

Concerned, Nuroc rose from his bench and started to move forward down the narrow aisle between the benches. Yordat, the old miner, reached out and gestured for him to sit down.

"But I have to see what my father is—"

"If he had wanted you ashore he would have said as much," Yordat scolded. "As it is, I've no wish to fall into the water here and see my brittle bones soaked and put to the twilight breeze. Sit down."

Nuroc reluctantly obliged as Peutor took his oar and used it to shove the boat clear of the docks. The other miners jabbed their oars at the water, guiding the boat out farther into the lake. Here the waves were far tamer than near the cove, and once their oar-play fell into rhythm the craft made good headway against the gentle pull of the tide.

The men rowed while facing the retreating camp, where Stromthroad continued to talk with the peddler Solat. Elsewhere, those soldiers not in a position to spend time with the traveling courtesans had resumed their positions and taken to various diversions from the boredom of their watch. Many fell into games of chance, like tossing cubes carved of bone in the dirt or hurling handknives at rounded targets on the trunks of trees, hoping to win sufficient lampich to stand a chance of earning time with one of the wenches during the latter rounds of bidding. Others made themselves comfortable at the base of other trees or large rocks and prepared to doze away the time until supper rations were distributed.

From the rudder, Fromm muttered bitterly, "I say *we* should stand guard against the hill raiders and let the army work the mines for a change."

"Good idea," Peutor hailed from the bow. "I'm tired of the way they lounge about while we slave away in the Kanghats. I say the king should add their pay to ours and let us defend ourselves. By the eye of Dorban, I'd wager I could outbattle any soldier at the camp, using my chisel against their fancy swords. Worthless, that's what they are!"

Tuledge, a fair-haired, clean-shaven man on the bench before Peutor, spoke up for the first time in a high, whining voice. "Not only that, but they also sneak across the lake to make love with our women!"

"Come now, Tuledge," Peutor chuckled. "It's not so easy to 'sneak' across this lake."

"But they do!" Tuledge protested. "I swear it. My

Lyiis has been acting strange since the troops came. I suspect she spends her days with a soldier."

The other miners laughed. Nuroc kept silent, however, feeling sorry for Tuledge, who was forever the brunt of jibes and insults from his fellow workers because of his slight frame and gentle features. He did not work the mines but rather tended to the horses that carried the ore carts to the loading docks at the end of the day.

"As I hear it," Peutor went on, winking to the rower beside him, "Lyiis's coolness is more likely due to your meetings with the school girl Hassiere."

"Liar!" Tuledge said petulantly.

"I've heard the same," Fromm countered from the rudder.

"I also," added Yordat.

"Lies! All lies!" Tuledge whimpered, close to tears. "I even know which soldier is guilty. The one with the red hair and no beard, who stands guard at the paymaster's tent. He eyes me each day."

Peutor grinned. "That might be because the affair he wishes is with you, woman face!"

At the insult, Tuledge threw down his oar and turned on Peutor. They grappled on the bench as the boat swerved slightly off course. The struggle was brief, for Peutor quickly overpowered the other man and flung him over the side, almost capsizing the boat in the process.

Tuledge thrashed to the surface, crying out curses on Peutor and the other miners, who continued to laugh as they rowed the boat away from him. Nuroc felt his anger rising, but held his tongue, knowing that any display of disapproval would only further the men's hunger for scapegoats and earn him a spot in the water alongside Tuledge.

Once Tuledge forsook his anger and began swimming in earnest, his firm, certain strokes made good headway in the calm waters. Still, as with Nuroc's earlier pursuit of the whoreship, his speed was no match for a bouyant craft. The men knew as much and lightened their oarplay to give him a chance to reach the boat.

"Yo," Fromm called out, looking past the rudder at Tuledge's approaching form. "Some sea beast is on our scent!"

Peutor stood up slightly and frowned as he glanced at the water. "Too slow for a sea lion," he mused. "Must be a river ox."

Fromm made no attempt to prevent Tuledge from grabbing hold of the wooden rudder cutting the boat's wake. He also made no effort to lend the other miner a hand onto the boat. He only smiled when Tuledge lost his hold and slipped back into the lake. Tuledge swore anew, spitting out more oaths between mouthfuls of water.

The curses seemed to have an effect. Aboard the rowboat, the men stopped laughing. Fromm, no longer grinning, took the oar handed him by Yordat and extended it to Tuledge bellowing "Look out . . . behind you!"

Treading water, Tuledge maneuvered about. Closing in on him was a chapyx, its caudal fin raised above the waterline. A deadly predator, more shark than eel and larger than either, the chapyx was the most feared creature dwelling in Dorban's inland lakes. Here in Wheshi, their schools for the most part kept to the uninhabited eastern shores, where sluggish sea cows and myriad fish made for the lake's best feeding. But occasionally a pack would stray from the feed beds and swim to other parts of the lake, menacing all who used the waters.

None of the miners bore arms, so they watched on in helpless horror as the chapyx converged on Tuledge.

"Noooooo!" Nuroc shouted out, bolting up from his bench, ripping his oar from its thule and lunging over the side of the boat toward Tuledge. He held the oar outright before him and rammed the blunt end of the handle into the tooth-lined jaws of the chapyx, just as those same jaws were about to clamp down on Tuledge.

Nuroc's momentum carried him over the other man's head and onto the waterbeast. He instinctively shoved the oar farther down the throat of the chapyx. The creature writhed viciously in the water, and with great swipes of its tail it attempted to thrash Nuroc away, but the youth sucked in one last lungful of air and clung all the harder to the beast as it plunged far beneath the surface. The water grew both darker and colder and Nuroc felt his breath being used up quickly in the effort to keep clear of the beast's jaws and tail without losing his hold.

As the pressure of the water began to throb against his temples, Nuroc gave one last shove of the oar and a trail of blood began to spew forth from between the lined jaws of the chapyx. After one final thrashing, the predator went limp in the waters. Nuroc let go of the beast and exhaled as he floated back toward the surface.

As the water about him began to clear, Nuroc saw fast-moving shadows approaching him from beneath the surface. To his shock, he realized it was a dozen more chapyx. There was no way he could fend off their assault, and he turned away from them and continued toward the surface in the desperate hope that he might outdistance them and reach the boat.

Once he could see the fading blue sky through the water, he stole a glance downward. The school had veered its course away from him, attracted instead by the blood of its own kind. They fell on the slain beast with merciless abandon, and the dead chapyx jerked in the reddening waters under the force of their jabbing bites.

With his attention on the raging pack, Nuroc did not notice the form swimming toward him until it was almost upon him. Caught off guard, he flailed out with the back of his hand and kicked his way to the surface, twenty yards from the longboat. Turning to face his attacker, Nuroc realized it was Tuledge, who now emerged and shook hair from his eyes. Blood trailed from where Nuroc had kicked him in the head.

"I kept diving for you," Tuledge gasped as he caught his breath. "I must have surprised you."

Nuroc nodded, then fell in beside Tuledge as they both began swimming back to the boat.

"I owe you my life," Tuledge said between strokes.

"You owe me nothing," Nuroc replied. "Let's get back before the other chapyx decide they've yet to have their fill."

Once they reached the longboat, several of the miners helped them aboard while the others leaned to one side to keep the boat stable. Both Nuroc and Tuledge glowered at the men, particularly Fromm and Peutor. They strode down the aisle to their benches. Someone handed Nuroc a spare oar and they all began to row.

Peutor finally broke the uneasy silence, looking to Tuledge and saying, "My apologies. It was an ill-chosen prank."

"Well put," Tuledge said, not looking up from his rowing. With a forced grin, he added, "Of course, it was no match for the ill-chosen prank your mother made, giving birth to you and your brother."

At this, the other miners snickered, relieving the tension. Even Peutor and Fromm were forced to laugh.

"So he's learned to dish it back," Fromm announced heartily. "Perhaps it was not a complete mistake."

As dusk continued to descend upon the horizon, the boat cut sleekly across the lake, away from the many fins that soon broke the surface near where Nuroc had slain the chapyx. Several of the creatures leapt into the air, letting the twilight glance off the wet sheen of their scales before they dove back into the tainted depths.

The men pulled harder on their oars, plying the craft against the rugged cross-current they encountered passing the point where Lake Wheshi flowed into the Targoan River. Beyond the delta lay the sand-strewn shores of their village, dotted with clumps of green wanyll reed and the bouncing forms of sandpipers.

"Faster, men!" Peutor called out. "I can almost hear singing in the streets! Pull those oars and think of the

75

heady ale and sweet women that await our pleasure in the tavern!"

Whoops of delight sounded amongst the others as the boat glided into the shallower waters near the shore. Nuroc thought of the women in the tavern, but it was not simple pleasure that weighed most in his mind.

Six

Dusk bled into the dark of night as the miners made their way along the roadway of paved flagstone leading to Wheshi. The small hamlet winked its lights far off down the road, but already the men could hear the singing and revelry that marked the first night of the Festival of the Black Moon, which would extend until the night that people throughout the land would witness the first eclipse since the cataclysm.

It had been King Pencroft's idea to mark the event as a time of celebration. He wished not so much to commemorate the cataclysm and the fall of sorcery as to glorify the birth of the nation he had forged together with remnants of the surviving militia he had commanded under Talmon-Khash. By decreeing that men and women rejoice in the coming eclipse, he further hoped to inspire a firm loyalty to Aerda and his rule. The rumors of war that Solat had whispered earlier that afternoon were mere echoes of the worried words that passed throughout the land, concerning Ghetite's designs on Aerda and the other kingdoms to the east. With the threat of foreign intervention so widely felt, Pencroft knew well the value of patriotic fervor on the homefront and hoped the festival might help fan the flames of that fervor.

In Wheshi, there were two sites, where the people were gathering to observe the event. Besides the town square, there was the games field at the edge of the hamlet, where the townsfolk staged sporting events and mock battles during the year for their leisurely amusement. The field was alive now with a scattering of bonfires, around which women and children danced in hand-held circles as they sang festive songs. While half the miners walked on toward the town, the others broke off and took an offshoot of the main road to the fields.

Nuroc ran ahead of the latter group, scanning the torchlit throng for his family. The closer he came to the site, the more his senses were bombarded with the impact of the celebration. Besides the songs and laughter and the sight of hundreds prancing about in carefree bliss, he could smell the vast quantities of food being readied for feasting. Whole pigs had been hoisted onto revolving spits over the smaller bonfires, and their scorched hides sizzled in the heat. Iron cauldrons, filled with chunks of meat and sliced vegetables boiling into a fine stew, rested on glowing coals. Women pulled loaves of fresh bread and cooked fowl from the outdoor hearths.

It was to the hearths that Nuroc went first. When he could not see his mother among the women, he asked someone where she was.

"Yonder, with the children," an old woman said, looking up from the table where she was slicing bread. "Here," she said, cutting Nuroc a sizable heel of the loaf. "You look as if you could use something to eat."

Nuroc nodded his thanks and excused his way through the clotted masses standing near the closest fire, waiting for a lutist and fifer to consult with each other over which song to play next. As he looked at the dozens of children playing at the edge of the crowd, he bit hungrily into the warm bread. It was soft in the center, filled with mild herbs and garlic. Three bites more and it was gone, leaving Nuroc with his appetite merely roused to full life.

Thouris sat amidst a group of younger children, holding an infant in her arms as she hummed a pleasant lullaby. Her eyes were closed and a serene smile was cast across her face as she rocked the sleeping toddler. The others were also asleep, or on the verge of it, laying in mounds of hay as they listened to Thouris. They seemed oblivious to the commotion about them, and none took notice of Nuroc's arrival.

There was a second woman sitting on the wooden bench with Thouris, and she took over the supervision of the children when Thouris finished her song and noticed her son. Stepping carefully past the children and pausing to stroke several of their upturned heads, Thouris joined Nuroc, still holding the infant, her daughter Ouella. The smile on her face faded as she took in Nuroc's expression and caught her first glimpse of the welts and bruises he had incurred during his struggle with the chapyx.

"What happened?" she asked worriedly. "You're hurt."

"I'm all right," Nuroc said. "There was a small accident at the mines."

"Where's your father?" Thouris looked over Nuroc's shoulder at the other miners who had fallen into a line before the long wooden table heaped high with foods ready for eating.

"He's across the lake still," Nuroc said. "There was a man at the camp with a condor. It flew after both Father and me, as if we were prey. I couldn't hear the man when he told Father why it happened, but I saw him point to Father's ring as he talked. Father stayed to speak more with him. It had to be important for him to have passed up this."

Together, Nuroc and Thouris walked away from the crowd to a grove of small fruit trees. The fruit had already been picked for the festival, but the odor from those overripe pieces that lay on the ground was pungent. An owl hooted in one of the branches, as if protesting the intrusion of his privacy.

"I don't care for the sounds of it," Thouris whispered. In her arms, young Ouella stirred and began to cry. Thouris rocked her gently until the baby fell quiet once more. "I've had strange sensations the past few nights," she went on. "The feeling that something uncertain lies just beyond the corner of my eye, lurking in the shadows. I thought perhaps it was mere imagination, triggered by the coming of the black moon, but now I wonder. It seems like an omen of some sort. . . ."

"I feel the same," Nuroc said, glancing up through the limbs of the tree at the partial moon. "There's more, too. Before the incident with the condor, I swear I saw Myrania. She was aboard the ship bringing women to Wheshi for . . ."

As Nuroc paused with sudden embarrassment, Thouris reached out and placed a hand on his arm. "Myrania? Daughter to Inkemisa? I can't believe she'd be among women of that sort."

"But I saw her!" Nuroc said, his voice straining. "I'm sure it was her."

"Then perhaps there is an explanation beyond the obvious," his mother said softly. "Nuroc, I know how you felt for her. It seems too much of a coincidence that she should appear the same day as this man with the condor. So many omens can only point to one thing."

"Talmon-Khash?" Nuroc guessed. "Do you think he is giving us a sign?"

"I'm sure that must have been your father's thought." Thouris said. "Where is this ship that you saw the woman on?"

"Docked here on the south shore. The women have been brought to town, for bidding in the tavern." Nuroc winced at his words, imagining his love upon a pedestal as men slavered over her as if she were a plow horse on the auction block.

"Then you must go there and make certain that it is

79

or isn't Myrania," Thouris said firmly. "Our oath to Talmon-Khash demands it."

Nuroc nodded and they turned back from the grove. As they approached the festivities, which ran on in a spirit of lively merriment, a young boy broke away from the other children and raced to them.

"Mother, Nuroc," the lad cried out. "I was afraid."

"We're here, Jahkums," Thouris said gently to the boy, who was in his fourth year. She took one of his hands and Nuroc grasped the other as they returned to the celebration. A few of the other townsfolk greeted them jovially, and both Nuroc and Thouris returned brief greetings with false smiles, not wishing to cause undue alarm or find themselves caught up in further explanations. Reaching the food table, Nuroc wrapped a thick slice of the herb bread around a slab of cooked ham and carried it off with a piece of fruit. As he came to the path leading back to the main road, he paused to kiss his mother and tousle the hair of his younger brother before dashing off, wondering for the first time if at last his destiny had come to claim him in Wheshi.

Seven

In town there was celebration as well, but it took on an aspect far removed from the pastoral festivity of the gathering Nuroc had left. Here there was an air of the dark and sinister in the streets. The infrequent light of torches threw long shadows across the stone pave as Nuroc made his way past small shops and vending booths closed for the evening. Tonight, those who ventured into the hamlet came, not for any of the various merchant offerings, but for drink, song, and the hoped for touch of soft flesh. All three were offered at the taverns, located at the far edge of town, and it was from that direction that Nuroc heard raucous cries and drunken howlings spilling out into the night.

He walked alone and warily, wishing he had his knife or sword. The darkened alleys between storefronts seemed to breathe with unspoken malice, like jutting maws waiting to swallow him. He'd heard numerous stories concerning miners found at dawn in these darkened niches, their throats slit and their belt-purses lying empty at their sides, victims of rogues who prowled the streets by night and fled to the hills at the first sign of morning.

As he passed the quarter of the city where the poor were sheltered, he glanced up to the second story of a poorly built brick building. Tuledge stood there near an opened window, staring down at the strings of his lyre as he plucked a melody that sounded mournfully off the sides of shops. Nuroc opened his mouth to speak, but held his tongue, deciding it was best not to disturb the man. Presently, a shadow moved across the ceiling above the man's head and Nuroc saw young Lyiis, Tuledge's wife, come up behind him. She placed her head on his shoulder and gently stroked his arm. Tuledge turned his head slightly and kissed his wife's hair while he played.

Nuroc walked on, feeling a sadness set upon him. For all his dreams of rampant adventure, there still crept through his heart the longing for the simple pleasure of shared love with Myrania. He hoped this evening's quest was futile, and that he would find at the tavern a woman who looked similar to Myrania but was not her. He would be content to never find her again rather than see that she had changed into a woman who could be had by the highest bidder. He paused once he rounded the corner and came into view of the taverns. Lights shone through the windows, and shadowy figures flitted unsteadily about the doorways. Several men fought drunkenly in the street, waving errant fists and swearing when they did not find their marks. Through the din he could hear the faint sound of bidding from within. Ten lampich. Twelve. Fifteen. The going price was as high here as at the mining camp.

"I can't," Nuroc moaned to himself at last. He turned about to leave the town, then stopped cold as a wave of terror washed over his spine.

Crazed eyes stared into his own from scant inches away. The eyes were clutched in wrinkled folds of flesh hanging from an ancient face. Stubble grew from a weak chin, and raised veins stood out like blue snakes on a bulbous nose. This startling visage was framed by a cowled hood that hid all but a few strands of limp gray hair. The breath that seeped out through twisted lips smelled of cheap rice beer.

All this Nuroc saw in a second of unbridled fright. Then jagged, broken teeth appeared in the old man's mouth as he stepped back and cackled in the voice of a madman. Nuroc saw that the man was taller than he, but thin and deformed beneath his cowled robe. His bare feet were filthy and several toes were missing.

Before Nuroc had a chance to react to his bizarre confrontation, the man before him raised an eyebrow knowingly and pointed up at the sky. In a broken voice, he gargled a brief song.

> *Wizards poked out Dorban's eye.*
> *Now just one moon in the sky.*
> *One day wizards poke the other.*
> *Death to you and me, my brother.*

Finished, the bent man cackled again and turned away from Nuroc, shuffling off into the shadows.

"Wait!" Nuroc said, shaking himself from his fear and stepping forward. When the man continued to walk away, Nuroc went after him. As Nuroc reached out to grab the man's cowl, he swung about and waved a hand before Nuroc's face. Several of his fingers were missing and the others were covered with swollen nodules.

82

"The curse!" the old man warned. "Would you carry the curse and watch yourself die, piece by piece?"

Nuroc stepped away, his mouth open with shock. The leper flashed his broken smile once more, then withdrew his deformed hand into the sleeve of his cowl and drifted back down the street, singing once again.

> Wizards poked out Dorban's eye.
> Now just one moon in the sky.
> One day wizards poke the other.
> Death to you and me, my brother.

Nuroc watched on until the man was gone from sight, feeling his pulse race with dread. Then, rather than continue in the same direction, he turned back to the taverns, certain that the hand of fate was leading him on.

The larger of the two taverns consisted of a single, cavernous chamber, supported by thick posts and overhead beams of jaunwood. Voices bounded and blended in the air above those gathered in the hall, increasing the considerable noise to a near-deafening uproar. Most of the activity was centered about a raised platform in one corner of the room, where Sphextay stood before the cluster of harlots he was auctioning off. Instead of the two giants and their Shangoran lions, the short whoremaster relied for protection upon several of the young boys, who stood poised with readied crossbows in their hands.

The woman standing on the small bench next to Sphextay was a dark-haired beauty in a flowing robe of dyed muslin, parted along one side to reveal the contour of her leg and the jeweled bracelet she wore about her ankle.

Nuroc entered the tavern as the bidding reached twenty-two lampich. He gave a start at the sight of the woman's hair, but quickly realized that it was not Myrania.

"Twenty-three lampich!" a portly merchant bellowed from his perch upon a stool propped near one of the

83

posts. His smooth fingers curled the tip of a curled moustache as he leered at the woman he was bidding on.

"The prize of the night and your last chance," Sphextay told the men crowded around the platform. "Think now. There can be no doubt this woman merits thirty lampich."

Despite his exhortations, no one came forth to top the merchant's bid. Nuroc worked his way through the crowd, seeing Peutor and Fromm standing with other miners close to one edge of the stage. From their expressions, Nuroc could tell that they had yet to claim a woman's time tonight. Fromm turned to his brother and whispered hastily in the other's ear. Peutor frowned at first, but then finally shook his head up and down and raised a hand to Sphextay. "My brother and I together bid twenty-five lampich!"

There fluttered through the crowd both murmurs and laughs. On the platform, Sphextay forced out his lip in a gesture of concentration, then turned to the woman beside him. She shrugged her shoulders as she looked over the twins.

"It's not my practice to take bids from groups," Sphextay said. "However, for the price of thirty lampich, I might consider a change of precedence."

The twins consulted once more, then Fromm called out, "Done!"

Eyes turned to the rotund merchant, who waved away any thought of raising his bid.

"So be it," Sphextay said, pointing to Fromm and Peutor. "She will be yours . . . but only for half the normal time."

"What?" Fromm protested.

"Unfair," Peutor added. "We should have twice the time, not half."

Sphextay shook his head, smiling thinly.

While the argument ensued, Nuroc looked at the other courtesans, feeling his heart lift with hope when none of them remotely resembled Myrania. It must have been the woman back at the docks that he had first seen, he figured. She must have changed her garb before the whoreship put into the docks.

Relieved, he began to retreat from the center of the crowd. Toward the back of the cavernous hall, he saw barkeepers drawing off foaming jacks of ale from large kegs. Making his way toward the kegs, Nuroc saw a number of the other miners he worked with, most of them already feeling the tug of inebriation, slapping one another on the backs and spilling their drinks as they toasted one another and the coming of the Festival.

He paid for his ale with the last of his lampich. Stromthroad still had Nuroc's pay for the past week's work. The dark-colored brew cut well through the thirst that caked his parched throat, and Nuroc emptied half the drink in a single draw. Wiping flecks of foam off his upper lip, he looked back to the platform.

With the bidding concluded, Sphextay bade the women to retreat through a back doorway set behind the platform, then told the men in his strident voice, "Lest those of you unable to secure my harlots' pleasures go unentertained, I have arranged for the pride of my collection to perform for all of you. Be forewarned, however, that any man who dares to breach the stage and touch this lovely shall die with four arrows pierced through his breast."

There was a rumbling of curiosity at this strange announcement, and even those who had come to the tavern with no thought of indulging in the offerings of Sphextay looked to the stage. The robed whoremaster raised a hand and snapped his fingers. At the base of each of the jaunwood columns supporting the tavern ceiling, more of Sphextay's boys raised long poles to which were attached bronzed cups that extinguished the mounted torches. Darkness swept over the tavern and the men mumbled anew with surprise.

A woman's voice sounded over the undercurrent of the men's conversation, carrying like the sound of a trumpet from the vicinity of the darkened stage.

85

Hear me, men!
Hear me tell
How lands were made
And how they fell.
The tale is old,
And each year retold.
On the day of the Festival,
Let the tale unfold!

Nuroc shuddered where he stood, defying his brain to deny what he heard. It had been five long years, but he knew the voice as if he had heard it only yesterday. Setting his unfinished jack aside, he stepped up on the shadowy form of a footstool so that he could see over the many heads that blocked his view of the stage.

On the platform, a single candle came to life, throwing dim light on a woman dressed in solid black, so that all but her face blended into the darkness of the background. Hers was a haunting visage. Her eyes were closed, and a mime's makeup exaggerated her features into a demonic mask with glowing pupils painted on her eyelids. She remained silent until the hushed, uneasy whispers from the crowd subsided and the tavern was quiet.

"Myrania," Nuroc gasped hoarsely from his vantage point.

As the men watched on, entranced by the sight before them, Myrania softly raised one arm before her and covered it from view with the other, then spoke again.

The waking dawn of time
Found lands the shape of beasts
Who ruled the pre-man climes
From barren west to sunbathed east.
Dorban was this land,
Named for the bird of prey
And the god most grand,
So the legends say.

Myrania lowered her foremost arm, revealing a condor perched upon the other, flapping its wings before

86

resting in profile. Again she raised her free arm, covering the bird from the men's view, ignoring their whispers of wonder. Nuroc blinked his eyes with astonishment and felt his mind reel as Myrania opened her eyes and stared out at the men with a gaze that seemed focused on that which no one could see.

The condor was gone when Myrania lowered her arm a second time. In its place was a clay replica of the bird's head distorted slightly into the shape of the Dorban continent. The upright statue balanced unwaveringly on the woman's cloaked wrist, and when she pulled her hand free, the replica floated in the air. She ran her slender fingers above and below the model to show that it hung in the air unaided.

In the ensuing silence she waved her hand slightly and, still untouched, the replica tilted to one side so that it lay parallel to the floor. With her hands closed into fists, Myrania held them out over the clay carving and continued her eerie oration.

> The god stared down
> From nightly skies.
> The world's twin moons
> Were Dorban's eyes,
> Bestowing powers strange and grand
> To sorcerers throughout the land.
> Wizardry was there for all
> Who knew the chants,
> Who knew the calls.

Myrania blew out the candle. There was only a moment's darkness before she opened her palms and revealed two small orbs that glowed with ethereal radiance. She slowly began to juggle the orbs so that they circled around the replica, all the while keeping her eyes fixed straight ahead.

> For magic there was costly toll
> As mages practiced far and wide
> They had no way to know

87

> *The moons held rule*
> *O'er Dorban's tides.*

Where light had previously shone from the candle, a thin stream of water sprang upward like a fountain until it pattered against the bottom of the replica. Near the edge of the platform, Fromm bent forward to steal a glance beneath the stage, seeking out the fountain's source. He could see little in the black shadow, but even by torchlight he would not have spotted anything but vacant space. He rose slowly and gripped his brother's arm.

"She's a sorceress," Fromm hissed. Peutor silenced him with an angry stare and turned his attention back to the performance.

> *With each feat the wizards chose*
> *Ocean waters swelled and rose.*
> *In orbit soon the twin moons closed,*
> *And man knew not the threat it posed.*

The shifting of Myrania's hands was indiscernible, yet the twin orbs circled closer together about the facsimile of Dorban. At the same time, the fountain rose higher, jostling the replica.

> *On this day five years past*
> *The tides against the shores did crash*
> *With force that made the land subside;*
> *'Twas magic made the moons collide.*

As her final words lingered in the chamber, the globes met in midair. As with the night of the cataclysm, there burst forth a flash of light so brilliant that all the men were temporarily blinded, shouting as they rubbed at their eyes.

"Witchery!"

"Spawn of Ghetite! She's blinded us all!"

"Treacherous Sphextay! He will die for this!"

The cursing ebbed as the men's sight slowly came back to them, and Sphextay stood alone on the stage before them, laughing with amusement before the relit candle.

"Come now, come now," he chortled merrily. "I've merely dazzled your eyes, not blinded them. Elsewhere men have paid a tidy sum to watch the illusions of my lovely. You watched for free."

There still hung in the air a building tension as the miners glared at the whoremaster. Those few who had a mind to lay hands on Sphextay gave pause as they saw the leveled crossbows held by the young boys who had slipped back onto the stage beside him.

While the other boys shinnied up the jaunwood columns to rekindle the torches, Fromm clapped his hands near the platform and cried out to the others, "Sphextay's right. Who can dare say they've seen a show such as that we've just witnessed?"

The others stirred where they stood, still unconvinced.

Peutor stepped beside his brother, adding, "And we all can see well enough now, right? Are we not men enough that we can have a clever prank played on us without whining like spoiled children because we were caught off guard." He turned to Sphextay and said, "Would that I could play so grand a trick. I applaud you, you and your clever illusionist."

The twins joined together in clapping their hands, and soon the others followed suit. Sphextay acknowledged the ovation, then said, "I regret that our enchantress cannot step forward to take a bow, but she is already back at her room in the lodge next door, along with the women who await the embrace of those who bid their favors. Let those men come forward and pay their wagers before my lads escort them to the chambers of bliss!"

And so the confrontation was deflated. The men fell back to their drinking, exchanging excited conversation about what they had just seen while Sphextay collected payments from the winning bidders. Nuroc slowly advanced through the milling crowd to take his place among those sorting through their coins for the price of their lust. He was confused, still absorbing the implications of Myrania's performance and her link to the diminutive whoremaster.

Once each man had exacted his payment to Sphextay, he stepped up to the platform and was led out through the rear exit by one of the loinclothed youths. Nuroc saw one of the lads open his mouth for a swallow from an untended skin of ale and realized the boy's tongue was missing. As he was staring, the boy looked up at him and smiled strangely, moving his jaw up and down obscenely as he tugged at the lower hem of his tunic.

"Embrose!" Sphextay shouted from the platform. The young boy cowered away from Nuroc and looked to his master with a shamed face. Sphextay waved him over and Embrose warily climbed up onto the platform. The whoremaster lashed out with the back of his hand, striking Embrose across the face. The youth's mouth opened in pain, but there was no voice to let forth his scream.

"Now lead this man back to the chambers," Sphextay snarled, jerking his head at an old merchant who had just paid his lampich to the whoremaster. Embrose bobbed his head obediently and sulked away. The merchant followed him from the main hall and Sphextay turned his attention to Fromm and Peutor, last in the line before Nuroc.

"There might have been a riot here had we not spoken up on your behalf, Sphextay," Fromm said. "Your crossbows would have claimed a few of us, but you would have died as sure as you're standing there."

"What is your point?" Sphextay grumbled irritably. "As if I could not tell."

"The woman we bid for and one other," Peutor put in. "We want them for the night, at no cost."

Sphextay smiled blandly. "I've allowed one bit of charity with the performance of the illusionist. That is my limit. However, since I must concede an indebtedness, I will allow you the favors of the woman you chose until midnight. You have a wife to see to some-time anyway, Peutor, am I right?"

Peutor narrowed his eyes suspiciously. "How did you know that?"

Sphextay sighed. "I know what I must. You've heard my offer. Take it or leave it."

Fromm and Peutor looked to one another, then nodded to Sphextay. The whoremaster sent them off with another of his boys, then turned to Nuroc.

"You made no bids," he said impatiently. "What do you want?"

"Myrania," Nuroc said, trying to keep his voice under control.

"What are you talking about?"

"The illusionist."

"She's not available," Sphextay said firmly. "I said as much once already."

"I know her," Nuroc replied insistently. "I wish to speak with her."

"No one speaks with her. She's mine," Sphextay answered, gloating. "I will have her while the others—"

Nuroc's fist swung out into the whoremaster's face, sending Sphextay reeling backward. Nuroc quickly grabbed the collar of the small man's robe and jerked him up to his feet, holding Sphextay like a shield between himself and the raised crossbows of the armed boys.

"Fire, and he dies first," Nuroc told them coldly, shaking Sphextay hard until he stopped struggling and stood still. "Put down your bows."

"Obey him," Sphextay told the boys.

From the crowd behind him, one of the miners called out to Nuroc, "What are you doing?"

"Stay out of this!" Nuroc shouted over his shoulder. "All of you!"

One of the merchants raised his voice from halfway across the room. "Get your hands off him, young man! Are you trying to ruin our source of pleasure in this godforsaken town?"

Nuroc kept his hold on Sphextay as he bellowed at

the merchant, "This swine deals in terror and abuse. You dare to call him a source of pleasure?"

"This is a tavern, not a temple," the merchant shot back. "Unhand Sphextay and take your preaching elsewhere or else I myself will teach you a few things about terror and abuse."

There was laughter among the other merchants sharing their spokesman's table, and even some of the miners snickered, finding the confrontation to be fine entertainment. One of Nuroc's fellow workers came forward to the edge of the platform and said, "Nuroc. You've made a mistake. I'm certain Sphextay will forgive you if you do the wise thing and let him go."

"Spoken true," Sphextay murmured, clutching at his collar where Nuroc was choking him. "Now let a man breathe."

Incredulous, Nuroc looked to the other men for support and saw that he had none. He angrily pushed Sphextay away from him. The whoremaster fell at the feet of his guards and they immediately raised their crossbows at Nuroc. Sphextay raised a hand to stop them from firing. He rose to his feet and took a step forward, looking up into Nuroc's hate-filled eyes.

"You're a fortunate young man," Sphextay said. "Few men insult me and live. But let me tell you this, if I ever lay eyes upon you again, you can be certain that you will die several times over. You have my word on it!"

Nuroc fought back the insane rage that tore through him, but refused to look away from Sphextay's squinting eyes. The whoremaster finally turned away and passed between his guards through the rear exit. The boys with the bows followed him and the door closed shut, leaving Nuroc alone on the stage.

Stepping down, Nuroc strode deliberately through the silent ranks of the drinkers, paying no heed to their sidelong glances. Once he was outside, he heard the sudden burst of a hundred conversations within the tavern. They would have much to talk about the rest of the evening.

"They're no better than Sphextay," Nuroc muttered angrily, coming around the front of the tavern and casting his eyes to the lit windows of the lodge, a two-story structure built of wood and stone set back off the street. He could see silhouettes through the cloth draperies and wondered in which room Myrania awaited Sphextay. From the look in Myrania's eyes, Nuroc suspected that the whoremaster was controlling her with proffax blossoms used by the oracles of Numeria to induce their prophetic dreams. It was the only possible explanation, he felt. There was no way she would willingly live by the whims of Sphextay and risk the swift death that would await her should a representative of the king see her performing and realize that she was not a mere illusionist, but rather the daughter of a sorcerer.

He decided to sneak into the lodge and try to find Myrania before Sphextay reached her. It was a desperate chance, but the only one he had. He started down the alley leading to the looming structure, but stopped when he heard a sound behind him.

Two of Sphextay's boys, each one carrying a glinting dagger, had followed him into the alley. One was older and taller than the other, but neither were Nuroc's match in size. He figured he could outrace them to the lodge, but once he turned and began to run, he saw two more of the youths emerge from the side of the lodge, similarly armed.

Silently, the four assailants closed in on Nuroc, who stood hemmed-in between the side of the tavern and a tall mortared wall surrounding the front courtyard of the lodge. He looked up to the top of the wall, but saw that barbed poles jutted up from the coping to prevent trespassers from gaining entry to the grounds within.

The tavern wall, however, had a narrow ledge running the length of the building from a height of ten feet. Seeing it as his only means of escape, Nuroc took several running steps toward the first boys he had seen, then leapt into the air. As he hoped, the youths' initial reaction was to stoop down and hold out their knives to impale him. Before they realized his plan, he had grabbed onto the ledge long enough to swing over their heads and land on the other side of them.

All four youths joined together and started down the alley after Nuroc, but he had gained his feet immediately and sprang forward to the street, where he broke into a run. His longer legs carried him along with a broader gait than the tallest of the youths, and he quickly gained ground on them.

As he turned and fled down the road by which he had entered this part of the town, Nuroc saw that Tuledge was still at the window of his quarters, playing his lyre tranquilly. Nuroc raced by, with the serene music sounding mockingly in his ears.

On he ran, long after the time when he ceased to hear the sound of racing feet beating on the pavement behind him. It was only once he was beyond the town and back into the hills that he allowed himself to slow his pace. Even then, he took the precaution of departing from the road, dashing into the brush until he came to a shortcut that would lead him home.

The ground pitched and varied, carrying him through thickets and past long stretches of rocky terrain until he finally reached the banks of a flowing creek that marked the boundary of his family's property. Exhausted, he slumped to his knees at the edge of the stream and splashed water at his face. He then cupped his hands and drank several mouthfuls.

Resting a moment on a nearby boulder, Nuroc looked up through the leaf-strewn trees and saw the position of the moon. He was startled. So much had happened since he and his father had left the mines earlier that afternoon, he thought for sure the night was half over. And yet, the moon's setting claimed that it was well before midnight. There was a good chance his family had not yet returned from the celebration at the sports field. The prospect depressed him, for he had pushed himself this far, wishing to talk with his parents and see if they could help shed light on the portentous swirl of events he had been caught up in the past hours. He particularly wanted his father's advice on the best way to see to Myrania's rescue from the clutches of the whoremaster Sphextay.

With great weariness, Nuroc dragged his frame along the path that followed the stream uphill to his home, a spacious affair of wood and thatch he had helped his father construct with the help of neighbors shortly after their arrival in Wheshi five years ago.

The house was dark, and Nuroc saw that both Stromthroad's and Thouris's horses were gone from the corral. Only his cream-colored mount paced slowly about the fenced enclosure, neighing and shaking its mane once it heard the approach of its master. Nuroc loaded more feed into the troughs and stroked the horse's massive head as it began to eat.

Nuroc's family lived on a scenic bluff overlooking Lake Wheshi, and from the corral he could see the sparkling reflection of the moon on the now-placid waters. Across the lake, the Kanghats rose darkly like the shoulders of some lumbering giant.

Once he stopped moving, the fatigue swept over Nuroc with a bludgeoning swiftness. Yawning, he bade his steed farewell for the night and went inside. There was a basket of fruit and a skin of fresh cheese on the table in the main room. He took the cheese and a pair of ripe yeago melons into the smaller room facing the lake. The room was normally used for entertaining guests, but during the summer Nuroc also kept his cot out here, preferring to sleep close to the sound and smell of the lake.

He sat on the cot as he ate the fruit and cheese, mulling over the puzzling fragments of the day. He had the same feeling as his mother, a sense that an explanation lay just beyond reach, shrouded in mystery. Except for the encounter with the chapyx, a common thread wove through the separate incidents. The spotting of Myrania, the strange behavior of the condor at the mining camp, the celebrations of the festival both in the city and at the edge of town—it was as if, after all these years in which men shied from speaking about

95

the old ways, the land were once again under the domain of sorcery.

Finishing the last of his meal, Nuroc tiredly got up from the cot and walked to the far wall. Moving over a roughly-hewn chair, he stepped on it and reached up to a thin recess carved out of the uppermost log. He pulled down a roll of thick burlap and took it back to the cot. Unraveling the coarse material, he uncovered the scabbard containing the sacred dagger of Talmon-Khash. It had been some time since he had looked upon the ornate weapon. He slowly pulled it free of the scabbard and admired anew the magnificent craftsmanship that had gone into its making. The carved head of the condor-hilt shone as if it had been polished only yesterday, and the stones that made up the eyes of the bird still seemed to glow of their own accord.

Nuroc gently placed the blade back into its sheath and lay back on the cot to wait for the arrival of his family. The last of his energy faded quickly and soon he was asleep.

Eight

The coming dawn breathed light through the opened window, but it was a sound rather than the light that wrenched Nuroc from his deep sleep. He bolted upright in the cot, seeing a man drop from sight through the window overlooking the sea.

"Who goes!" Nuroc shouted, shaking off the daze of his slumber and the aches that coursed through his body. Swinging his legs to the floor, he reached for the dagger he'd left at the foot of the cot.

96

"No!" he gasped as his hands fell on the empty scabbard.

"Nuroc?" his father shouted from the other room, where the rest of the family was sleeping. "What is it?"

Nuroc did not answer in his haste to reach the window. Before he could clear the distance, however, the blurred shaft of an arrow hissed through the opening, missing him by inches before imbedding itself in the wooden wall that framed the main room of the house. Ignoring caution, Nuroc stared out the window, seeing the retreating form of the archer vanishing into the brush just beyond the corral, where his parents' horses joined Nuroc's in galloping short, panicked circles around the compound.

"Thieving coward!" Nuroc shouted angrily.

Behind him, Stromthroad strode into the room.

"What goes on, Nuroc? We let you sleep when we returned, because . . ." Stromthroad's voice trailed off as both men looked to where the fiery tip of the arrow had showered sparks along the main wall. Flames licked at the dry timbers, and a larger blaze burst forth in the straw that lined the cot.

Together they struggled to put out the blaze. Nuroc snatched up the length of burlap and slapped at the cot while his father risked his hands on the burning wall. They succeeded in snuffing parts of the blaze, but it was growing faster than they could control it. Stromthroad finally backed away, rubbing at his blistered palms.

"Come on, Son! It's no use! We have to leave!"

Nuroc nodded and his father dashed into the main room, waking the rest of the family. The children screamed with alarm.

Nuroc remained behind, however, fiercely determined to save the house. As he continued to flail at the cot, smoke filled the ceiling and worked its way downward, choking him and stinging his eyes. Everything in the room was dry and the flames spread out like the tentacles of a vengeful squid, framing the doorway and crawling across the loose straw on the floor.

"Get out, Son!" Stromthroad shouted from the main room. "Use the window! Forget about the house!"

Nuroc stubbornly battled the blaze until the burlap he was whipping about came alive with the scorching flames. He dropped it and looked to the window, which was also veiled with fire. Reaching for the scabbard that was meant to hold the condor-dagger, Nuroc grimaced as the heat absorbed by the metallic design burnt through the callus of his hands and stabbed at raw nerves. Still he kept his hand on the scabbard and took long strides across the flaming floor before flinging himself toward the window. In the smoke he misjudged his leap and caught the edge of the window frame, but it was so eaten through with the voracious blaze that the charred wood crumbled on impact. Head-first he burst into the open air, twisting his body to cushion the force of his landing on the hard ground outside. He rolled in a somersault and came to his feet.

The heat from the burning house drove him from its walls, and he looked back to see that the thatched roof was aglow with a fiery brilliance that surpassed the rising sun behind it. Dropping the heated scabbard to the grass, he charged toward the now vacant corral, searching the grounds for those responsible for the attack. In the back of his mind, he was certain that this was an act of Sphextay, who undoubtedly had learned where he lived from one of the drunken miners. He craved to find the whoremaster alone, but knew that the torching would have been handled by an accomplice. The man he had seen leaping from the window was much taller than Sphextay or any of his youthful lackeys.

When he could see no one about the corrals or the surrounding brush, he followed the hoofprints in the dirt to the side of the house. He stopped short as he rounded the corner, his stomach in knots.

"It can't be!" he raged, staring at the sight before him.

Bodies lay in the tall grass, pierced with arrows. His brother was closest to him, lying in a grotesque sprawl

98

where he had been felled. Although he had breathed his last, his eyes were still opened in a look of bewilderment. Blood trickled out the corner of his still lips. Thouris lay face down nearby, twice-struck in the back. She had dropped the infant, and young Ouella wailed on her back, kicking in the air for several seconds before a feathered shaft stilled her.

Speechless, Nuroc traced the last arrow's flight to a lone rider on the path connecting the family land with the main road. The rider sat upon Stromthroad's mottled steed, and he stared coldly at Nuroc as he placed another arrow into his longbow. Contrary to Nuroc's suspicions, he was not a hireling of Sphextay at all. The deep olive color of his skin and the green weave of his jupon placed him as a Ghetite, disciple of the sorcerer-king Augage.

Before the archer could draw his bowstring, there came a curdling roar from the grass as Stromthroad staggered to his feet, several yards away from his slain family. An arrow jutted out from his left shoulder, spilling blood but not preventing him from clutching at a sword with his other hand.

"You will die for this!" Stromthroad howled, charging through the grass toward the assailant.

As the rider was changing his aim to Stromthroad, Nuroc saw his father bring his fingers to his mouth and impart a shrill whistle. The mottled stallion responded to its master's call and reared in the air, kicking out its hooves as it threw the unsuspecting Ghetite and galloped off into the brush.

Both Nuroc and Stromthroad rushed to the fallen raider, who lay stunned in the grass. Nuroc reached him first and grabbed him by the collar, shaking him violently with one hand. With the other he grabbed the fallen arrow and placed its tip against the Ghetite's neck.

"Why?" Nuroc spat in the man's face. "Before I slay you like the animal you are, tell me why!"

The Ghetite turned his icy gaze on Nuroc, showing

99

no sign of fear, although he winced when the arrowhead pricked the flesh of his neck.

"He's mine!" Stromthroad shouted, pushing his son to one side and wielding his sword with such rampant fury that the blade's cleaving arc beheaded the swarthy-skinned assassin.

Nuroc stumbled back from his father, his eyes widening as he saw the severed head roll to a stop in the grass, even as the body continued to jerk in the contortions of death. Stromthroad stood over the corpse until it ceased moving, then stepped away, clenching his teeth as he ripped the arrow from his shoulder.

Father and son at last met each other's gaze and Nuroc felt fear at the uncontrolled passion that burned in Stromthroad's eyes. The older man was mad with rage, and he drew in heavy breaths as he looked at the blood on his sword.

Hoofbeats sounded down the path and soon three more horsemen appeared. Two were Ghetites, similar in appearance to the one slain, but the third was Shangoran, smaller of frame and of lighter skin than his companions. They were armed with swords and lances and, seeing the fate of their fourth member, they quickly fanned out to surround Nuroc and Stromthroad.

Two more riders appeared from the far side of the yard, but they were neighbors astride Nuroc and Thouris's horses. Behind them, others from the town began to emerge from the brush, attracted by the fire and cries. Most were miners who Nuroc had seen at the tavern the previous night, and they seemed far from recovered after their long stint of drink and debauchery.

Stromthroad shook off his mad trance and reached down for the fallen Ghetite's sword, unsheathing it and handing it to his son. There had been numerous occasions in the past when they had stood on this same stretch of ground and traded blows as they practiced their swordsmanship, but now they turned to fight in earnest, fueled on by a grief-stricken wrath.

Many of the miners were armed, and they closed in warily on the scene of the confrontation, but held back from stepping in to aid Stromthroad and Nuroc in battle. The others stood their ground nervously, watching with mute disbelief, as if they were caught up in some nightmare that would pass once they awoke.

Nuroc moved toward one of the Ghetites, waving the sword lightly in the air to gauge its weight and dexterity. It was much heavier than the blades he was used to, so he held it in both hands as the horseman suddenly tugged on his reins and rode forward, sword extended before him.

Nuroc saw in a glance that the rider had the ceremonial dagger of Talmon-Khash tucked into a sash tightly wound around his waist.

"It was you, then!" he called out hatefully, tightening his grip on the broadsword. As the rider thundered toward him, Nuroc fixed his gaze on the opponent's blade. He timed the anticipated blow well, and was able to lunge forward and away from the cutting edge, at the same time swiping upward with his own sword.

The Ghetite screamed as blood gushed from the stump that had once been his swordarm. Clutching the reins with his remaining hand, he slumped over the horse and rode toward a group of startled townsfolk.

"Stop him!" Nuroc shouted to the people, but they fell away from the approaching rider, letting him escape past them into an overgrowth of foliage.

Nuroc turned away from them angrily and saw his father holding the other two horsemen at bay with manic waves of his sword. However, the raiders were nudging their horses in closer between swings.

"This way, butcherers of women and children!" Nuroc taunted as he strode through the grass. "Dare you face a foe man to man?"

His insult drew one of the horsemen his way. The rider leveled his lance at Nuroc and bore down on the youth. Nuroc held his ground, letting the lethal tip come to within several feet of him before he moved, slashing out with his sword enough to deflect the lance's course away from him. The same motion brought him into the horse's path, and he swiftly arced his back to avert a collision. The rider pulled tightly on his horse's reins and it rose at once on its hind legs and swung about, catching Nuroc by surprise. A hoof to the head sent Nuroc tumbling into the grass, stunned. His sword fell to the ground beside him.

His vision blurred as he rose to his knees and grappled through the grass, desperately seeking out his sword. As his searching fingers fell upon the thick hilt, he heard a sickening thud in the air above him. He awkwardly brought the blade up before him in hopes of warding off a blow that never came. The raider plummeted limply to the ground beside him while his horse ran off with a flurry of hoofbeats.

When the streaks faded from his sight, Nuroc saw that his would-be slayer had died from a thrown sword that had impaled his side. Nuroc recognized the sword and quickly jumped to his feet, crying, "Father!"

It was too late, though. Unarmed, Stromthroad was cut down by the remaining Ghetite across the yard.

"Vermin!" Nuroc wailed in anguish as he ran through the grass. The Ghetite, angular-faced with a dark goatee, smiled menacingly at his new foe. He was about to ride forward and engage in battle when an arrow whisked past his face. Turning his horse about, he saw the peddler Solat standing next to his donkey amidst the townsfolk, fitting another quarrel into his crossbow.

Slapping the flat of his blood-stained sword against the hindquarters of his horse, the final raider rode off through the cover of fruit trees growing in neat rows at the edge of the yard.

Nuroc chased after the horseman, but gave up when the Ghetite reached the open space of the main road and thundered off at full gallop. Seething, he returned to his yard and glowered defiantly at the men of Wheshi.

"Spineless worms!" he ranted at them. "You murdered my father with your cowardice!"

Peutor was among those in the group Nuroc accosted. His face was white and his voice trembled as he spoke, keeping a cautious eye on the sword Nuroc still held in his grip. "We could do nothing. Except for the peddler, we had no arrows to use for a distance."

"You had no courage!" Nuroc retorted. "Better to watch the best of your lot be cut down than risk your worthless hides!"

Peutor could only mumble, "We could do nothing."

Nuroc spat in Peutor's face and hurled the sword so that it bit into the dirt between the miner's shaking knees. Striding hastily away, he grabbed the man astride his horse and pulled him from the saddle before climbing into the stirrups.

As Nuroc started to ride off, Solat came forward, waving his arms pleadingly, "Wait, lad. I must speak to you. It—"

His words were lost in the play of hooves on the dirt path as Nuroc urged his horse through the townsfolk and after the distant figure of the fleeing Ghetite. Behind him, the blazing roof of his once-lovely home crumbled into the charred ruins of its burning foundation.

Nine

South of Wheshi, the soft roll of the terrain was scarred by a treacherous pass formed during the earth's buckling in the grips of the cataclysm. A seam of ripped ground exposed stratified layers that marked the passage of time. Newly grown weeds sprouted from bands of earth that had not seen the light of day for centuries before the rupture of earthquakes had folded them to the surface.

It was to the pass that the one-armed Ghetite fled.

Sweat matting its brown coat and froth wetting its bit, the raider's steed cleared the final series of crags that led to the hidden camp. Rock formations jutted outward in overlapping directions, providing cover from view of any casual observer. The location served merely as an added precaution, for few traveled the pass or its surrounding land, rendered useless for farming or inhabitation.

Once onto the level ground of the camp, the rider stilled his horse. His face was pasty and he was bathed in the sweat of fever, barely conscious from the pain of his gaping wound. Swinging one leg over the saddle, he dismounted and fell to the ground, screaming at the jolt. The sacred knife fell from his sash and clattered across the hard ground.

He lay on his back, building his strength to the point where he could struggle to his feet and fumble through his saddlebags for a waterskin. Thirst assailed him, and he drank faster than he could swallow, sending rivulets cascading from his face as he shook off death's course and held the skin high so that the water splashed off his heated brow.

The horse stayed in place as the man leaned against it for support and reached back into the saddlebags for a small stone jar, tightly sealed with brass clasps. Holding the jar, he stumbled into the shaded area of the camp, where a hot spring bubbled forth in a naturally formed pool and gave off a sulphurous stench.

At the edge of the pool he dropped to his knees, blinking the sweat from his eyes as he concentrated on opening the jar. It was closed in a way that required two hands to open it, and after several futile attempts to prop it between his knees for a better hold, he despaired and dashed the jar against the rocks, cracking the frame enough so that he could pry the shards apart.

Inside was a thick purple salve, fragrant with a sweet scent he could smell even through the sulphur of the spring. Acting quickly, he collected as much of the salve as he could on the tips of his fingers, then brought the hand to his still-bleeding stump and rubbed in the ointment. His eyes rolled at the contact and his screams echoed off the cavern walls as the pain sent him twisting to one side and toppling headlong into the yellow-tinged waters. The pool was turbulent as the man thrashed about, then the surface settled over him.

A condor shrieked overhead, piercing the silence. The untethered horse whinnied and clopped its front hooves nervously at the ground. Behind it came the rustling of twigs, followed by the sound of footsteps. A man reached out and stroked the horse's mane, quieting the beast. After a pause, the footsteps retreated and the camp fell silent once more.

A hand suddenly burst forward from the surface of the pool. The raider lifted his head from the water and gasped for air as he reached out for a large rock protruding from the pool's edge.

As he pulled himself to his feet and emerged, he stared down at the new arm and hand that had been regenerated from the severed stump. Smiling with amazement, he flexed the fingers and splashed the water with them as a child might. Not only had the limb been reproduced; the pall of death, which had almost settled over him, had now been lifted. He was as whole and vital as he had been before Nuroc had sliced off his arm.

His exultation faded at the sound of a second horse making its way up the rocky escarpment. He quickly lifted himself from the pool and took cover behind a boulder set near the mouth of the cave. A lance was propped along the rock wall beside crude baskets filled with provisions. He secured a firm grip on the weapon with his rejuvenated hand.

It was the other survivor of the attack on Nuroc's family who coaxed his steed up onto the ledge.

"There you are, Barris," the rider said gravely.

"Yo, Quidantis!" the lancer cheered, lowering his weapon as he stepped clear of the cave.

Expecting a cordial rejoinder, he was taken aback when Quidantis bolted forward on his horse, at the same time extending his booted toe so as to catch Barris full in the stomach. Barris reeled to the ground, his lance thrown clear. Quidantis dismounted and strode over to Barris, sword drawn.

"You deserted us, Barris! Both Examore and Corjoiis were slain!"

"My . . . my arm!" Barris cried out, wheezing to regain the wind that had been knocked from him. "Didn't you see? The youth clove it at the elbow!"

Quidantis looked hard at his companion. "It looks well enough for a missing limb!"

Exasperated, Barris stepped back near the pool and picked up bits of the broken jar, holding them toward Quidantis. "I used the salve and recited the Chant of Healing as Augage taught it!"

"You lie!" Quidantis countered, stepped forward.

"Look," Barris gasped, holding the arm out, "See if you find any trace of the scars from our battle last month . . . by the gods!" Barris stared incredulously at his regenerated forearm, where the poorly healed wounds from a previous skirmish had been reproduced.

Keeping his blade pointed Barris's way, Quidantis walked over to his cohort's horse and began searching the saddlebags. "Where is the dagger, Barris?"

Barris reached to his sash, realizing for the first time that it was missing. He frantically looked around for it, but it was nowhere to be seen. "I could swear I still wore it this far." He turned back to the pool. "I must have lost it when I fell in the spring!"

"A likely story," Quidantis said coldly, moving away from the horse.

"You must believe me, Quidantis!" As he spoke, Barris moved slowly toward the fallen lance. Before Quidantis could stop him, he picked up the weapon and held it before him. "Put down your sword."

"You left us to be slain," Quidantis said, stepping toward Barris, his blade at the ready. "You wanted to claim sole reward for bringing the dagger to Augage. No doubt you would have said it was you alone who slew all those who carried the blood of Talmon-Khash as well."

"Untrue!" Barris said. "Quidantis. For years we have been in Augage's service. I have come to love and trust you like a brother. How can you make such a charge?"

Quidantis sneered, "Examore, my true brother, is now dead because of your greed and cowardice. Tell me where the dagger is, Barris, and I'll see that you die swiftly and with mercy."

Barris stiffened, his features transformed from fear to rage. He charged Quidantis with the lance, shouting, "Join your brother in hell!"

Alas, a lanceman afoot is out of his element, and Quidantis easily sidestepped Barris's charge. When he riposted, the lance was snapped in twain, leaving Barris with no more than a broken staff.

"The dagger, Barris," Quidantis said coldly.

Barris turned and broke into a run. Quidantis followed in chase. There was a precarious footing to be had along one of the jutting outcrops, and Barris scrambled to it, climbing like a man possessed. His pursuer advanced more cautiously, and the distance between them grew slowly. Still, once Barris had cleared the outcrop, he found himself trapped on a flattened peak that reached out over the pass.

All around, the horizon stretched unbroken in the morning sun. He could see the scattered ruins of a town that had been destroyed by the force of the quake five years earlier, lying flattened like bleached bones in the desert.

Quidantis climbed up to the peak and the two men faced off. Barris looked in Quidantis's eyes for mercy, but saw only the promise of a slow, torturous death. He had seen the way Quidantis handled prisoners in the days when they helped Augage earn the allegiance of the Ghetite hill tribes. There was no act too brutal for his taste, no whimper from broken men that could make him ease up on his tortures.

"Your last chance," Quidantis said with grim finality.

Barris braced himself, then sprang forward at Quidantis, swinging mightily with the broken lance. Quidantis ducked the blow and sent his blade into Barris's ribs. Barris's momentum brought him in collision with the swordsman, however, and together they toppled to the edge of the peak. Barris was dead before he landed, and Quidantis pushed the corpse away as he clawed at the rock to prevent himself from slipping over the edge. That fate befell Barris, who bounded off the jagged sides of the ruptured fault before landing in a grisly heap at the base of the pass.

Struggling to his knees, Quidantis edged in from the lip of the peak. His breath came in short gasps, but he was uninjured from the encounter.

"I'll find the dagger somehow," he told himself. "Then I'll track down the last man who carries the blood of Talmon-Khash. I'll bring his head and the dagger to Talmon-Khash, and the glory will be mine!"

So determined, he made to his feet and brushed himself off. Before he started back, he looked up, seeing a lone condor streaking across the deep blue sky. He grinned with pleasure at the sight.

Ten

Nuroc spent the entire day combing the land in search of his family's killers. He rode along the edge of the Targoan River, asking questions of the women who washed clothes along the banks. At sprawling farms he inquired of the men who tilled the soil. Up and down the dusty road that wound from Wheshi to points beyond he accosted strangers. He saw more new faces that day than he had in his five years as a miner, and every one of those faces listened sadly to his story, then wagged reluctantly to confirm that they had not seen the men he sought.

Darkness soon settled over the territory, but still Nuroc drove his horse on, straining eyes and ears in hopes that he might come upon some clue, some indication that the direction of his search was not in vain.

He came at last to the first split of faultline acting as the border between Wheshi's outskirts and the wilderness left barren by the cataclysm. A row of twisted trees grew out from the uplifted earth, and at the base of one of the trees Nuroc could make out two figures lying in the grass. As he rode closer, the figures began to move quickly.

Slapping his steed's flanks, Nuroc hastened toward them, grabbing for the sword he had received from a sympathetic blacksmith farther down the road. Hopeful that his long-sought vengeance was close at hand, he reined his horse to a disappointing halt when he realized the couple were a young shepherd and a girl, both struggling into their clothes with looks of great fear.

"Forgive me," Nuroc said, keeping his distance as they finished dressing. "I mean no harm."

The couple stood together, clinging to one another for support as they stared at Nuroc's sword. He sheathed it and remained in the saddle. "I am looking for two men. One is wounded, missing an arm at the shoulder. The other—"

"You're not sent by my father?" the girl asked anxiously.

Nuroc smiled wanly and shook his head. The shepherd stepped forward, relief already showing on his face.

"The wounded man," he said, "was he on a black mount?"

"Yes!" Nuroc cried out. "You saw him?"

The shepherd nodded and turned, facing the badlands.

"This morning, shortly after I took up my post near here, I saw a man break from the main road and race his horse across the pasture." The shepherd pointed and Nuroc saw that down the slope beyond the tree there was a field of broad-leafed grass hugging the last of the good soil before the stretch of ruined terrain. "He sent the sheep running in fear, and I shouted for him to stop. When he didn't, I took to my horse and rode after him. When I saw that he was Shangoran and that he was missing an arm, I became frightened and pulled back. He rode off toward the pass where the city of Tharue once stood. I rode to tell my master, but he would not believe me. Several others told me I was imagining things, so I stopped talking about it."

The girl beside the shepherd pulled tighter on his arm and murmured, "I would have believed you. Why didn't you tell me?"

"I was going to," the shepherd insisted.

"Is there a route through the badlands?" Nuroc asked.

"There are foot trails," the shepherd said, "but the terrain is too rugged for horses, especially at night. I was amazed to see the Shangoran ride in without hesitation. The badlands are littered with the skeletons of horses that failed the journey. If you value your steed, you will take the main road around the pass, or at least wait until morning to attempt the same course as the Shangoran."

"I appreciate the advice," Nuroc said, stroking the mane of his horse. "Still, I have no choice but to go on. If the paths are as bad as you say, I will lead my horse on foot. Can you show me the safest route?"

The shepherd pointed again, saying, "You can see the path that winds across the pasture. It leads into the badlands as well, and merges with the way taken by the Shangoran."

"I can show him," the girl volunteered, and Nuroc

110

saw that she was looking at him coquettishly as she adjusted her hastily-donned tunic.

"That won't be necessary," Nuroc said. He thanked the shepherd and gently guided his horse down the steep pitch of the faultline. As he reached the designated path and started across the pasture, the scene about him conjured up visions of his own former life as tender of the royal flock. How long ago that seemed. He felt a twinge of envy for the shepherd who had given him directions. Never would he be able to be so carefree and foolhardy. The nostalgia bit harshly into his present sense of loss, reminding him of his purpose. Reaching the edge of the pasture, he rode his horse a few dozen yards into the badlands until the way became too uncertain.

Dismounting, he led the way and walked on slowly, gauging the lay of the terrain before him in the dim moonlight. His horse was more sure-footed than most, but he chose not to tempt fate by rushing. In the back of his mind, Nuroc knew that he stood only the most remote chance of finding the men and he would do that only if they camped for the night and gave him time to make up for the day's worth of travel they had managed before he came upon their scent.

When he came to the point where a second path merged with the one he was traveling along, Nuroc crouched over and inspected the dirt. There were three sets of tracks visible in the moonlight and, more important, a dried trail of blood undoubtedly left by the wounded Shangoran's severed arm.

Spurred on by the discovery, he continued across the crippled landscape. All around him, the ground began to rise and fall with increasing regularity, and the path zigzagged around obstructions, both natural and man-made. A former temple lay in ruins nearby, with most of its columns down and fractured into bits like large teeth. In the moonlight, the once-polished stone almost seemed to glow with a ghostly light, and he felt as if unseen eyes stared out at him from behind the few standing pillars. He moved on, wondering what it must

111

have been like the night when the temple fell and the land ripped apart, swallowing victims into the black chasm of the triggered fault.

In time his steed began to tire from the constant negotiation of bolting escarpments and the relentless turns of the thin, winding trail. Several times its hooves skidded over a stretch of gravel, almost causing the horse to lose its balance. Nuroc was equally exhausted and keenly aware of his untended hunger. Last night's snack of cheese and melons had been his last meal.

As they reached the swollen formations of the rocky pass, Nuroc felt relief at the sight of a trickling creek surrounded by bushes ripe with edible negoti, whitish berries the size of grapes. He tethered the horse to a sapling that grew near the stream bed and let it drink as he helped himself to the berries, taking care not to eat too many and risk the outbreak of itching splotches that came from the negoti's high acidity.

He felt better after sitting down a moment, then decided it would be wise to climb the nearby cluster of rocks and survey the surrounding badlands for a trace of fire that might betray the camp of the raiders. If he spotted such a fire, he would move on. If not, he would put up for the night and accept that the killers had eluded him for the time being.

Taking off his sword and sheath to make the climbing easier, Nuroc began to circle the base of the rock formation, looking for the best footing. As he rounded a large boulder, he suddenly stopped and leaned back behind the rock's cover, forcing down a wave of nausea. Twenty feet away, a pack of four kildwolves were crouched over a human corpse, tearing at what was left of the flesh with their powerful jaws. In the dim light, Nuroc saw that the ripped clothing was similar to that of the Shangoran he had wounded, but this body had two arms.

Not wishing to investigate further, he backtracked on light feet, thankful that the wolves had their sensitive noses buried deep in flesh and blood so that his scent went unnoticed. Once he was beyond sight of the kildwolves, he turned about and scurried back to his horse and the security of his sword.

"It *is* you, then," a voice called out of the darkness behind Nuroc.

Nuroc whirled about, cutting his sword through the air before him. The figure who had addressed him stood beyond its range, however, to one side of the negoti bush.

"One step closer and I'll cut you down!" Nuroc warned, his voice firm despite his trepidation.

"That would be unfortunate," the man said calmly. He stepped forward despite Nuroc's warning, and the young man recognized the man as the peddler his father had spoken with the previous afternoon. "You are Nuroc? My name is Solat. You can lower your sword. I have no wish or reason to harm you." He held his hands out to demonstrate that he was unarmed.

"What are you doing here?" Nuroc demanded suspiciously.

"The same as you, although I have been both more and less successful," Solat replied cryptically. "I tracked down the camp of the raiders, but I broke my leg and lost my donkey stealing to cover when the last of them arrived."

Nuroc saw that the old peddler was leaning for support on a length of broken lance. "Their camp is here?" he asked, less vehemently.

Solat nodded and pointed to the rock formation. "Help me up onto your horse and I'll show you. There are provisions there, and one can light a fire without being seen from below."

"Why should I trust you?" Nuroc questioned. "What if you are in league with the Ghetites and luring me into some trap? You could be pretending to be injured."

Solat forced a laugh. "To what end, Nuroc? To overpower you? Look at me. I am no threat to an old woman, much less a youth of your bearing."

"But what of your condor?"

"Enough, lad!" Solat said impatiently. "Providence

113

has sent you to me when I was unable to seek you out. I come by the orders of the sorcerer Inkemisa. Three months I have sought you and your family out with the aid of his daughter Myrania. Augage had his people on your trail as well. They killed your family, and now only you can assist us in what must be done to stop Augage from realizing his plans for domination over Aerda and all of Dorban. Now, have I said enough to earn your trust? We have much to discuss, and time is crucial. Already the moon races toward eclipse at twice its normal speed."

Each of Solat's words stung Nuroc like slaps in the face of hysteria, and for the first time he realized that his destiny was at hand. Lowering his sword, he stepped forward to help the peddler, seeing the vile bruise that marked where his leg was broken.

"Myrania," Nuroc said excitedly. "I saw her in the tavern at Wheshi, performing at the wish of the whoremaster." He made a cradle of his clasped hands and bent over so that the peddler could support himself as he climbed onto the back of Nuroc's horse.

"There was good reason for such desperate measures," Solat said as Nuroc untethered the horse and led it toward the rock formation. "I will tell you all I know once we reach the camp. Until then, we will both need our breath to scale the rise."

Indeed, the climb would have been a challenge to Nuroc without the added burden of dragging his reluctant steed up the incline. There would have been no chance of clearing the initial slope had there not been a length of vine for him to pull himself up by. He guessed that the vine had been laid along the footholds by the raiders to help them make the climb while carrying provisions to the camp.

Once they had made their way up two of the formations, Solat stopped Nuroc's horse with a suddenness that almost jerked Nuroc off the trail.

"Let me know when you want to stop, damn you!" Nuroc cursed. "It's your leg that's broken, not your mouth!"

114

"Forgive me," Solat apologized. "But my saddlebags are down in the narrow space between those overlapping rocks."

Nuroc reached into the crevice Solat pointed to and pulled out the bulging leather bags. He handed them to Solat, who said, "I had the good fortune to take these off the donkey moments before it plunged over the side."

Hearing strange sounds off to one side of the path, Nuroc leaned forward to see where Solat was staring. Down a drop of fifteen feet, the donkey was wedged on its back between two boulders. Another set of kildwolves were feasting on its entrails.

"It lost its footing when I pulled off the trail to seek cover," Solat said, looking away from the grisly carnage. "It died cushioning my own fall, but I still struck the rocks with my leg. It took me the entire day to crawl back up to the path here and drag myself to level ground. I passed out near the creek some time before you arrived. Fortunately, the kildwolves prefer dead meat to living or else it might have been my bones they were cleaning their teeth with. But come, the camp is just up this last rock."

The final slope was the least difficult to clear, and soon they were on the flattened clearing of the raider's hideout. It was vacated, although Nuroc stared suspiciously at the bubbling pool near the edge of the cave. He had his sword out and searched the shadows, a small part of his mind still braced for treachery and ambush.

"From where I fell I could hear the two raiders argue, then fight," Solat said, awkwardly dismounting so that he put no pressure on his wounded leg. Nuroc helped him to a crudely made bench of stone near a rounded firepit. "Only one of them rode back down, with the other's horse trailing behind. I am certain the one whose arm you clove was slain by the other, though I don't see his body here. Perhaps it is—"

Nuroc interrupted, "More kildwolves are feeding on

115

a Shangoran at the bottom of the pass, but he possessed both his arms."

"One was regrown through the aide of a powerful ointment," Solat explained, leaning over and picking up a fragment of the broken jar. He sniffed the dried salve and made a face. "A rare substance. Augage gave his highest priority to their mission in providing them with it."

Nuroc looked about the campsite, seeing a stockpile of wood in the recessed cave, along with rations of dried meat and fruit. He retrieved pieces of the wood and arranged it in the firepit, which was already layered with cold ash and snuffed embers. He then took his fire stones from his belt and worked them together until the wood took flame and began to send out its welcome heat.

Returning to the cave, he brought out the food rations and sat on the ground next to Solat. Together, they chewed silently on the tough meat, working it to a soft consistency as they watched the fire grow.

"A sad day for you," Solat finally said.

"Savages!" Nuroc spat, voicing the anger that had been building all the day within him. "They cut down my family like cornered game. By the eye of Dorban, I'll make them wish they'd slain me as well!"

"They mean to do just that, Nuroc," Solat said gravely. "Their mission is not completed until you are dead."

"But why?"

"You know well enough why. You are the last link between Talmon-Khash and life among the living. If you die, Talmon-Khash is trapped in the nether realm forever, where he can pose no threat to Augage."

"They have the ceremonial dagger, though," Nuroc said. "Without it, I can do nothing to revive Talmon-Khash."

Solat smiled enigmatically as he reached for his saddlebags and began to untie a row of knots firmly securing the largest pocket. Nuroc watched the peddler, swallowing the last of his meat. It was salty and dry, but it served to tame his hunger some.

"What of Myrania?" he asked, starting on the fruit. "You say she is aiding you, and yet it seemed to me she was a prisoner of Sphextay."

"I will get to that," Solat said, unfastening the last knot while holding down the loosened flap. "Now be silent and do not move, on your life."

Confused, Nuroc obeyed the peddler and stared at the saddlebags as Solat began to hum a haunting dirge, softly and flawlessly. Once he removed his hand from the leather flap, there was motion within the bag. Nuroc watched on in dumbfounded awe as a full-grown cobra slithered from the pouch and immediately coiled itself between Solat and the saddlebag. Solat continued his song and the serpent reared its head, fanning out its lethal head and swaying to and fro. Ever so slowly, Solat reached past the snake and withdrew from the pouch the ceremonial dagger of Talmon-Khash. Setting the knife in his lap, Solat changed the pitch of his humming and the cobra pulled away, bending back to the ground and returning to the pouch. Solat pressed down the flap and began securing the knots, one by one.

"An elaborate precaution, to be sure," Solat said once he stopped humming, "but the stakes are high. I followed the Shangoran here and stole the dagger from him. It had been my plan to retreat and track you down, but his companion returned too soon. I've told you the rest."

"But how did you know to follow the Shangoran here?" Nuroc asked, reaching over for the sacred dagger.

"The condor," Solat said. "I train the birds for a living, and am better at my trade than any man that breathes. Inkemisa and Myrania sought me out three months ago and confided in me their purpose. They wished me to train a condor to seek out the rings and dagger of Talmon-Khash. The pieces each contain an essence from the marrow of the first condor to fly the

117

skies over Dorban. Kind knows kind, and it is possible for the condor to detect both dagger and ring from afar, as it did yesterday afternoon at the mining camp."

"That is how you knew who we were," Nuroc guessed.

Solat nodded, tying the last knot. "Now I must tell you what I told your father, and send you on your way to—*Aaaeiieeee!*"

Solat jerked as he screamed, and Nuroc saw that the cobra had forced its way through a space between knots and imbedded its fangs in the old man's wrist.

Taking the ceremonial dagger, Nuroc lashed out and quickly severed the cobra's head. Solat reeled back to the ground, clutching his arm above the wound. Nuroc used the blade to pry the serpent's deadly jaws from its target, seeing venom drip from its fangs.

After tossing the head into the fire, Nuroc turned to Solat, whose jaw was trembling as sweat rolled a wet crown around his forehead.

"Potent devils they are," the peddler gasped through the pain that set his body afire. He licked at his lips and his voice grew thick as he tried forcing words out. "You must go . . . to . . . go to Cothe. . . . Myrania goes there . . . to . . . tomorrow. . . . She will b . . . b . . . be at . . ."

Spasms racked the old man violently, cutting off his words. Nuroc reached for him and tried to hold him still.

"Where in Cothe?" Nuroc cried. "Where will she be? How can I rescue her from Sphextay?"

But it was of no use. Solat was dead. Nuroc let the body fall lightly to the ground. He took the dagger and carefully wiped the blood of the cobra off its blade, turning up to the sky, where the moon shone down on the camp.

"Why?" he wondered aloud.

Why was the road to his destiny paved with death? Why was his loved one among the company of whores and a man without virtue? Why was the burden of an entire civilization heaped upon his shoulders?

The questions plagued him until late in the night. When sleep finally came to him, it was accompanied by nightmares. He relived the past two days in countless variations, each one vivid with horror and intrigue. It would be some time before the string of tragedies would cease to prey on his mind, weighing his thoughts with grave torment.

Eleven

In the morning Nuroc slung Solat's body over the back of his horse and led it down to the base of the pass. The kildwolves had ravaged most of the Shangoran's corpse, and smaller beasts and birds of prey had gathered to fight over what was left.

A single set of tracks led away from the pass in the opposite direction from which Nuroc had arrived the previous night. Mounting up, he rode on, following the prints. The terrain along this stretch was less formidable than the land he had already crossed. Brush and spindly trees were more common, and Nuroc saw countless species of small creatures scurrying about the rocks that baked in the early sun. The day promised to be as hot in the badlands as it had been cold during the night.

There were more ruins tossed about the land, and after many miles the tracks led to the remains of what had once been an amphitheater. Most of the curved rows of stone seats were still intact, facing a simple stage where poets had once told the old tales and musicians had wooed the citizenry with song. Nuroc frowned at the sight and guided his steed down one of the aisles and around the stage.

119

Several campfires still smouldered in pits, and the beaten dirt was marred by the prints of several dozen horses. The fragile bones of small beasts lay in scattered heaps around the fires, along with rinds from fruit that were now dried and curled from the sun.

A whole force of raiders, Nuroc reflected. It seemed impossible they could have roamed so far within Aerda's boundaries.

Concerned, Nuroc drove his horse on, until at last he was clear of the badlands and riding along surer paths that parted vast meadows lush with tall grasses and summer flowers. At one point, the sets of tracks he had been following since the amphitheater strayed off into the meadow, and he could see the subtle bend in the grass where they had gone.

He was about to follow in pursuit when, out the corner of his eye, he saw the watery sparkle of the sun's reflection off the Targoan River, less than a mile downhill. Peering hard against the sunlight, he realized that he faced the riverpost marking the junction between separate forks of the Targoan.

Continuing down the path, Nuroc saw crudely built shacks lining the banks of the river. The largest was a trading post where local hunters, craftsmen and miners brought their goods for sale or transport to Cothe and points beyond. There were also shanties stocked with provisions for the crews of the merchant vessels, who, as a rule, preferred to gather rations as they were needed in order to leave the holds free for the storage of trade cargo.

The closer he came to the post, the more Nuroc could see of the river. It was wide and placid here, with a faintly visible current carrying loose sticks and other objects downstream. A craft was drifting down river away from the port. Nuroc realized it was the whoreship.

"Myrania!" Nuroc called out. The bend in the river was half a mile away, however, and his voice was lost in the rampant overgrowth. Lush as the meadow was, the growth along the river looked brown and brittle, com-

120

prised as it was with the conti reeds that thrived best in the rains of the winter season. The stiff dry blades rustled in the breeze blowing over the river as Nuroc rode as fast as he could and still keep the Solat's body secure slung across the horse.

The post was watched over by Aerdan soldiers serving the same purpose as those who watched over the mines. Piracy was infrequent along the river, but the presence of troops along its shores acted as a further deterrent, assuring any violators of swift reprisal should they breach the peace of the king's waters.

Nuroc did not approach the post unobserved, and as he rode to the bridge that spanned the river and led to the docks, he was greeted by a dozen archers in Aerdan garb who trained their shafts on his chest.

Slowing his horse, Nuroc looked past the grim reception to the docks, where the merchant galley he had helped load with ore the previous day was now moored. Youths younger than Nuroc were walking down the docks and boarding the ship, taking places along the oar benches that lined the ship's interior. Many of them looked up toward him curiously.

A corpulent officer appeared before the archers and addressed Nuroc. "Stay your horse, boy, and give your purpose!"

"I've followed foreign raiders across the badlands," Nuroc said hurriedly. "Their trail leads through the meadow to the banks of the Targoan farther downriver."

The officer laughed heartily and looked to the archers, who also snickered. He turned back to Nuroc and chortled, "Are you a jester in search of a court, boy?"

"I am Nuroc, bound for Cothe," Nuroc answered firmly.

"Cothe is on the verge of battle, though not with your imagined raiders," the officer said, no longer laughing. "You've no business there. Who is the dead man?"

"A peddler, slain by the fangs of a cobra. I wished to see him properly buried among his fellow man."

121

"How touching," the officer said drily.

Behind the officer and his coterie of archers, another man crossed the bridge in long, steadfast strides. He was tall and muscular, wearing the crested Shield of Aerda emblazoned on the chest of his jupon. Nuroc recognized him as captain of the ore galley.

"Your ship carries ore I helped mine and load with the men of Wheshi," Nuroc told the captain.

The captain furrowed his brow as he looked Nuroc over, then nodded his head, "Yes, I recall you now. What brings you to this post?"

"I wish to go to Cothe. Let me join the cargo's guard."

"Are you of age, boy?"

"As much as the rest of your crew, as I see it."

The captain grinned, though not happily. "More guards I don't need," he said. "Can you bend an oar?"

Nuroc exposed his calloused palms, saying, "As I told you, I am from Wheshi, where men row each day as a matter of course."

The captain conversed with the other officer, who then signaled the archers aside and waved Nuroc across the bridge. As he rode, the captain walked alongside him. "I am Neupitt and I run a good ship. Help keep it that way and I'll get you to Cothe. If not you'll be off at the next port. Fair enough?"

Nuroc nodded.

"And what of the dead man?" Neupitt asked.

"I will bury him yonder, where I see the graves of others."

"There's no time for that. Our ship leaves as soon as we board. Already we are half a day behind schedule."

"I'll tend to the body," the other officer said, falling in behind Neupitt. He asked Nuroc, "What's your price for the horse? You can't take it with you."

Nuroc patted the steed's neck, reluctant to part with it. "I'm not sure of its worth," he admitted.

A restrained smile came over the other officer's face as he looked over the beast as it walked. "Eighty lampich," he pronounced finally. "A fair price to be sure."

"Twice that would still be a bargain for you, Mordzai," Neupitt said from behind. "Don't cheat the lad."

Mordzai shot Neupitt an angry glance, but the ship's captain was grinning at him. Grumbling to himself, the portly officer went to his pockets and sorted through a handful of coins. He thrust all but two of them Nuroc's way. "One hundred and fifty lampich."

Nuroc looked over to Neupitt, who bobbed his head approvingly. Dismounting, Nuroc handed the reins over to Mordzai and followed Neupitt across the bridge and down a weathered path to the docks.

"I am grateful for your help," Nuroc told the captain.

"Unless I miss my guess, you are the lad whose family was slain by raiders," Neupitt said. "I think you deserve a show of kindness."

"But how did you know?"

"No word travels faster than that of ill news, lad. We were delayed because the men came late to the mines yesterday. They saw to the burial of your family and spent time seeking you out."

"I was pursuing the raiders," Nuroc said. "There were only a handful that attacked us, but as I rode here from across the badlands I spotted the tracks of a larger force. They were heading toward the banks downriver from here. I tried to tell Mordzai but he laughed as if I were telling jokes."

"Mordzai is a swine," Neupitt said. "Ten years I've dealt with him along these waters and I'll venture he's swindled himself a king's fortune from those who fall prey to him. Look at him now, the jackal!"

Nuroc looked back to the bridge, where Mordzai was feverishly tugging at the rings on Solat's fingers. Instinctively, Nuroc felt to his waist, where his hands touched the condor-hilt of the ceremonial dagger. Sheathed in his plain scabbard, he hoped it would not draw overdue attention.

"These raiders you saw," Neupitt asked, showing obvious concern. "Were they Ghetite or Shangoran?"

123

"I only saw those who slew my family, but there was one Shangoran among three Ghetites," Nuroc said as they continued to the galley. "Is it true what Mordzai said about the war? Will Cothe fall under siege?"

"That is the word. My fear is that Augage is sending these small raiding parties into points well beyond the capital, in hopes that Pencroft will spread apart his troops. That is why you see my ship is filled with recruits younger than yourself. They're from upriver, at Thutchers. Two days they've camped here, waiting for us to arrive and take them to Cothe, so they can take up arms and help defend the capital."

Reaching the galley, the two men boarded and the plank was pulled away from the docks. As he walked the main deck behind Neupitt, Nuroc could feel the eyes of the youths following him. Besides the recruits, there were also a dozen guards already dressed in the uniform of the militia.

Above the sounds of activity on the ship, there came the sound of a loud splash in the river. Both Neupitt and Nuroc turned about. The waters surged by but they could see nothing out of the ordinary on its rugged surface. Then their eyes strayed up to the bridge, where Mordzai stood beside Nuroc's horse. Solat's body no longer was draped over the steed's back.

"There's your burial, lad," Neupitt muttered bitterly. "Come, let's be gone from here before I go back and wring that wretch's neck!"

Neupitt pointed out a vacant bench and Nuroc climbed down to it, taking up his position behind the oar. As the ship was slowly maneuvered out into the flow of the river, he looked at the water for a trace of Solat, but the old peddler never surfaced.

"You'll be avenged," Nuroc whispered. "Augage will pay for your death and that of my family with his own blood!"

Twelve

Because the galley's course was downriver, the twenty young men hunched over their benches were not hard-pressed to work their oars. Most of the labor came from the behemoth dark-eyed Cothian manning the rudder, who guided the craft around occasional snags and the more frequent bends in the river. Nonetheless, an olive-skinned youth, clad only in sandals and loin-cloth, strode the deck between rowers, tapping a rhyth-mic beat on his tabor as he droned a rowing dirge. Some of the oarsmen joined in, while others were con-tent to remain silent and let their minds drift forward to the day when they would have the chance to take up arms against the dreaded Ghetites.

Nuroc shared his bench with Tudier, the oldest of the recruits but still a few month's Nuroc's junior. He was short and wiry, with a thin wisp of moustache scratched above his thin lips. High-spirited and gregari-ous, Tudier's almost ceaseless banter was welcomed by Nuroc, as it kept his mind from dwelling on his situa-tion. Already they had wisked by two ports without his seeing the whoreship, and he felt certain that it must be proceeding directly to Cothe, at a pace that would bring it into dock well before the galley. His odds of rescuing Myrania seemed precarious enough on open waters; to seek her out at the capital would be im-measurably more difficult.

". . . most of us are shepherds," Tudier was saying. "I myself spent half my years in the fields, staring at infernal sheep and longing for the day I could do something more. I was always glad when wolves or foxes would raid the fields and give me a chance to escape the boredom. I mean to tell you, Nuroc, that there is no one in all of Thutchers more skilled than I with the slingshot."

Tudier paused to catch his breath and Nuroc smiled at his new-found friend. Tudier sounded to him like the Nuroc of old, in the carefree days before the cataclysm, or even as recently as his last day at the mines, before grim realities had made a bitter travesty of his dreams for excitement.

Tudier went on, "And so, when word reached our hamlet that the king sought more men to take arms against the Ghetites, we all decided to enlist. More thrills to be had in battle than minding sheep, don't you think?"

Nuroc nodded slightly, staring out at the passing scenery. The banks still swarmed with conti reeds, interspersed with the sweeping branches of willows and an occasional thick-trunked scenoak with fiery leaves. Small birds could be seen flitting amongst the flora, and some ventured out over the water, diving toward the surface for a stab at floating insects or small fish.

"What a weapon!" Tudier said, noticing the hilt of Nuroc's dagger. "May I see it?"

Nuroc hesitated, then figured he would draw more attention to the weapon by maintaining secrecy about it. He unsheathed the blade and handed it to Tudier, who whistled low in admiration as he rubbed a finger over the intricate carving.

"Where did you come upon this?"

"It was my father's," Nuroc said, not bothering to elaborate. He cringed anxiously as Tudier waved the blade through the air, attracting the attention of the recruits on the nearby benches.

"I've never felt a knife so well-balanced," Tudier commented, returning the dagger to Nuroc. "You're lucky to own so fine a piece."

As Nuroc slipped the sacred dagger back into his sheath, the rower in front of them bragged, "I've seen finer weapons. Back at my home I have a half-sword of metal so well-polished I can see my face in it."

"What does that matter, Bordo?" Tudier sneered contemptuously, "Especially with a face so homely as yours. If I were you with that blade, I'd keep it in the scabbard lest I frighten myself."

Bordo ignored Tudier's insult and boasted further, "Each year, Thutchers holds a gaming festival. The past two years I've won matches of swordplay against others in my age group. I can't wait to pit myself against some scurvy Ghetite!"

"As I hear it," Nuroc cut in, slapping his oar idly into the river, "in battle they don't take the time to match you up evenly."

"Fine with us," Tudier countered, now siding with his hometown friend. "We'll match our swords against any."

"What about three swordsmen at once, or an archer who strikes from beyond reach of your blade?" Nuroc asked them both.

For once, both youths from Thutchers had no ready reply.

As the galley rounded a bend and entered a wide span of the river, the current waned and they took to their oars. The craft wavered from side to side until their strokes fell into a steady rhythm. Along the upper decks, which ran the length of the ship, archers were positioned at strategic points, scanning either shore for signs of suspicious activity.

One of the archers near Nuroc and Tudier suddenly turned upward and loosed a shaft toward the sky.

"What are you doing?" Neupitt shouted to the archer, striding down the deck toward him.

"I was just practicing my aim on that condor," the archer said, pointing at the bird of prey that soared in the air above the vessel. "It's been following us since the riverpost, begging to be shot at."

"Fool!" Neupitt cried into the archer's face. "Do you know the fates you tempt in slaying a condor on the coming of a black moon?"

"Surely the captain does not believe in Ghetite superstitions," the archer said, lowering his bow.

"Do not confuse the ways of Dorban and the folly of Ghetite," Neupitt warned the archer. "Stay your arrows and leave the bird be, else we'll tie you to the prow and let it eat your liver!"

Neupitt walked off and the archer looked to the bowman nearest him, sharing slight smirks. From his bench, Nuroc looked up at the condor, rubbing the talon ring about his finger. He was certain it was the condor of Solat, perhaps the same bird used by Myrania in her performance at the tavern in Wheshi. But why did it stay aloft instead of flying down after the ring, he wondered to himself. The ways of sorcery had always mystified him. It was as if practitioners of the black arts dwelled in a separate world from that of normal men; a world based on another set of rules far beyond his ken.

As Nuroc puzzled further over the trailing condor, another set of eyes were on the outstretched wings.

"Well done, my feathered friend," Quidantis murmured from astride his horse, hidden under cover of a wooded fringe along the southern banks of the Targoan. "Again you have led me to those I seek."

Quidantis was not alone. Twenty fellow horsemen, comprised equally of Ghetites and Shangorans, stayed their mounts behind him, watching Quidantis for a signal.

Turning his eyes from the bird to the ship, Quidantis slowly raised a hollowed goat's horn to his lips. Moments later, when the galley had passed through to a narrowing of the river, a shrill bleating broke the air, and from the north banks the heads of Ghetite archers peered above the cover of conti reeds and a shower of their arrows descended upon the ship.

The tabor player was the first to die, with shafts pierced through his heart and the taut skin of his drum. Two of the Aerdan bowmen aboard the ship also fell under fire. One was the man who had sent a shaft speeding after the condor only moments before.

"Dorban and Wondelf!" Tudier gasped, dropping his oar as the archer slumped over him. Nuroc helped the youth shove the bowman aside, then leaned forward to glance over the side of the boat. He saw Quidantis bolt from cover, leading the other horsemen in storming the southern banks, waving their weapons.

Farther downstream, yet another small group of raiders worked the final ax strokes on a huge scenoak before pushing it into the river, where it lodged itself firmly into the embankment and formed a barrier the galley would not be able to circumnavigate. Half of the horsemen rode to the newly laid obstruction while Quidantis led the others in the opposite direction, keeping the woods between them and arrows being fired by archers on board the galley. A few of the shafts whistled through the cover and found their marks, sending horses plummeting through the conti reeds and into the water, both with and without their riders.

Charging down the deck of his ship, buckler raised against the opponent's arrows, Neupitt shouted down at the recruits, "Drop the oars and take up your weapons. Let's see what kind of soldiers you are!"

The current had begun to pick up, and the galley drifted toward the fallen scenoak, now aswarm with dismounted Ghetites and green-garbed Shangorans grasping swords and battleaxes in anticipation of lusty massacre. The river at this point was shallow, and Quidantis led his men into the waters, boxing the galley in.

Across the river, the enemy archers were being selective with their targets, and the Cothian manning the rudder was next to fall. A constant hail of shafts kept any of the Aerdans from taking his place, and the unguided boat began to drift toward the southern bank.

"Show yourselves, devilspawn!" Neupitt screamed at the north shore assailants, grabbing a bow from the dead archer beside him and loosing a quarrel into the

129

foliage. He was answered by a volley he could not dodge. Twice pierced, he tumbled over the row of shields lining the edge of the ship and plunged into the brooding depths of the Targoan.

The archers on the ship attempted to retaliate, but their targets remained unseen and elusive. Some turned to take aim on the more visible enemy in the waters and on the fallen scenoak, but did so at the expense of their lives. Any Aerdan who turned his back to the north shore exposed himself as a target and was quickly struck by the deadly accuracy of the bow-wielding snipers.

Half of the oarsmen had followed Neupitt's final command and risen from their benches. The others, Nuroc among them, chose to remain less obvious a mark until they were in reach of foes they could raise a sword against. The horseback raiders were plodding closer to the ship each second.

Nuroc was the first to realize a means of countering the north shore offensive. Squatting low on his bench, cursing an arrow that thunked into the boat's thick siding, he quickly worked free his firestones from his belt. The floorboards were lined with dirty straw to provide a matting for the rowers' feet, and Nuroc made a pile of the driest pieces before showering them with sparks coaxed from his stones.

"Tudier," he cried out without taking his eyes off his desperate task. "Are there torches in the hold?"

Understanding Nuroc's plan, Tudier relayed the message amidst the death and confusion on deck. By the time Nuroc had raised a small fire on the bench, a handful of pitch-tipped torches had been brought to him. One by one he ignited the staffs and passed them up to Tudier, who in turn hurled them into the foliage on the north shore.

The dried conti reeds burst into an immediate blaze, and the undercover assault from the hidden archers ceased. Because the reeds extended directly to the embankment, the rebel bowmen were forced to either retreat or take to the river. Some attempted the latter course and befell the same fate their volleys had dealt.

The galley was sweeping headlong into the fallen tree. Nuroc rushed to the forecastle, an oar slung over either shoulder. Tudier followed him and took one of the oars as Nuroc continued to bark orders, none of which were questioned.

"Give us some cover! If we ram that tree, we'll go under! Beat back those horsemen trying to get aboard! Show these swine that we can deal death as well as they!"

Using the oars to push against the tree and the bank, Nuroc and Tudier eased the docking of the galley against the southern bank, pushing aside the water-bound horsemen in the ship's way. A few of the raiders managed to fight their way aboard, however, and the hand-to-hand combat began in earnest.

With hearty cries and little restraint, the youths, armed with whatever they could snatch up, poured along the decks to join the fray, eager to prove themselves. Meanwhile, the Aerdan bowmen continued to hold the blazing north shore offensive at bay, although some of the enemy managed to work their way to the unruly span of the fallen scenoak.

The two forces were close to matched in number. The more war-trained raiders, however, held a slight edge, as their weapon-handling brought death with fewer blows than the relentless flailing of the recruits. Tudier and Bordo, the boastful Thutcherian, were exceptions. Tudier dropped his oar and began battling with an ax plucked from the corpse of an Aerdan officer. He fell each man he faced in the course of several blows, while Bordo wielded his sword with a deftness that left three men dead or wounded in as many swipes.

Nuroc was less willing to part with his oar, as it provided a range he could not have with his dagger. Though awkward to handle, it served its purpose well, sweeping two men from the tree into the water, one dead from a caved skull and the other helpless, his swordarm and half his ribs shattered.

As he battled his way onto the scenoak and continued to wreak deadly swaths with the oar, he saw one of the horsemen dismount from the waters and wade ashore. It was Quidantis.

"You!" Nuroc shouted, dispatching several more foes as he scrambled down the slick bark of the fallen tree to the embankment, where Quidantis awaited him, sword in hand.

"That's it, boy!" Quidantis growled, a gleam in his eye. "Come and die!"

The oar was too awkward for handling on the bank, so Nuroc tossed it aside in favor of the ceremonial dagger. Ignoring the advantage against him, he lunged at Quidantis, his short blade hissing through the air. The glint of metal coruscated in the sunlight and the air sounded loud with the exchange of blows. All around the river was a din of shouts and clashing weapons.

Quidantis fought with finesse, his swordplay swift and measured. But against the sheer force of Nuroc's parries and ripostes his arm began to weaken. Any other blade Nuroc's size would have snapped at the hilt from the abuse, but the onslaught did no damage to the edge of the condor-dagger.

"I mean to have that sword, boy," Quidantis snarled. "It means much to me. Hand it over and I'll call off our attack."

Nuroc pressed on, laughing, "You've no attack to call off, Ghetite! Your men fall like grain at the harvest!"

Though Nuroc exaggerated, the Aerdans had indeed turned the course of battle. The raiders were beginning to retreat, leaving their dying comrades to bleed the river red. One of them, however, saw the duel between Quidantis and Nuroc and splashed through the shallow waters toward them, ready to lend his mace to Quidantis's aid. Nuroc saw the approach of the second Ghetite and maneuvered the course of the fighting so that Quidantis stood between him and his new aggressor.

His footwork was done hastily, however, and without a proper bearing on the odd pitch of the embankment. Backing into the raised root of another scenoak, he tumbled off-balance into the dirt.

As the two Ghetites raced forward to capitalize on Nuroc's brief incapacity, a feathered blur flew down from the sky, and the mace-wielding raider screamed as powerful talons ripped into his arm and shoulder. The condor pecked fiercely at the man's face, sending him back into the river in hopes of forcing the bird loose from his shoulder.

The distraction gave Nuroc time to recover his footing and fend off an overhead swipe by which Quidantis had hoped to split his skull. Instead, the Ghetite found himself committed to a futile blow that left him unprotected as Nuroc's dodge brought him within striking distance. Before Quidantis could bring his sword around to his defense, sharp metal ripped through his chest and stilled the rapid beating of his heart. Nuroc had to grit his teeth as he yanked his dagger clear and pushed Quidantis away from him.

Nearby, Tudier was making quick work of the man with the mace. Nuroc looked to the skies above the river and saw the condor flying off, blood trailing from beak and talons. Its throaty shriek sounded shrilly as it soared through the blackened smoke of the burning conti and was gone from sight.

Nuroc looked about the gruesome scene before him, seeking out another foe, but soon realized there were none save for the wounded. Above their moans, the air resounded with the first cries of victory as the recruits saw that they had routed the enemy and sent their few survivors fleeing into the brush.

"By the Shield of Aerda!" Tudier howled with delight, paying no heed to his many surface wounds. "We've done it! Victory is ours!" The rangy Thutcherian made his way to shore and beamed at Nuroc. "It was your thinking that turned the tide, friend!"

From the blood-drenched decks of the galley, another of the recruits called out, "Lo! Only we from

133

Thutchers survived the battle. All those from the militia have been slain!"

Tudier grasped Nuroc's swordarm and raised his hand high so that the ceremonial dagger pointed in the air.

"Then I say we have a new captain!" Tudier hailed the others. "Nuroc will lead us to Cothe!"

Still dazed from the battling, Nuroc stared out with disbelief as he saw the other recruits rise from the midst of the bloody carnage and cry out in affirmation.

"Hail, Nuroc!"

"Hail, Captain of the Young Recruits!"

Thirteen

The tasks at hand dealing with the aftermath of battle put an end to the displays of euphoria. No sooner had the wounded been treated than predators began to descend upon the site for a go at the carrion. By water, land and air they came, beasts and creatures of all shapes and sizes, casting their hungry eyes on the victims of the battle. It was quickly decided that those Aerdans who had died, recruit and officer alike, would be loaded in the hold along with the ore for transport to Cothe. There was no time to see to the enemy fatalities, and it was hoped that the slain Ghetites and Shangorans would keep the scavengers well occupied while the skeleton crew hacked away the fallen scenoak and eased the galley past so that it was once again on open waters. There was considerable relief when all were aboard and the ship drifted from the scene of battle.

It was not too long afterward that the sun dipped

low in the sky and threw long, rippling shadows across the river. From his post at the helm, Nuroc turned to Tudier, who was pounding the punctured tabor to give the oarsmen a beat to row by.

"With a crew this small I think we're best off staying on board for the night," Nuroc said. "Do you think we should moor at a likely place or keep moving?"

Tudier replied, "It's been some time since we've passed one of the ports. Perhaps we'll come upon a place where we can dock for the night. If not, it'd be best to stay clear of the banks. There might be survivors from the battle bent on revenge or more animals that come out at night to feed."

On they went, and the sky began to change from blue to the grays of night. It seemed that with the coming darkness, the banks of the river grew increasingly loud with the chatter of wildlife. Monkeys could be seen swinging through the upper reaches of scenoaks, and brightly colored macaws and parrots squawked from their perches at the passing craft. Other beasts could be seen only in the rustling they made against the tightly grown bushes that replaced the conti reeds as the primary growth along the embankment. Fish splashed the water as they fed on bugs, and bullfrogs began to compete with crickets to see who could put forth the most persistent wall of sound.

After a series of sharp bends that required all those aboard to lend a hand in keeping the boat clear of snags and sand bars, the craft was ushered into a long stretch of river so wide that the current was reduced to an imperceptible drag.

"Look, yonder!" one of the rowers cried out, pointing down the river.

Nuroc looked up from the rudder and saw a length of dock reaching out from the banks a hundred yards ahead. As the craft drew nearer, he could make out a raised guard station perched on stilts above the treeline. Another building was half-hidden in the foliage, dark and silent.

"Yo!" Tudier called out through his cupped palms. "Let's have a greeting meant for heroes!"

There were louder sounds from the monkeys in the trees, but no response from the riverpost save for the gentle lapping of water against the posts rising from the river.

"I don't like it," Nuroc muttered.

"Nor I," Tudier said. "I wish there was more light. My skin is beginning to crawl."

The others were equally in the grips of apprehension. Hands were transferred from oars to weapons, and those on the benches leaned behind the cover of the shields that lined the boat. Nuroc kept one hand on the rudder but grasped a mace with the other, keeping his eyes on the post. Tudier grabbed up a bow and fed an arrow into the taut string.

"Who's minding the post!" he called out again, taking aim at the abandoned docks. His voice echoed slightly off the buildings, but there was no other answer.

To the fore, one of the recruits warily tossed a lasso about one of the dock's uprights and began pulling the ship in. Nuroc left the rudder and bade for Tudier to follow him forward and up onto the docks. He paused and turned back to the others, seeing the uncertainty in their eyes.

"At the first sign of trouble," he said lowly, "cut free and row as best you can. We'll catch you if we can, but there's nothing to be gained in throwing this small crew against a larger foe." To Bordo he added, "If need be, you take command."

Walking slowly alongside one another, Nuroc and Tudier advanced down the dock, listening through the innocent play of sounds for something that might betray the threat they sensed lay before them. Although Nuroc was unfamiliar with the ways of the militia, it seemed unnatural to him that a port along the Targoan would be left untended during so crucial a time. The only explanations for the absence of Aerdan troops he could think of filled him with further dread.

The docks were old, and the boards creaked and sagged beneath their steps, playing havoc on tensed nerves. As their eyes adjusted to the growing darkness, they could see no trace of damage to the weathered buildings, no sign of bloodshed on the banks. Tudier's fingers began to ache, but he refused to let up his hold on his drawn arrow. Nuroc held the mace in his right hand and kept the left near the hilt of the ceremonial dagger.

There was a sudden sound from the tower. Tudier jerked his bow upward and sent the arrow into the woodwork of the raised guard station. Nuroc sprang forward, clearing the last few planks and bounding up the rungs of the ladder built onto the tower's stilts.

"W . . . w . . . wait!" someone stammered from the tower in a startled voice. "Hold your fire. I am on your side."

"And what side is that!" Tudier shouted, reaching to his quiver for another arrow.

"Aerdan! Loyal to the death!" the man wailed.

Nuroc quickly reached the tower box and slipped over the side, landing behind the man. Shrieking with fright, the man spun about, falling over a strung hammock stretched out the width of the station.

"Don't kill me!" he cried out.

"Who are you!" Nuroc demanded, leaning over the man threateningly. "Where is the rest of the guard?"

"I am Struc," the man said, looking with terror at the tip of the mace. "King Pencroft has drawn back all forces to the capital, leaving me to give word to passing ships that the harbor at Cothe is off limits to all but military craft. It is the truth! Believe me!"

"Why didn't you answer our calls?"

"I was asleep," the man confessed. "I expected no ships to pass down the river after dusk."

Nuroc stared at the man, then slowly eased his grip on the mace and offered Struc a hand. "Here, stand up like a man. I believe you." He shouted down to the docks. "It's all right, Tudier."

Tudier lowered his bow and let the string loosen in his hand.

Nuroc looked back to Struc, asking, "What do you have by way of provisions?"

Fourteen

Fire ate through the largest log and it collapsed in the heap of glowing embers at the bottom of the fire pit. The recruits had set up camp around the fire, and most of them were now asleep in the shadows just beyond range of the flickering light. Nuroc was awake, along with Struc, Tudier and a few others. One of the youths had brought along a lyre, and he played out a soft melody as he leaned against the base of a jaunwood.

The night was still young. Struc had shown the recruits where the post's provisions were kept, and a feast had been prepared from the best of the rations. With full stomachs, it was easy to crawl off and let their exhaustion carry them into the arms of heavy slumber. The music of the lute was punctuated by varied snores and the continued sounds of the nightlife that surrounded the camp.

The moon's march across the night sky finally carried it above the treetops, and Tudier frowned as he observed it.

"That's strange," he whispered. "Last night, almost half the moon shone. Now it is already in its final quarter."

"Strange indeed," Struc agreed, sharing in the view. "The king's stargazers claim the black moon approaches with unnatural speed, which can only mean

138

that strong chants are being spoken in Ghetite. That is the reason the guards here were called back to Cothe. Pencroft fears that Augage has readied his offensive and is urging on the black moon so that his troops can ride full force across the border under cover of the darkness."

"But that seems far from likely," Tudier argued. "The moon is blotted out for too short a time to be of use as cover."

"The stargazers believe that if Augage can speed the black moon's coming, he can also prolong its stay," Struc said.

Nuroc listened on as Struc and Tudier continued to debate the meaning of the moon's swift waning, fighting back an urge to divulge what he knew. For so many years he had carried his secret, and it seemed as if the urgency of the situation demanded that he seek out whatever aid he could in seeing to his uncertain mission. How could he alone be expected to thwart Augage in matters of sorcery he knew so little about? There had to be a flaw in such a destiny, for he felt that events beyond his control were propelling him along, when it had always been his notion that he would be the master of that fate which awaited him.

But Nuroc recalled the oath of secrecy he and his parents had sworn to Talmon-Khash, and he remained silent, staring into the dying fire as he toyed with the blade of the sacred dagger. Across from him, the recruit with the lyre began to sing, retelling an ancient song of soldiering, handed down from a hundred generations of warriors.

> *Fair is my love,*
> *Her eyes like no other.*
> *I pray while I'm gone*
> *She won't love another.*
> *Her voice I'll hear*
> *As I sail to war.*
> *I'll hold her near*
> *When I'm back to shore.*

For fair is my love,
Her eyes like no other.
I pray while I'm gone
She won't love another.

For Nuroc the song brought on feelings for Myrania, and he felt both anger and a wrenching pain as he thought of her aboard the whoreship, forced to share the embrace of the treacherous Sphextay. He turned to Struc, who had finished talking with Tudier and now leaned before the fire, rubbing his hands over the last of the flames. Tudier had crawled off into the shadows to sleep.

"Struc, at what time did a craft carrying harlots and small boys come past the post today?"

Struc cocked his head toward Nuroc. "I saw no such boat," he said.

"It left the fork post just before our galley this morning," Nuroc said. "It should have reached this point by midday."

Struc shook his head and picked up a stick to stir the coals with. "Five ships passed by before yours today. Three were merchant galleys and the other two were private vessels. None carried boys or women." Struc moved away from the fire and rose to his feet, yawning. "Good night, Nuroc. I'll sleep in the guardhouse. The night sounds keep me awake."

Nuroc nodded to Struc and watched him walk back to the main building and disappear inside. The lute player finished an instrumental passage and continued to sing.

Love, guide my swordarm.
Love, guide my steed.
Love, bring me back
To the love that I need.
For fair is my love,
Her eyes like no other.
I pray while I'm gone
She won't love another.

The song was disturbing, and Nuroc tried to keep his mind off the lyrics. He looked to the young recruit and saw the longing in his eyes as he sang. He could not bring himself to ask that the youth stop, so instead he nodded and smiled, then rose to his feet, figuring to walk along the docks until his mind was settled enough for him to sleep.

As he left the circle of dim light cast by the fire, he heard a rustling in the brush behind the guardhouse. There had been similar sounds elsewhere in the dark most of the night, but something about this sound made him uneasy, because in its wake the other noises faded to silence. He knew from his years of shepherding that the only thing that stilled the voices of nocturnal creatures was the intrusion of a threat into their presence.

Unsheathing his dagger, Nuroc slowly approached the guardhouse and circled around the side. The rustling continued, and he wished there were some way he could alert Struc inside the structure to help investigate. In the back of his mind, he tried to calculate the distance they had traveled since routing the ambushers upriver, thinking the survivors might have finally caught up with them.

As he came to the back of the guardhouse, he carefully peered around the corner, knife ready. The darkness here was close to all-consuming, and he had difficulty making out shapes. But at last he saw something move. A figure was backing out of the rear door to the guardhouse, dragging something. Holding his breath, Nuroc dared to stick his head out farther for a better view, and realized with a chill that it was a body being dragged along the ground.

Certain that a raider had slain Struc and pulled him from the guardhouse, Nuroc kept silent and still until the figure moved off into the brush. He would have to see how many more there were before he decided upon a course of action.

There remained only one source of rustling in the thickets, and Nuroc finally stepped around to the back

141

and crept along to the spot where the figure had disappeared. He was about to follow in stealthy pursuit when he suddenly froze.

The man he pursued was coming back.

Nuroc leaned into the cover of the nearest bush, crouched in a position from which he could leap into action if need be. He tensed with apprehension as the figure walked directly past him and headed back toward the rear door of the guardhouse.

Once he could make out the man's features, Nuroc sprang from cover. The man whirled about and reached for his sword, but Nuroc was too fast and slammed him into the guardhouse wall and held the blade close to his throat.

It was Struc.

"Nuroc!" Struc cried out in surprise, trembling where he stood. "What is this?"

"I ask you the same question, Struc!" Nuroc countered, pressing cold metal against the flesh of Struc's neck. "Who was that you dragged out into the brush?"

"I dragged no one—"

"I'm tired of your lies!" Nuroc hissed, grabbing Struc by the collar of his jupon and pulling him away from the wall. Before Struc could secure his balance, Nuroc shoved him back through the thickets to a small clearing where a body lay half submerged in a gloomy marsh.

"Who is it?" Nuroc demanded, keeping his blade pointed at Struc.

Struc did not answer, but guilt and shame flooded across his face, replacing the look of fear he'd had from the moment Nuroc had surprised him. Keeping his dagger pointed at Struc, Nuroc bent down and dragged the body from the water. Even before he turned the corpse over to see the face, Nuroc knew it was one of Sphextay's boys. The youth's face was discolored and frozen in a look of confusion. Nuroc could see no wounds at first, but then saw the blood staining the front of his tunic below the belt. The boy's legs slumped apart, riding up the hem of the tunic to reveal the slashed, mutilated flesh between his thighs.

"Animal!" Nuroc shouted at Struc. "Sphextay *was* here after all, and you procured this boy for some grisly pleasure, then slew him. Or was that what gave you the pleasure, you foul—"

Struc bolted toward Nuroc, grabbing at the ceremonial dagger. Nuroc was ready for him, though, and pulled the blade away from Struc's grasp. Struc fell upon Nuroc and dragged him into the marsh. Struggling for his life, Struc fought with a vicious frenzy, knocking the knife from Nuroc's hand and grabbing at his throat. Nuroc's rage gave him strength enough to keep Struc's fingers from crushing his windpipe, and when he broke the other's hold they both tumbled into the deeper waters of the marsh. Nuroc was unprepared for the sudden drop and lost his hold on Struc, who quickly pushed away and swam off through the lily pads and cattails that rose from the surface.

Nuroc was about to dive out in further pursuit when, out of the corner of his eye, he saw something move along the lower branches of the scenoak that reached out over the marsh. He stopped where he was and could soon make out the swaying head of a full-grown python dangling his way. Swallowing hard, he remained still in the chest-high water as the large snake extended itself farther out of the tree.

Struc continued to thrash his way across the marsh, and the python changed its course, sliding into the water and heading away from Nuroc. A full thirty feet of snake dropped from the branch before Nuroc saw the great serpent's tale disappear beneath the surface of the marsh.

Letting out his breath, Nuroc waded back to the edge of the marsh. As he was pulling himself from the murky waters, he saw several of the recruits pouring through the brush toward him. They stopped before the corpse of the slain boy and looked at it uncomprehendingly.

"What happened?" the lute player asked, his instrument shaking in his hands as he stared at Nuroc.

Behind them, there came a scream from the marsh as the python closed its coils around Struc. The guard managed two more panicked shrieks before his voice was smothered by the depths of the marsh.

"Never mind," Nuroc said wearily, brushing himself off. "Let's get back to the camp and sleep. We leave at dawn."

Fifteen

Dawn found the galley once again cutting its wake down the Targoan. Two of the recruits had been left behind to man the post and pass word of the day's traffic regarding the state of affairs at Cothe. The current was sufficient to keep the craft moving, so the young recruits manned their benches with weapons at hand, watching the banks for signs of raiders.

As he paced the helm, Nuroc wondered if the whoreship would succeed in harboring at the capital, or if it would proceed further south to the open sea and the coastal towns. He knew that his destination was to be Cothe, regardless. There, he would have to concoct a plan for dealing with the menace of Augage without delivering himself into the service of Aerda's militia. He could not risk discovery by the king, who would easily recognize him as the son of Stromthroad and Thouris. However bleak his prospects might seem, he was determined that it would not lead to finding his head severed and placed upon a stick in the royal courtyard.

The journey was uneventful for much of the day,

and all those aboard the galley were thankful for the lack of activity. Few of them had slept well, and the aches from their exertions the previous day were far more pronounced after hours of lying on cold, hard ground. They came to a riverpost early in the afternoon and docked long enough to take advantage of the stockpile of medical supplies the lone guard told them was stored at the station. They also took from the storerooms several heavy canvas sails, using them to cover the bodies of the dead and stave off the foul stench of their decomposition.

They had been back on the river for several hours when they encountered their first semblance of danger that day. As they drifted into another of the wide stretches of the river where the current waned considerably, the crew tensed at the sight of two dozen thick-bodied gnus. Unprovoked, the wildebeests were splendidly beautiful creatures, with wide faces splashed with bright colors and curled horns white as bone. However, when the beasts were antagonized, their fury was uncontrollable and their sturdy horns became twin instruments of piercing death and destruction. Galleys twice the size of that the recruits were aboard had been known to sink after crazed gnus battered gaping holes in their thick hulls.

At first sight of the beasts, bathing in the shallow waters near the north bank, Tudier let up on the tabor and quickly paced the deck, whispering for the others to raise their oars clear of the water and to make no sound. The armed youths walking the decks also froze in position and the ship became instantly silent, save for the ripple of the river against the prow and the faint wake trailing from the rudder.

Slowly the ship glided toward the herd. One by one, the magnificent beasts looked up from their feeding and cast their dull eyes on the sleek form of the galley. None of them moved, however, aside from swaying their tails at the hovering riverflies attempting to light on their sensitive hides.

The galley was soon cutting through the water

directly alongside the gnus. Any one of the recruits could have touched the animals with the tips of their oars. Nuroc could even smell the distinctive odor of their wet hides. He stilled the rudder as best he could and still navigate around the herd.

The tenseness aboard the ship began to ease once they were past the herd and approaching the next bend. However, Nuroc dwelled too long on watching the gnus and turned his gaze back to the way before them too late to avert the ship from crashing through the thin branches of a low-hanging scenoak. The brittle limbs splintered against the prow in a series of loud snaps.

From behind the ship there came next the howling of the lead gnu as it tilted its rainbow head upward and bared rows of firm, bone-crushing teeth. As the crew looked back, the wildebeests raised a splatter of waves about them as they charged through the waters after the ship. Behind their leader, the rest of the herd let out similar cries of aroused rage.

"To the oars!" Nuroc shouted to the youths as he steered the ship away from the banks.

Tudier and the others walking the decks scrambled to the benches and aided their comrades in plying oars against the surface of the river. The galley slowly picked up speed as they rounded the turn.

The gnus continued their pursuit through the deeper waters, but their pace slowed once their hooves lost contact with the riverbed. Still, they moved along, heads raised above the surface of the water, shooting off geysers of water through their flared nostrils in demonstration of their fury.

Burdened with the weight of the ore and the dead, the galley quickly reached a point at which it could move no faster through the waters. It seemed for a moment that the persistent stalking of the gnus would bring their piercing horns within striking distance of the ship's hull.

"Ho!" Tudier cried out, "Nuroc, steal a quick glance over your right shoulder, toward the shore!"

146

Nuroc swerved his head and saw, on the banks of the north shore, the slithering forms of crocodiles making their way down the muddy slope and into the Targoan. There were close to a dozen of them, half the number of the gnus that were on the trail of the galley.

As Nuroc turned back to check on the craft's pursuers, he saw that the lead gnu had changed its course and begun heading toward the approaching crocodiles. Again those beasts behind him took up after him. Soon the gnus gained footing on the riverbed and shook their shining black hides, then let forth with their fearful cries before ducking their heads and jabbing horns at the assaulting crocodiles. The latter beasts at once submerged, slapping at the water with their massive tails as they set upon the gnus. The waters around the converging foes began to rage white from the ensuing battle. Hideous cries broke through the loud splashing as wounds fuelled the gnus' violent rage.

"Man or beast," Nuroc commented as the galley went into a turn that took them from view of the carnage. "They are one and the same when it comes to survival. No doubt we looked just as savage yesterday when we clashed with the Ghetites."

"Aye," Tudier agreed solemnly. "We are beasts in clothing, but beasts nonetheless. It is the way of life."

"And yet, I would have to say it takes more than a beast to create the likes of that," Nuroc commented, pointing over Tudier's shoulder, past the prow of the galley.

Tudier followed Nuroc's fingers and his face lit up with a special sense of awe as his eyes fell on the distant walls of a city rising above the dense foliage of the riverbanks. Beyond the walls, there rose even higher the spires of a palace and, in the background, the multisided edges of a towering obelisk.

"Cothe," Tudier muttered. "At last we come to Cothe."

Sixteen

The harbor that nestled its waters close to the walls of Cothe was a product of the cataclysm a generation before, when the earth's upheaval had diverted a fork of the Targoan River into the shallow valley once used to harvest grain for the city's populace. That grain was now grown on the other side of the capital, as the waters had never receded from the basin. With the existence of the harbor and the ready access to the city by way of water, Cothe's rebirth following the abdication of the sorcerers had been marked by a rise in mercantilism in the capital. Cothe was now ruling seat and trading center for Aerda, dealing in the import of goods from all the coastal kingdoms save for Ghetite and Shangora, while also serving as a point of departure for the country's exports.

Nuroc and the band of recruits labored to pull their craft free of the river's current and into the calmer waters of the inland harbor, where they found themselves surrounded by a plethora of ships widely varied in size and construction. Sleek ketches skimmed the waters with seeming ease, their sails swollen with the wind, while larger galleys and triemes propelled themselves more slowly by the tug of oars worked by whip-driven slaves. Gulls shrieked in tight circles overhead, their wings fixed in position as they rode the currents of air. The Targoan Sea was still half a day's travel to the south, but oceanic smells had made their way inland over the years, carried in part by such coastal wildlife as barking seals and the gray-furred otters that taunted a flock of herons and other winged predators raking the shores for nourishment.

Nuroc was dumbstruck by the sight. He stared over the side of the galley and into the deep waters, amazed that paths and roadways he had traveled during his childhood now lay beneath the harbor.

"This is incredible," Tudier murmured from the deck, taking in the surroundings. "There are more people aboard ships in this harbor than in all of Thutchers."

"Aye, Thutchers and Wheshi combined," Nuroc added, turning his eyes to a bulking ship, five times the size of the one he captained, scudding through the waters close to them, shifting its position slightly in order to cut more easily into the narrowed waters of the river. The decks were aswarm with citizens of Cothe, and their faces were uniformly grave. Those men that Nuroc could see were mostly old or deformed, vastly outnumbered by women and children.

Nuroc strode to the fore and cupped his hands around his mouth, calling out to those aboard the other craft, "What goes with you?"

A woman, old and heavyset, called down to him, "We leave the city by the king's orders. Cothe braces for battle. We are being sent off to lodging elsewhere so that arriving soldiers might have a place to bed. The barracks and Coliseum are already overflowing with troops. None but men of war and those tending to the needs of the military are allowed to remain."

"Then it's true," Tudier cried out excitedly as he came up behind Nuroc. "We are on the verge of the great battle! Our swords have only whetted their appetite for Ghetite blood!"

As the two ships drifted away on their separate courses, he brooded silently over the busy waters. The sight of so many families, however grim their manner, filled him with a renewed sense of loss. The citizens of Cothe would soon return to their homes to make the best of whatever lot befell them, assured that, for better or worse, the fate of their city had not deprived them of each other. Nuroc had no one to go back to. His past had been wiped from the earth, leaving him in the grips of an ever-changing present and uncertain future. His only link to the past was the dagger sheathed at his side, and he rested a hand on its ornate hilt as he turned his gaze to the skies, which were turning a leaden gray as the late-afternoon fog rolled in from the coast. A chill rode on the wind and he felt it to his bones.

Behind him, Tudier began shouting orders as the galley made its way toward the docks. Scores of the wooden structures reached out into the bay like weathered fingers, clutching at the many ships still tied to their moorings. The waves slapped noisily at the barnacle-encrusted poles that supported the docks, competing with the sounds of activity along the wooden planks and on the decks of ships. Beyond the pier, a long walk stretched the length of the shore, fronting a small city that had grown on the banks outside the walls of the capital. There were more than a dozen buildings, each one tending to the needs of sailors and traders who wished, for whatever reason, to handle their affairs away from the city. The wharves were not a place of wealth. Although the structures were only a few years old, they were ill-kept and poorly constructed against the force of the elements. As the boat weaved through the bevy of departing vessels and sought out its own place of mooring, Nuroc marvelled that such squalor could thrive in the shadow of the wondrous city that lay beyond the imposing walls of Cothe.

A man in a faded leather jerkin, in his middle years but still possessing a lean, sturdy frame, pushed his way through the throng of women and children crowding toward the wide plank that led to a massive trieme moored on the other side of the dock from Nuroc's galley. He took hold of a coiled rope and tossed the line to Nuroc, who in turn wrapped his end around the ship's capstan.

"That's Neupitt's galley," the man on the docks said with concern as he tugged on the rope and pulled the ship into position alongside the docks. "Where is he?"

150

"Slain," Nuroc said. "We were set upon by a force of Ghetites and Shangorans when we were halfway downriver." He proceeded to tell the other man of their encounter. The dockmaster shook his head sadly at the revelation.

"This news will not set well with the king, I fear," he said at last as a few of his aides helped dock the vessel. "Bad enough that he must learn the enemy has already crossed our borders. To tell him his nephew is dead from an ambush will only compound the situation."

"Neupitt was the king's nephew?" Nuroc said, feeling his heart jolt.

"Aye, his favorite at that," the dockmaster answered. "By the way, I am Builcule."

"Nuroc," the young man from Wheshi said tersely. His mind was still reeling with the latest twist of events.

There were shouts along the dock and the citizens of Cothe were told to hasten their boarding of the other ship. A work crew was waiting to come forth with several horsedrawn carts to help in the unloading of the ore galley.

The recruits disembarked from the galley and stood on the docks with their eyes turned toward the city walls. Awe and wonder filled their faces. They remained with their attention riveted on the capital until the work crew had brought the carts alongside the galley. Then the Thutcherians joined in helping the others begin the difficult task of unloading the ship. They formed two groups, each comprised of a human chain extending from the carts to the hold. The first group passed the raw ore hand-by-hand up to the docks, while the others engaged in a similar task, although with a more grisly haul—the slain victims of the ambush. The carrion scent bloomed forth from the hold with a reeking intensity. Several of the recruits swooned at the odor and dropped to their knees, retching over the side of the ship. On the docks, women covered the eyes of their children and held

151

their breath, hurrying up the plank to the refuge of the other ship.

Tudier and Nuroc worked side by side as Builcule stood nearby, overseeing the operation with a look of profound sorrow and displeasure.

"Tell me, Builcule," Tudier asked as they loaded the last of the corpses. "Why is the king so certain that the Ghetites mean to strike first at Cothe? After all, we've already witnessed their aggression elsewhere. Is it not possible that they might continue to make war elsewhere, in hopes of smaller, more certain victories?"

As the horses began to haul the carts back toward shore, Builcule replied, "You do not seem to understand, lad. The Ghetites could win a hundred small battles and be left with less of a gain than they would have by seizing Cothe. By conquering the capital, they not only have the chance to seize the crown from Pencroft, but Augage would regain access to the sorcerer's gardens and the obelisk. Away from Cothe, his powers are limited. But should he return and learn more of the highest chants, it is feared he might become invincible. Need I say more?"

Tudier shook his head as he and Nuroc followed the dockmaster ashore, where another group of women and children stood, their eyes wide with grief as they stared upon the carts piled high with the casualties from the ambush. Nuroc and the others stepped back as the women and children converged upon the carts and frantically began sorting through the twisted limbs and looking over the recruits as if seeking familiar faces. Nuroc realized that these were the families of the dead, who had undoubtedly been waiting along the wharves all day for the arrival of the galley. It didn't take long for them to come to the despairing conclusion that their loved ones, to a man, were all dead, their faces and bodies already decomposed beyond recognition.

The women and children dropped to their knees and began to wail disconsolately, reciting hysterical, eerie chants of mourning meant to cleanse the spirits of those departed as they began their ethereal ascent to the heavens. Nuroc tried to close his ears to the mourning, but it was impossible. His own grief rose again to the surface of his emotions, and he turned away from the others a moment to compose himself.

Beyond the scene of the mourning there wound a trail up to the walls of the city. Amidst the steady progress of those using the beaten path to make their way to and from the city, there came forward a horseman who rode with reckless speed, sending those around him dashing clear of his way.

"Palem, the king's aide," Builcule told Tudier as the horseman reached the carts and dismounted. He pushed aside the women and children and stared wild-eyed at the bodies. Nuroc had rejoined the others by the time Palem turned from the carts and strode over to them. He was several years younger than Builcule, golden-haired and dressed in the jupon of a general. His face was flushed with anger and his blue eyes darted swiftly back and forth as he glared at the recruits.

"Who has the explanation for this!" he demanded hotly. "Who stands in for Neupitt?"

Tudier stepped forward, gesturing to Nuroc. "It was Nuroc here who led us in defeating the Ghetites," he boasted proudly. "We appointed him our captain."

"As if you were so empowered," Palem said icily. He took a step forward and stood before Nuroc. Nuroc did not recognize Palem from his days in Cothe, and hoped that he would likewise seem unfamiliar to the general. "Why is it only men of rank are among the dead?" Palem asked Nuroc.

"Some of the Thutcherians were among the dead," Nuroc said evenly. "They were placed in the bottom of the carts."

"But no officer survived," Palem said suspiciously, glancing over Nuroc's shoulder at the gathered recruits. "In fact, I see no member of the Aerda militia among the survivors. How is that?"

"We were ambushed," Nuroc replied. He did not care for Palem and his tone of accusation. "The enemy

153

archers took aim on all officers and soldiers first. Their aim was good."

Builcule found humor in Nuroc's answer and stifled a snort of laughter. Palem eyed the dockmaster brutally. Still smiling, Builcule returned a gaze no less malicious. Palem turned back to Nuroc.

"And when our soldiers were slain, you took command," he said cynically. "How do I know you are not a Ghetite yourself, trying to infiltrate our ranks?"

"You don't," Nuroc said, holding back his temper.

Tudier was less restrained. He said, "Had Nuroc not acted when he did, we all would have been slain and this ore would now be in the hands of the enemy!"

Palem ignored Tudier's outburst and pointed instead to Nuroc's dagger. "That looks like a Ghetite weapon to me. Let me have a look at it."

Nuroc placed his hand over the hilt of the condorknife and stepped back, his patience strained to its limits. "I have not risked my life for Aerda to be rewarded with insults and abuse," he said firmly. "I am loyal to my country and will not tolerate accusations to the contrary."

Palem and Nuroc faced off for a tense moment as the general's body trembled visibly with a rage that immobilized him. Before Palem could take action, Builcule swiftly intervened, pulling Nuroc aside and taking his place.

"Stay your temper, Palem," the dockmaster said calmly. "You know the youth is right. Your anger comes from dreading the news you must give the king. Don't make matters worse than they are already."

Palem continued to stand mute with his hands clenched into fists. At last he turned about and strode back to his horse. Mounting, he looked down at the recruits and said, "Fall in alongside the carts and follow me to the city." With his menacing stare fixed on Nuroc, he added, "The king will wish to see you all once he's learned of the incident upriver. You will tell him what you know personally."

As the other recruits slowly moved forward, Nuroc
154

stood riveted with dread. Had he survived countless brushes with death only to reach Cothe and be handed over to the king and certain recognition? How could he hope to convince Pencroft of the true reasons for his being in the capital, especially once the king learned that he had so brashly assumed the captaincy of a ship once commanded by Pencroft's favored kin? He watched his comrades take their positions alongside the cart, then grimly stepped forward, certain that he was about to march to his inevitable execution.

"Wait here," Builcule whispered hoarsely, reaching out to stop Nuroc. "I wish to have a word with you."

Nuroc looked to Builcule, for the first time dwelling on the dockmaster's features. There was something haunting in the man's face, as if Nuroc had seen it before. The eyes in particular gave him an uncomfortable feeling of déjà vu.

Palem rode over to them and shouted down at Nuroc, "I gave you an order, soldier."

Builcule once again interceded on Nuroc's behalf. "I'll see that he catches up with you, Palem. We have business to see to first."

"His business is with the king," Palem insisted.

Builcule sighed impatiently and moved closer to the general, lowering his voice. "How have you been enjoying the favors of Pencroft's mistress?"

Palem stiffened in the saddle. "I have no idea what you speak of."

"I speak of the nights you and the king's lover share embraces behind the royal stables," Builcule whispered. "Perhaps Pencroft might wish to know of your dalliances, to see if you've mastered some technique that would be of—"

"Enough," Palem said, pulling his horse away. He glared at both Nuroc and the dockmaster, then rode back to the head of the column formed by the loaded carts and the marching recruits. Slowly they began to move up the path toward the gates to the city.

Nuroc turned to Builcule. "I am indebted to you, but I don't understand why—"

155

Builcule reached for Nuroc's hand and held it up, his fingers closed around the talon ring. "This and the dagger," the dockmaster said lowly. "They can mean only one thing."

Nuroc's renewed fear at being discovered quickly diminished once he realized why Builcule looked so familiar.

"Do you have a brother?" Nuroc asked.

Builcule nodded, saying, "It was Solat who found you then?"

"Yes, he told me to come as quickly as I could."

"And he did not come with you?"

Nuroc could see from Builcule's expression that he suspected the worse. Taking a deep breath, Nuroc told the dockmaster of his brother's untimely death in the badlands, and of the whole chain of events that had brought him to Cothe. Builcule's face sagged with grief at the revelation, and once Nuroc had finished speaking, the dockmaster remained silent and walked off.

Nuroc followed behind, taking in the hectic activity along the docks. There were mostly sailors rushing about, dressed in faded cloth and leather cracked and whitened from the bite of saltwater, just as their features were ruddy and etched by the elements. Here and there small groups of soldiers mingled about, wearing their woven jupons with the embroidered Shield of Aerda on the back and chest and the ringed stripes on their sleeves declaring their rank. And there were still more citizens forming great clots along the docks as they waited to board their ships. Nuroc felt as if everyone's eyes were on him, holding him in judgment. He avoided their gazes and looked instead to the buildings they were passing; open markets filled with the aroma of fish and other delicacies from the sea, raw and smoked, neatly stacked for sale. Nuroc's appetite stirred into life, and he parted with a few coins in exchange for a side of smoked whitefish and a clump of ripe grapes.

Builcule had recovered somewhat from his grief and

he rejoined Nuroc as they continued down the main walk.

"Solat was my older brother," the dockmaster said. "I looked up to him since my youth. When Myrania confided in us as to the meaning of the black moon, he was the first to volunteer to help go in search of you and your family. I wanted to go as well, but he insisted that I remain behind. Perhaps he knew there was a good chance he might not return and wanted to make sure one of us was here to lend a hand when the time came."

"Why did Myrania come to you two?" Nuroc asked between bites of the fish. "I don't recall you or Solat from the days I lived in Cothe."

Builcule looked around to make certain no one was listening to their conversation, then said, "We are not from here originally. We came to work the docks after years spent working the harbor of Eliska, to the south coast. On the days we did not work, we would go hunting along the cliffs, Solat and I. One day we came across Myrania and her father, who were living in hiding in the caves that riddle the face of the cliffs." Builcule paused a moment, then asked Nuroc, "What of Myrania? Where is she?"

"I had hoped she would be here," Nuroc said. "The last I knew, she was among the women aboard a ship owned by a rogue who thrived—"

"Sphextay!" Builcule said bitterly.

"Yes!" Nuroc cried. "You know of him? Did his boat arrive here, late yesterday or perhaps this morning?"

The dockmaster nodded his head bleakly, then pointed down the shoreline. Nuroc looked and saw the whoreship moored before a lavish wharf situated a few hundred yards away from the main docks.

"Each year that animal takes his ship up and down the Targoan. He leaves with an empty craft and returns with a fortune and a throng of battered women he dresses prettily and offers to rich merchants seeking love-slaves. How is it that Myrania fell into his hands?"

157

"Solat died before he could tell me," Nuroc confessed. "I only know that we must free her before we go on."

"That is easier said than done," Builcule said. "He guards the wharf more heavily than he does his ship, and I trust you know the extremes he goes to there."

"But we have to do something, and soon," Nuroc said. "The black moon is almost upon us."

They had almost reached the end of the main boardwalk. Builcule gestured to the docks, where a handful of men were laboring along the decks of an expensive-looking galley, unloading cargo. "Let's give a hand to these men. They're unloading goods for the king, the sort of things that might help to take his mind off the grief for his nephew. Perhaps we can think up a plan while we're working."

The merchant overseeing the work on his vessel was yellow-skinned, wearing princely robes and an elaborate turban of peacock feathers. His wrinkled face was a mask of concentration as he stared at the men before him, making certain that nothing was improperly handled.

"How goes it, Oyphrom?" Builcule called out to the merchant.

Oyphrom turned and greeted Builcule and Nuroc with a perfunctory nod. "I'll feel much better once this load is off my hands. Twice I was almost overtaken by pirates sailing across the sea from the Tavkyd Islands. Five men on the crew I had to see executed and tossed to the sharks for attempting to steal items from the hold."

"Wealth has its price, Oyphrom," Builcule said.

"Sometimes I wonder if it's worth the price," Oyphrom wondered aloud.

"I'm certain you don't wonder much beyond the time it takes for you to count your take," Builcule said with a grin as he and Nuroc boarded the ship. Oyphrom stayed on the docks, brooding darkly as he watched them.

The ship was the same size as the galley Nuroc had

158

commanded into port, but it was better constructed, made to withstand the rigors of the open sea as well as inland rivers. All visible woods were glossy with a waxed sheen, and albino slaves in tunics of burlap scurried about the decks with fine cloths to rub at spots where the luster had begun to fade. Those unloading the cargo were also white-skinned and blonde-haired but they wore only loincloths and boasted rippling biceps and scarred shoulders that betrayed their normal functions as the ship's oarsmen. Few of them bothered to look up from their work, but those pink-pupilled eyes that rose to gaze at Nuroc and Builcule were filled with a dull lethargy that thinly-veiled an inbred contempt for their captivity.

The hold was dark and dank, musty with the smell of damp furs, which filled huge woven baskets being passed up. Besides the furs, there were ivory tusks from a dozen breeds of beasts, all destined to be carved into prized daggers or pieces of jewelry for the king and his nobility. The horns and a few skulls from other creatures were stocked in huge barrels and chests, some opened for inspection but others closed against further temptation to the slaves.

Nuroc and Builcule walked over to where four men were already gathered around the largest of the chests, which was equipped with sturdy poles lashed across the top for easy carrying. They lined up, three men on each side, and strained their muscles to lift the burdensome load and carry it across the hold. They moved slowly, stopping on occasion to counter the swaying of the ship in the waters of the harbor.

Oyphrom ducked his head through the doorway and hissed at the slaves, "That's the most valuable cargo we carry. Skulls and skeletons of rare Tavkyd beasts, adorned with gems by their voodoo priests. Drop the load and your own skulls will be added to the chest."

"Hold your threats, Oyphrom," Builcule called out. "We'll manage this load once you step clear of our way."

The merchant withdrew himself and the six men

made their way up the steps from the hold with the utmost of caution. The large chest barely fit through the opening, and Nuroc sighed with relief once they had it out on the decks, where more slaves hurried over to help it the final distance to a flat cart waiting on the docks.

The chest was the last of the cargo to be unloaded. As the goods were tightly secured to the carts that would transport them into the city, Builcule watched the slaves who were resting from the toll of their exertions.

"Tell me, Oyphrom," the dockmaster said, "do you recall the favor you've been meaning to repay me for the change I negotiated in your trade route?"

"As often as you remind me of it, I'm not apt to forget," Oyphrom responded.

"Well, I think I'd like to collect on that today, if I may."

"What is it you want?"

"The use of your slaves and their freedom once I'm through with their services."

"Not a chance!" Oyphrom said, visibly upset.

"I beg your pardon?" Builcule said, stealing a wink at Nuroc. "I don't think I heard you correctly, Oyphrom. Did you just say you prefer your old trade route? I can arrange it easily enough . . . ."

Oyphrom stewed on the decks, pacing before the loaded carts, staring at the sort of goods he would lose access to if the trade routes were changed on him. He finally turned to Builcule and said, stubbornly. "It's hardly a fair trade."

"I know," Builcule replied, "but I'd be willing to say you don't owe me more."

"That's not the way I meant it!" Oyphrom cried with exasperation, his cool resolve shattered by Builcule's cunning.

"We don't have much time," the dockmaster said. "Doust will be arriving soon with his ship and his usual complaints for a better route. I need to know how to answer him."

Oyphrom threw up his hands with resignation. "Take them," he said angrily. "And, by the gods, I'll never ask a favor of you again, mark my word!"

"Gladly," Builcule said. "Gladly."

Seventeen

Busy as the waters of the harbor were, there were still vast spaces where no ships traveled. Because the docks huddled along only a scant portion of the overall shoreline, the further reaches bore little traffic save for a smattering of small rowboats used by old fishermen who found that the activity in the central harbor drove the fish to the tranquility of the waters surrounding their baited hooks.

Sphextay's wharf lay along the far reaches, and aside from the moored whoreship, there were only a few skiffs docked in front. It would not be until Sphextay sent off a messenger to the main docks that word would go round that the wharf was doing business. At that time, men would begin to make their way by foot and ship to the wharf in hopes of sampling the whoremaster's illbegotten slaves of passion.

And yet, one particular vessel swerved off course from the other ships and pointed its prow toward the eastern bank. It was an ancient rig of bulky design and bleached woods, showing crude patches where punctures in the hull had been nailed over with mismatched boards. Unseen oarsmen rowed the craft slowly toward the wharf, and no one roamed the dreary deck. Like a ghostship it moved through the fog-filled air of the harbor. The few anglers fishing the nearby waters looked up at the approaching vessel and hurriedly drew in their lines before taking to the oars, muttering to the gods for protection.

Aboard the ship, Nuroc and Builcule peered cautiously over the battered edge of the forecastle, taking in the wharf, which loomed larger before them with each pull of the oars from below.

"You're certain they won't recognize the ship?" Nuroc asked.

"I've had it lying idly at port for years now," Builcule said. "Sphextay has no idea who owns it, not that it will matter. There's little he could do to stop us. We're almost close enough to take action, so look quickly while I tell you what must be done. . . ."

It was not long before there were signs of activity along the docks in front of Sphextay's wharf. A gateway opened in the high walls of vertically strapped logs that surrounded the infamous compound, and the two giants emerged with their snarling lions. Several youths strode out with them, holding crossbows. Down they came to the edge of the docks, where they stared out at the approaching vessel.

Nuroc went to work quickly, striking at his firestones until he ignited a bed of kindling under a layer of damp leaves filling the front end of the ship. The kindling was dry and brittle, and the fire spread with a surge of fury, sending up a thick cloud of blackened smoke from the smoldering leaves.

Rising from his crouch, Nuroc then ran back to the onager mounted on the central deck. Builcule and two of the albinos were grunting as they pulled back the arm of the catapult and hastily tied it into place. Nuroc quickly wrapped lengths of cloth around his palms as he straddled the cradled hold of the catapult and braced himself precariously.

Builcule reached for a coiled rope and handed one end to Nuroc. The other end was tied securely to a thick bolt fit into an oversized windlass mounted next to the catapult. The large crossbow was aimed toward the top of a wooden tower that rose above the walls surrounding Sphextay's wharf.

"Are you ready?" Builcule asked Nuroc.

Nuroc grinned nervously. "One is never ready for the likes of this."

Arrows began to hammer into the deck about them as the boys on the docks fired through the smoke. By now the framework of the ship's prow was also afire, adding to the smoke and further screening Nuroc and Builcule.

The giants bellowed out threats to the burning ship, but when it became clear that their cries were unheeded, they tugged on the leashes of their great beasts and backed away from the docks.

Builcule leaned to one side to see through the smoke. When the ship was within ten feet of ramming the docks, he quickly moved to the trigger of the long-bowed windlass. Beside him, Nuroc pulled himself into a ball and clutched tightly to the end of the rope. The albino behind him raised an ax, and at the same time that Builcule let loose with the crossbow, he severed the taut rope of the catapult.

With deadly accuracy, the fired bolt rammed into the wooden frame of the rising tower. Tumbling through the air on a parallel course, Nuroc felt the line in his hands growing rapidly tighter as he was flung past the tower facing. His speed was such that he faced certain death on impact with whatever obstruction lay in his path. It seemed that his course was about to send him slamming into a brick wall when the line he was holding reached its full length and jerked him clear of the thick wall with a force that tore at the muscles in his arms. Sheer momentum swung Nuroc in a wide arc that brought him down into the flower beds of an open courtyard. He rolled with his fall and staggered to his feet, shaken and covered with rich upearthed soil but otherwise unharmed.

He pulled free his dagger and prepared himself to fight off any number of aggressors, but his fantastic entry to the compound had gone unnoticed because of

163

the splintering collision of the burning warship into the docks, which had brought all hands rushing from their posts to investigate.

From the bowels of the dying ship, the albino slaves foamed forth with frenzied zeal, armed with battleaxes and gleaming swords. They fell eagerly upon the astounded defenders of the wharf, knowing that victory would earn them freedom. Even death would be a better fate than the continued enslavement they had experienced under Oyphrom.

The giants had shouted commands to the Shangoran lions, but the widespread fire and sounds of collision had driven the beasts berserk, and they broke free of their leashes and bounded off the docks. The giants resorted to scimitars and urged the youths around them to abandon their slow-loading crossbows for knifes and daggers. Together, Builcule's light-skinned force and the lackeys of Sphextay clashed amidst the flaming docks, battling to the death as they tried to avoid the spreading fire, which now swept across the docks and began to feed upon the strapped poles of the main wall.

Within the compound, Nuroc rushed across the open courtyard to the base of the tower. He was about to enter the unguarded doorway when a third giant, this one even larger in size that his counterparts, strode out to meet him, brandishing a length of chain, which ended in a ball of iron covered with pointed spikes.

Nuroc ducked as the giant lashed out with the chain. The lethal ball whooshed within inches of Nuroc's skull before biting into the wooden pole supporting the handrailing that reached around the base of the tower. The pole splintered under the ball's impact.

As the giant lowered his aim in dragging the weapon back toward his smaller intruder, Nuroc jumped upwards, clearing the whistling swath and grabbing onto the sloped roof that extended out over the doorway. He kicked forward with all his might, striking the giant in the chest with a force that sent him reeling off balance. Before the giant could recover, Nuroc let go of

164

the roof and landed with a crouch before springing forward. The giant's eyes widened as it saw the condor-dagger pierce his chest. Howling in agony, he swiped at Nuroc with his free hand and sent the youth flying into the frame of the doorway, knocking him senseless.

The wound did not seem to hinder the giant aside from the pain, but when he reached down and pulled the dagger free, the life went out of his eyes in an instant. He slumped to the ground next to Nuroc, dead.

Nuroc stirred and shook his head to clear his vision. He looked at his foe, panting for breath as he pushed the giant clear of the ceremonial dagger. With the weapon back in his hand, he rose to his feet and cautiously entered the tower, eyes searching the darkened shadows for the sign of any others who might wish to foil his attempt to save his lover.

The steep-rising staircase was vacant, and he started up it two steps at a time. Reaching the first floor, he looked down the corridor that connected the tower with the adjacent hall. The corridor was lined with doors, most of them closed. One was opened, however, and a woman stared out, terrified at the sight of Nuroc.

"Don't slay us, please!" she cried out.

"I don't intend to," Nuroc told her. "I am seeking Sphextay to add to his blood to my dagger."

The woman's eyes looked up toward the upper floors.

"He is in the top room, with Myrania," she said. "Be careful, though. I heard screams from there only moments ago. When he is angered, no beast can match the rage of Sphextay."

"He has yet to face my fury!" Nuroc said grimly, turning away from the woman and continuing up the last flight of steps.

The door to the uppermost chamber was watched over by a giant ape that paced angrily about, tugging at the chain that kept it shackled to the wall beside the door. Snorting its displeasure, the simian did not see Nuroc at first. Remaining several steps down from the top floor, Nuroc kept low as he wondered how he was

165

going to pass by this final obstruction. There could be no doubting that the door the ape guarded was also locked. Nuroc might be able to sneak past the animal as it was turned away, but he would surely be set upon before he could work the lock free or try to break the door down. He considered hurling the dagger at the gorilla in hopes of killing it, but it seemed that the beast was too thick-chested for his blade to reach the heart or slay it before he would find himself crushed by monstrous arms.

Nuroc heard cries from below as the body of the slain giant was discovered. He had to act soon or he would be trapped where he stood. Holding onto his dagger, he cleared the final steps and crossed the planked floor to the door. As the ape saw him and turned around to attack, Nuroc stood firmly before the door, timing his motions so that he could move forward and lash out with his dagger at the same time he moved clear of the beast's sweeping arm.

The ape fell back, grunting in pain as it reached for the bleeding slash across its face that had left it blinded. One hand swung madly about while the other dabbed at the wound that ran red with blood.

"Here!" Nuroc called out tauntingly to the ape as he stood before the door. "Come and get me!"

The ape cried out and charged forward, berserk with rage. Unable to see, the beast lashed out with its fists and Nuroc ducked as the first blows fell upon the door with so much force that the door was knocked loose. Nuroc goaded the ape a second time, and the resultant pummelling on the door brought it crashing down into the room.

Nuroc rushed in, moving beyond range of the wounded ape's frenzy. The inner chamber was strewn with silks and satins that covered the walls like fabric rainbows. The ceiling was layered with polished gems positioned like stars against a black background. A wealth of trophies and art objects filled the room, leaving barely enough space for the finely woven rugs that surrounded a plush bed adorned with the skins of rare

166

beasts. In the midst of this splendor Sphextay sat in a lavish chair of carved wood and ivory trim, with his hands resting calmly on his lap. He was seated against the wall opposite Nuroc, and Nuroc stopped, seeing the unnatural serenity in the whoremaster's eyes. The short man had an odd smile and Nuroc was instantly on his guard, suspecting that Sphextay was about to spring some unseen trap.

"Where is she?" Nuroc shouted above the roar of the gorilla clamoring in the doorway behind him.

Sphextay began to lean forward in his chair, and Nuroc acted swiftly, snapping his wrist to send the dagger flying out at the whoremaster. His aim was off, and the blade thudded into the frame of the throne. Nuroc rushed forward, bounding off the top of the bed and throwing himself at Sphextay. His hands reached out before him, landing on the other man's neck.

Nuroc began to squeeze Sphextay's throat, but suddenly stopped, realizing that his hands gripped cold flesh. Sphextay was already dead. He slumped from the chair to the floor, and Nuroc saw the blood seeping through the fine material of his satin robe. Lying next to Sphextay was a dropped sword with half its blade red with drying blood.

"Myrania," Nuroc muttered, stepping up from the body and looking about the room for a trace of the woman. He heard a feverish struggle outside the door and could see the great ape tugging madly at his bonds as he raged after the boys who had rushed to the top of the stairs, carrying their crossbows.

There was one window in the chamber, and Nuroc ran to it, seeing a length of silk rope tied to a brass sconce and dangling out the opened sill. He grabbed at the rope and looked out the window, seeing where it reached all the way down the outside of the tower to a corral filled with horses. The gate to the corral was open, and Nuroc hurriedly looked down the path that led away from the wharf and harbor and toward the meadows where he had once watched over the king's sheep. He first saw a raised cloud of dust, then the retreating outline of someone in the saddle, driving on a steed along the roadway.

"Myrania!" Nuroc shouted, but she was too far away.

Elsewhere, the fire had begun to consume the entire wharf, and smoke swirled up around the base of the tower. Nuroc looked to the courtyard long enough to see Builcule and the albinos driving back the boys of Sphextay and the one surviving giant. Then an arrow rammed into the windowframe from behind him and Nuroc realized the boys had slain the gorilla and entered the chamber.

Without looking back, Nuroc bounded out the window, holding onto the silk rope as he lowered himself to the corral. The horses shied away from him, and he ran in pursuit after them, leaping onto the one closest to him and riding bareback as it bolted from the corral and carried him away from the growing inferno that had once been the domain of Sphextay.

Eighteen

The imported goods brought by Oyphrom from the Tavkyd Isles were set in a large chamber adjacent to the palace, alongside other purchases the king had recently made but not had the chance to fully appreciate. Perhaps he would come and glance them over, but it would not be until after the looming battle that he would take the items from their chests and barrels and put them to use in adorning the rooms of his palace. For now they would wait in storage.

Oyphrom was in the chamber now, calmly inventorying the stock to make certain that all the pieces were accounted for. He moved about calmly, in no particular hurry, as another, younger trader paced before him, poorly concealing his anxiety.

"But, Oyphrom!" pleaded the other merchant. "Our trade routes are almost identical. Why compete when it only hurts the price we take for our goods? As partners—"

"Why compete?" Oyphrom interrupted. "Is there competition here, Doust? I deal in quantities four times your own. I have first choice of the best goods at every port, while you make the best of what I leave behind. No, Doust. You have much to gain by joining me, but I only stand to lose by such a deal. Don't be wasting my time with your foolish pleas."

Doust, Cothian born and modestly dressed in contrast to the clothing of his adversary, attempted to sneer threateningly, but the gesture seemed little more than a look of petulance. "Very well, Oyphrom," he said with false bravado. "I have made my offer. You have refused. You leave me no choice but to sell my goods at a loss to steer away your business. Come two years' time and you will be the one begging my way. Mark my words, Oyphrom. I'll see you in ragged tatters, pleading for alms, and spit in your cup!"

Oyphrom looked up from his counting and smiled with amusement. He casually walked up to the younger merchant. His hand suddenly shot out from his robe, grabbing Doust by the collar of his tunic and dragging him forward so that their faces were only inches apart. He spat in Doust's face and pressed the blade of his drawn dagger against the youth's trembling throat.

"From this day on, you'd best find a new itinerary for your business, Doust," Oyphrom said coolly. "Run any trade along my routes in the future, and you'll wish it was pirates instead of my crew that fell upon your ship. Understood?"

Doust nodded his head feebly, his wide eyes gaping at the dagger stroking his throat.

"Now leave me be or I'll carve a smile on your throat!" Oyphrom warned, shoving Doust away from him. The young merchant fell over a load of furs, then stumbled to his feet and prepared to retort, but Oyphrom cut him short. "And don't threaten me or I'll skin you alive and sell your hide with my next lot."

Oyphrom moved forward, dagger still clenched in his fist. Doust backed away, then turned and fled from the chamber.

Oyphrom followed him as far as the entryway, where he closed the thick wooden door and bolted it shut from the inside.

Striding back across the room, he stopped before the large chest Nuroc and Builcule had helped unload from the merchant galley. With the dagger he cut away the heavy ropes wrapped about the chest, then reached inside his robe for a key with which to spring the elaborate series of locks further securing the lid. The locks gave way with dull snaps, and the lid creaked on its hinges as Oyphrom raised it to have a look at the valuable cargo.

Inside, the chest shone brilliantly as the torchlight reflected off the myriad gems that artisans had used to adorn the white bone of skulls and skeletons used by high priests among the voodoo tribes of the Tavkyd Isles.

"Exquisite," Oyphrom marveled, picking up the skull of a kildwolf cub. Diamond dust sparkled along the surface of the bone, and large polished opals were set in the eye sockets. Stunning as the piece was, it was far from the most treasured piece. Oyphrom guessed that the entire collection held within the chest matched the value of everything else in the chamber combined. Forty high priests he had slain with the help of a mercenary force to steal these contents from the Tavkyd's main temple. He had then gone to the islands' king in secret and betrayed the mercenaries, who were massacred by irate troops as they were about to set sail from the islands in their own ship.

Oyphrom set the skull on top of a nearby barrel, then leaned over the chest to sort through more of the contents.

A hand suddenly burst forth from the chest,

reaching out to the merchant, who backed away in fright. Delicate skulls and bones clattered over the edge of the chest and broke into fragments on the marble floor as a figure emerged from amidst the trophies, half-hidden in a white cowl. Slender, almost bonelike fingers reached to the hood and pulled it away so that Oyphrom could see the face of the man who now stood before him.

"Augage," Oyphrom muttered feebly. Although he knew the sorcerer-king had been secreted in the chest, he still was held in the grips of a nameless terror at the sight of Augage. The wizard was bald, and not so much as a stubble of hair marked his chin or cheeks. Browless, Augage's pallid countenance seemed more made of bone than flesh. Even to the large eyes of ebony sunk deep in their sockets, the Ghetite's face took on the appearance of a skull, like those of the beasts that surrounded him. Oyphrom felt as if Death were staring him full in the face.

As the sorcerer climbed the rest of the way out of the chest, more of the invaluable pieces shattered down to the floor at his feet.

"I . . . I trust your journey was not too unpleasant," Oyphrom stammered, beginning to have doubts as to the wisdom of his decision to deal with the king of Ghetite.

"It is not a means of travel I relish," Augage said, rolling his shoulders and flexing his fingers to loosen the stiffness in his joints. "Still, it served its purpose well. I am within Cothe's walls without notice."

"But you have yet to gain entry to the sorcerers' gardens," Oyphrom said. He did not like the look in Augage's eyes, so he kept his dagger in hand, hidden in the folds of his robe. "There is a full contingent charged with guarding all entrances."

"That is my concern, not yours," Augage intoned. "You have served your purpose in getting me this far."

"For which you will name me trade minister once you've claimed the throne of Aerda," Oyphrom said, as if to remind Augage.

171

Augage did not reply. He looked down at the merchant's side and calmly said, "Why is it you hold a knife secreted in your robes?"

Oyphrom smiled wanly and exposed the blade, looking to it as if unaware he had been holding it. "I was using it to cut the ropes around the chest," he explained nervously.

"Perhaps there are other things you might wish to cut," Augage said. "Perhaps you mean to slay me and call in the guard. Pencroft would be pleased to see that. He might make you trade minister himself for accomplishing my murder."

"You mistake me, Augage," Oyphrom said. "I am a man of my word. You have bought my loyalty."

"I think not," the sorcerer said. Raising one hand, he reached behind him and waved his palm over the top of the opened chest.

"We have an agreement," Oyphrom said. He tried to sound insistent, but he was already broken. His voice bore the same emptiness that had made the threats of Doust sound so futile.

"No more," Augage said with an air of finality. He turned away from Oyphrom and began to walk across the cold marble floor toward the rear of the chamber.

Oyphrom watched him, livid at the thought he had been duped. Clenching his jaw, he shook off his fear and raised his dagger as he took a step toward the retreating figure of the Ghetite. There was a sudden sound behind him and he stopped, alarmed. He looked over his shoulder in the direction of the chest.

"Noooooooo . . ." he croaked hoarsely.

The sound came from within the chest, where the gem-studded skeletons of two kildwolves rose from among the heap of other bones and turned their sapphire eyes on Oyphrom. The merchant, mesmerized with terror, dropped his dagger and watched on helplessly as the skeleton predators leapt from the chest, spilling more bones. They landed on the run and pounced full force at Oyphrom's unmoving form, dragging him to the ground. A scream died in his throat as

172

the aberrations of skull and bone snapped their exposed jaws and began tearing at the merchant's flesh.

Across the room, Augage paid no heed to the unnatural death of Oyphrom other than to smile to himself at the wonder of his power. Just to be this close to the obelisk filled him with a sense of omnipotence that in turn gave greater force to his charms. The curse of the Tavkyd skeletons was well known to him; he had only to wave his hand and think of the last words spoken by the dying high priests to see that the curse was carried out.

But he had little time to dwell on Oyphrom's sealed fate. He reached the far wall and ran his hands along the surface of a tiled fresco depicting the earth's creation according to the old beliefs. When his fingers pressed against specific tiles, the fresco magically pivoted on a central axis, acting like a doorway that led Augage to a staircase. The steps led down to the catacombs, which in turn led beneath the city to the obelisk.

Nineteen

Sheep still grazed those parts of the rolling meadow that lay above the harbor. Like tufts of cotton they stood out against the backdrop of coarse, hearty grasses, bleating at the darkness that came on the heels of the fog. Night was falling fast. Nuroc drove his horse onward, blocking from his mind the fierce pain between his thighs from riding bareback. His only consolation had been the steed's fine temperament. After a brief protest at the mounting of a strange rider, the stallion had fallen into an effortless gait that was at last making headway toward the elusive wake of dust that marked Myrania's position on the roadway ahead of them. Several times Nuroc tried calling out, but in each instance his words were lost to the wind blowing in from the coast.

For more than an hour he had ridden, and now his sweat began to chill him as the drop in temperature told him they were more than halfway to the sea. It struck him as odd that he had yet to see anyone else traveling the road but himself and Myrania. It was understandable that none of the fleeing citizens would choose to seek out safety in the direction of Ghetite, but Nuroc thought that the military would be widely present along this reach against the chance of invasion from the south. His concern proved to be misinformed, though, he realized, for a number of campfires began to appear in the distant mountains, indicating where Aerdan outposts had been established near the several passes by which Ghetites might hope to cross the Kanghat Mountains onto Aerdan soil. The roadway had been abandoned as being too far from the potential point of entry to worry about.

Nuroc's steadfast pursuit at last bore fruit. As he rode over the final rise and started down the long, gradual slope leading to the cliffs, he saw that Myrania had pulled her horse off the main road and was inspecting one of its front hooves.

Nuroc leaned forward on his steed and slapped its hindquarters with his heels, crying out, "Come, one last burst of speed!"

As his horse thundered down the hillside, raising its own trail of dust, Nuroc saw Myrania turn toward him. At once she took the reins of her horse and leapt into the saddle. Her horse started off down the road, but it was favoring one hoof and its gait was off-stride. She cast a look over her shoulder and Nuroc could see that she was terrified, thinking him to be one of Sphextay's avengers.

"Myrania!" he shouted at the top of his lungs. "It's me, Nuroc!"

If Myrania heard him, she did not acknowledge his cry. She desperately reined her steed on, closer to the

174

cliffs. Its hobbling became more persistent, and finally the beast's leg gave out and it tumbled forward off the road, throwing Myrania from the saddle into a ditch.

"Myrania!" Nuroc cried out again as his steed brought him down the last stretch of the slope.

Myrania's horse rolled over once and clambered uncertainly back to its hooves, neighing in pain from the obvious break in its front leg. Myrania, however, lay face down on the ground where she had fallen.

Nuroc was off his horse before it fully stopped, and he rushed forward down the incline of the ditch, demanding his eyes not to believe what they saw. Myrania lay still, sprawled unnaturally from the force of her fall.

Speechless with grief, he leaned over and extended a hand toward her unmoving form, then recoiled with shock as she suddenly spun about and pointed the tip of a half-sword toward his face.

"Stay where you are or I'll slay you just as I did . . ."

Her threat hung unfinished in the air as she finally recognized the man before her. Her eyes stared at him incredulously and her mouth hung open in shock.

Nuroc found himself equally stunned. Without the makeup she had worn for her performance in Wheshi, she was lovely beyond his most far-fetched dreams. The way the wind had swept back her hair and put color on her fair cheeks gave her a spirited look, and the cobalt depths of her searching eyes made him ache with desire.

"Nuroc," she finally managed to murmur, lowering the blade of her half-sword. "Nuroc."

He was still without words, consumed with profound ecstasy. He took her by the hand and raised her to her feet, letting his joy show through a smile that pulled his mouth to its limits. She stepped forward and they embraced one another tightly, letting their heartbeats sound together with the hurried pulse that measured their racing passion. The love they had held back for so long, at first by choice and then out of necessity, now washed over them, blotting out all concerns for the troubled state of the world around them. They were Nuroc and Myrania, lovers united in embrace for the first time, their touch charging one another with the urgent desire for more. They could not have enough of one another. His lips sought her out, crushing her mouth as they kissed longingly and felt themselves drifting down onto the lush grass. She stroked his face and neck, then, still mingling her lips with his, she reached through the rips in his tunic and felt the firmness of his chest, moved her fingers along the trim muscles of his stomach to his waist. He moaned pleasurably and let his own hands gently rove the smooth flesh that lay beneath her loose garb of spun silk.

"By the gods, I love you," he whispered in her ear.

"I never thought I'd see you again," she said softly, taking his hand and guiding it inside her kirtle so that he could feel her flesh directly. "Love me, Nuroc. I want you so much."

There in the grass, beneath the hanging fog, under the closing eye of Dorban, they made love. Frantically, desperately, until the passion was spent and replaced by a lingering bliss. Naked in each other's arms, they continued to lie in the grass, letting the elements about them slowly return them to the harsh realities of the present. But, whatever else might happen, they had sealed their love, and nothing could take it from them again.

Twenty

Augage stood at the base of the obelisk, basking with a sense of the triumph so close at hand. As planned, he had reached the seat of power without being discovered by the Aerdan force that so diligently stood guard over the surface entrances to the sorcerers' gardens. He still had much to do, and his time would have to be spent in full concentration if he were to succeed in this, his long-planned scheme to achieve domination over the continent.

As he lit a torch and started toward the winding stairway, he looked over the ground floor, noticing the minute changes that had occurred since the night he had left the obelisk five years before. There were crumpled bodies, now decayed into dishevelled heaps of bone sprawled along the floor where they had fallen under the trampled press of the panicked citizens Talmon-Khash had driven away in horror. Bits of would-be plunder were strewn about as well, now layered with dust that hid the luster which had dazzled the eyes of the looters.

Augage paused at the massive bench of petrified jaunwood, noticing immediately that several volumes of handwritten chants were missing, as well as various obscure ingredients used in the concoction of salves and ointments similar to those he had given Quidantis and the other members of his raiding expedition. He wondered in passing about the fate of that expedition. The night before he had taken to hiding in the chest containing the Tavkyd treasures, Augage had received word by carrier hawk that the raiders had succeeded in slaying all but one member of the family that carried the lifeblood of Talmon-Khash. Quidantis had written that the sole survivor was under surveillance and soon would be slain. Delivery of the sacred dagger was also promised, but Augage was no longer concerned with its recovery. The dagger was of no consequence unless it was wielded correctly before the altar of Dorban by one carrying the essence of Talmon-Khash. Augage could see the altar before him, round and cold, unattended by anyone who could stand between his dreams and their realization. Talmon-Khash was trapped within the stone, and would remain so forever once Augage assumed his full powers. The thought gave him

177

great pleasure, and he smiled as he went to the steps and began the slow ascent.

At each level he neutralized the protective powers of the guardian jewels, and presently he had risen to the level from which Talmon-Khash had plunged into the nether realm. Snuffing his torch so that its light would not be seen through the open portal, Augage looked out and could see the lid of darkness drawing tighter over the lone eye of the constellation Dorban. He had hastened the moon's waning just enough. It would be several hours before the moon went black. By then he would be ready to recite the one chant that would make him the most powerful sorcerer to have ever walked the face of the earth. Even the legendary powers of the great Noj Syb would be dwarfed by the prowess of Augage.

So inspired by his dreams of glory, Augage proceeded up the next two flights of steps. He hesitated before the last of the guardian gems and pulled from the folds of his cowl a scroll of parchment. Unrolling it, he looked over five years of calculations and patient decipherings, comparing his notes against the hieroglyphics on the wall beside the jewel. Satisfied that he had translated them as best he could, he looked up from the scroll and placed a hand over the mounted gem.

"Achel halizedective powfedian," he whispered cautiously. Then, taking a deep breath, he took a tentative step up the stone staircase. Had he misjudged his knowledge of the magetongue and mispronounced the chant, the gem would unleash its lethal bolt and snuff his life and dreams. Sweat came to his brow in large drops as his eyes watched the gem. A faint, almost imperceptible glow began to emanate from the heart of the jewel, filling Augage with a sense of abject terror. Then, just as swiftly, the light faded.

Letting out his breath, Augage continued up the steps to the uppermost level of the obelisk, where no sorcerer in the history of recorded time had ever stood before. He strode to the wall before him and relit his torch, setting it in an ancient holder forged into the shape of a condor. The light fell upon the many rows of carved inscription. Augage concerned himself with the uppermost series of symbols and strange letterings, chiseled into the very pinnacle of the obelisk. Five years ago, he had attempted to copy down the chant from his vantage point several levels down. This close, he could see at once the many symbols that had been obscured in shadow or scratched too close to the surface for him to see from far below. There could be no wondering why the chant he had subsequently recited had failed so miserably, unleashing a cataclysm instead of bestowing him with the means to invincibility.

Now the mistakes would be corrected. He took his scroll once more and held it up beside the inscribed chant on the slanted wall. With calm deliberation, he went to work.

Twenty-One

"My father awaits me in the caves," Myrania said as Nuroc fixed the straps of the saddle onto the back of his horse. Myrania's steed lay nearby, slain by a merciful stroke of the sword.

Nuroc helped Myrania into the saddle, and she squirmed back to make room for him. Mounted, Nuroc snapped the reins and his stallion started down the road toward the coast.

"I still cannot figure out how you fell into the hands of Sphextay," he said.

Myrania held him tightly and spoke to him over his shoulder. "It was after Solat and I had spent months searching for you and your family to tell of the news about the black moon. It had been our hope that the trained condor would lead us directly to you, but its tracking abilities were far too limited. We had to think of other ways.

"We were in Thutchers, resting after having roamed the whole northern range of the Kanghats without success. Solat saw Sphextay's ship and was inspired with a new strategy. It was decided that I would take myself to Sphextay and convince him to let me travel with his ship to the various ports along the Targoan. Rather than offering myself as a simple harlot, I would perform magic tricks for the entertainment of the men. It was our hope that if I were to perform an act that had to do with the coming of the black moon and make it as stunning a show as possible, the men would spread word of what they had seen and perhaps you or Stromthroad would overhear and guess at the true meaning.

"Sphextay agreed to my proposal—though of course I told him nothing of my true intent—but only if I consented to share his bed as lover. Solat was against the idea from the first, but I did not see as we had any choice. The black moon was coming far swifter than anticipated, and you had to be found, whatever the cost. So I agreed with Sphextay's terms."

Myrania tightened her hold on Nuroc and kissed him behind the ear. "Each time he came to me with his lustful cravings, I would numb myself with proffax blossoms against the shame I felt in his embrace. Had I not done so, I could not have gone through with the charade. No doubt I would have slain him earlier, in which case I would have also been killed and the fate of Aerda would be sealed. Already we will be fortunate if we can act in time to thwart Augage."

They rode on silently a moment as Nuroc mulled over the grim experience his lover had gone through. The two of them had been tossed along cruelly by the hands of fate, and their mutual trials had further bound them together in love.

"What is it that we must prevent Augage from do-

180

ing? He can't be planning to unleash another cataclysm," Nuroc surmised. "He has only to lose by destroying the land he hopes to conquer."

"When we fled from the obelisk," Myrania replied, "my father took with him several large books concerning the chants of sorcery. For him, most of our exile in the caves has been spent in studying the texts and trying to learn the meaning to Augage's actions the night he forced the moons to collide. It was always thought that Augage had deliberately started the cataclysm in hopes of turning sentiment against Talmon-Khash and usurping his throne. We felt that he had merely misapplied the chant and wreaked more havoc than he had intended, forcing himself into exile rather than risk the wrath of the populace.

"But early this year my father finally determined that the chant Augage had recited that night had nothing to do with its unfortunate results. Rather, Augage had been attempting to recite the Oath of Summoning, a chant so powerful and forbidden that it has never been spoken by mortal man."

"I don't understand," Nuroc said.

As the horse carried them on in the chilled darkness, Myrania went on, "You know the teachings regarding the black moons, and how they are a time when the gods are set free from the stars to come down to earth."

Nuroc nodded.

Myrania paused a moment, then said grimly, "The Oath of Summoning is a chant by which the gods can be called down during a black moon and materialized in the form of their carved likeness. Inkemisa says it was Augage's intention to summon forth Dorban himself and trap the god inside a statue of clay he had taken with him from the obelisk. Had he succeeded, the mightiest of the gods would have become his slave, and Augage would have become as powerful as the gods themselves!"

None of Nuroc's darkest imaginings approached the true meaning to the menace posed by Augage. Think-

181

ing back on the trail of death and bloodshed that had brought him to this time and place, he understood the odious reasoning behind the slaughter of his family and why his destiny had become one steeped in trauma and adversity. And it was not over yet.

"And what now of Augage's plans?" Nuroc asked, glancing up at the shrinking slice of moon that shone through breaks in the cloudcover.

"My father fears that Augage has mastered the chant and will attempt it in the obelisk, where he might trap Dorban within the stone idol that rises from the ground floor."

Nuroc pulled hard on the steed's reins, stopping it in the middle of the road. "Then we must head back and make our way to the obelisk at once, before it is too late."

"No, first we must seek out my father," Myrania insisted. "Or do you recall by heart the chant you must know to bring back Talmon-Khash?"

Nuroc cursed his thoughtlessness. During the first few years of his exile from Cothe, he had recited the Oath of Revival daily to make certain he did not forget it. But as time went on he had spent less and less time recalling the strange words of the magetongue, until now he knew only bits and pieces of the chant. Incomplete, the chant was useless, or even dangerous if recited.

So on they rode, until the edge of the cliffs came into view. Although he had not been here since the cataclysm, Nuroc knew at once that something was wrong. He could hear the waves of the sea thrashing violently, but the sound was not faraway as it should be.

"By the gods!" he suddenly cried out, seeing a shower of spray crash over the top of the cliffs. It seemed impossible, for the cliffs normally rose more than two hundred feet above the level of the sea.

Myrania was the first to jump down from the horse and run to the edge of the cliffs. Nuroc dismounted and quickly followed after her. Their worst fears were confirmed. Another wave sent spray foaming over the rocks of the cliff, and they could see that the Targoan had indeed risen two hundred feet. And the depth was not of the sort brought on by a tidal wave. It was constant and certain.

"Father," Myrania cried, breaking away from Nuroc and rushing across the jagged topography of the cliff until she reached a cluster of rocks. Moving the top boulder aside, she stared down a narrow shaft and gasped at the sound of water lapping up to the top of the vertical tunnel.

There was a cranny chiseled into the upper reach of the tunnel, and Myrania quickly reached into the cavity and withdrew a handful of soaked staffs with the thicker of two ends wrapped with a material Nuroc was not familiar with. Myrania set down all but one of the staffs. She ripped off the covering to the staff in her hand and the tip burst brightly with a flame-dripping glow. Shaking the stick until the loose flames were knocked free, Myrania was left with a burning tip that gave off a steady, bluish light. Even when she held her breath and dropped down into the watery shaft, the end of the stick she carried remained lit.

Nuroc took in a deep breath and lowered himself down the vertical passage as well. Five feet down, the tunnel opened out into a large cave that normally looked out over the sea. Now that the sea had risen up past the cave's mouth, however, the cavity was completely filled with water. Nuroc knew at once that he was in the lair where Inkemisa and Myrania had shared their exile.

The water was icy cold and dark. The light at the end of Myrania's staff bobbed before Nuroc's opened eyes like a luminous fish, but he could barely make out Myrania's figure as she swam about the chamber in search of her father. Nuroc groped about in the darkness until his lungs were about to burst. Fortunately, there was a pocket of air just above the water level in the cave, and he reached the surface for another breath at the same time as Myrania.

183

"Perhaps he fled when the waters began to rise," Nuroc suggested hopefully, but Myrania shook her head, taking another breath and diving back down in the water. Nuroc dropped back in the water and began swimming along the irregular contours of the cave wall, feeling around in the darkness. Whenever something grazed him, he shrank from its touch involuntarily, filled with a wracking dread. Once his hands fell upon a thick book, but as he tried to pull it toward him it crumbled into waterlogged fragments, rendered useless by the saltwater.

It was on their fifth dive when they simultaneously found Inkemisa. Myrania's sorcerous light revealed him in a back corner of the cave, where he bounded eerily off the walls with the supple roll of incoming waves. Inkemisa stared out at them, his face already distended from the effects of the water. Although the body was lifeless, his limbs moved grotesquely about in the water.

Fighting back his revulsion, Nuroc swam forward and helped Myrania secure a hold on the drowned sorcerer. Together, they dragged the body between them to the surface. As they took in air, Nuroc looked at Myrania, knowing the measure of her grief.

"I'm sorry," he said between gulps for air.

"I want to leave him here," Myrania gasped. "He would prefer it that way."

They were about to let go of the body when Nuroc felt something sharp scrape across his side. He reached down and realized it was the edge of a scrap of parchment clutched in the old man's fist. Carefully prying the paper loose, Nuroc kept a hold of it as they dropped Inkemisa and let him drift back to his watery grave.

They swam over to the tunnel and floated back up it to the cliff top. Nuroc climbed out first, then helped Myrania to the rocky edge of the precipice. He held her close, stroking her hair as they both shivered in the cold air pushing inland from the sea.

"I'm okay," Myrania finally said.

They turned and started back to the horse. It was only then that Nuroc bothered to inspect the scrap of parchment. There were unfamiliar symbols and letters scrawled in blood on the yellowing paper.

"The chant," Myrania said, staring at the scrap. "The Oath of Revival. He ripped it from the book of chants."

"His last act," Nuroc said with grave admiration. "Dying, he has given us a chance to live. If only we have enough time to reach Cothe. . ."

Twenty-Two

Trying to find the secret entrance through which Nuroc had seen Augage and the rebel sorcerers flee years before proved to be difficult. As Nuroc and Myrania rode along the contour of the rugged coastline, he saw that the reach of meadows where he had witnessed the clashing of the twin moons had been as radically transformed as the badlands outside of Wheshi. The force of the tidal wave had compressed the land into tight folds that were smothered with a top layer of broken rock that slowed their progress considerably. Various clumps of vegetation rose from between the rocks, obliterating any trace of paths.

"We can't spend much longer looking for it," Myrania said over Nuroc's shoulder. "I think we should return to Cothe and try to seek out one of the entrances in the city."

"But you yourself said those entrances were all within buildings that would be heavily guarded," Nuroc said. "The risk is too great unless we have no . . . wait!"

He stopped his horse and they both looked down at a deep gash that cut through the earth like a canyon. From where they sat in the saddle, it was more than thirty feet down a steep-pitched wall to the base of the chasm. Nuroc pointed to the base. "Do you see it?" he asked Myrania.

Dark as it was in the lower reaches of the chasm, Myrania could also make out one area where the blackness was more pronounced than its surroundings. Reaching into the saddle, she pulled free one of the torchsticks they had taken from the entrance to her flooded refuge in the cliffs. She ripped off the husk of covering, igniting the tip and throwing the staff down into the chasm. The initial burst of light was sufficient for them to see that the darkened area at the base of the defile marked a portion of manmade tunnel.

"Praised be Dorban," Nuroc muttered as they dismounted from the horse. "We're not lost yet!"

Myrania tethered the horse to a nearby sapling, then took several of the remaining torchsticks from the saddle. Nuroc led the way toward the belt of shrubs that lined the upper edge of the canyon. As he was about to push his way through the overgrowth, Myrania reached out and held him back.

"See the blossoms?" she said, pointing her finger to the brightly colored flowers growing on the bushes. "Proffax, the dream-bringing petals. Hold your breath and try not to stir the pollen."

So warned, Nuroc sought out a space where the proffax shrubs grew farthest apart and eased his way carefully past the vibrant, wavering blossoms. Myrania followed and they made their way without incident to the lip of the canyon. They stood ankle-deep in a riot of creeping vines and ivy that spilled over the edge of the vertical precipice like a green waterfall. Bending over, they ran their fingers through the trailing plants until they found a sturdy, inch-thick vine that extended far down the sheer wall of the chasm.

"I'll go first," Nuroc said, testing the strength of the vine. "If it supports me, it will hold you as well."

186

"Be careful, Nuroc," Myrania said, laying a hand on his shoulder.

Nuroc nodded and let himself over the side. The drop was precipitous, but he had scaled pitches just as steep in the Kanghats near his home in Wheshi. Here, too, the meshing of the vines and ivy provided an occasional foothold as well, allowing him to temper the strain on the vine he was holding. In a matter of minutes he was on the canyon floor, slightly scraped from the jagged leaves of the ivy but otherwise unharmed.

He called up to Myrania, "There's an outcrop halfway down that rubs against the vine, so be careful."

Nuroc watched her begin her descent, stepping back from the trickle of loose stone that worked its way through the webwork of vine and ivy. She handled herself with an agility that surprised him until he paused to consider that she had spent much of the past few years subsisting off the treacherous coastline. Her lithe grace filled him anew with desire.

When Myrania was a few yards from the base of the cliff, the chafing of the outcrop against the vine weakened it so that it snapped in her hands. Caught off-balance, Myrania fell back from the wall. Nuroc was there to cushion her fall, catching her in his arms. They embraced momentarily, but then pulled away from each other to contend with the situation at hand.

The fallen torch still emitted a faint light, and they could see that the floor of the chasm was layered with sand that formed sloping drifts along the far wall. Nuroc crouched down and rubbed the fine granules between his fingers, amazed.

"Sand from the base of the cliffs," he said, letting it sift back to the ground. "It seems so incredible."

"It makes me afraid to think what might happen if Augage were to attempt the chant again and fail," Myrania said. "My father said the coastal land is so fragile after the cataclysm that another tidal wave would crumble much of it into the sea."

Nuroc rose to his feet and kicked aside a few shattered fragments of shells, splintered slats of wood from broken hulls, and even scattered bones that shone dully through the silt—all of it cast up from the Targoan Sea years before.

"If Augage attempts the chant, he will either enslave the land or destroy it," Nuroc murmured. "Is that what you're saying?"

Myrania could only nod her head.

"Then I suggest we head into the tunnel," Nuroc said, "I'm sure this is the route I was pushed along by the floodwaters. We can only hope that the walls haven't collapsed . . . ."

Nuroc fell silent before the opening, his muscles tensed. He glanced over at Myrania and she whispered, "I heard it, too."

From within the blackened tunnel came an inhuman, guttural sound that echoed hauntingly off the walls of the defile. A rank odor wafted out from the hole and they heard scraping sounds of movement within the earthen maw, like the sound of countless boots grinding soft gravel underfoot. Without mistake, Nuroc knew that something inside the cave was making its way toward them. He slowly stepped back from the orifice, slipping the sacred dagger from his sheath. Behind him, he heard Myrania unsheath her sword as well.

The sound in the cavern suddenly ceased, and for a seeming eternity Nuroc and Myrania held their positions, afraid to move. The fallen torchstick flickered with the last of its light, then went cold so that the chasm was lit only by the lopsided sickle of the waning moon, and even that illumination was obscured by the fog that seeped down the vine-laden canyon.

Then, from out of the blackened hole there came an ethereal hiss. A grotesque shadow-figure oozed from the cave and rose up before Nuroc, moving with such bone-chilling swiftness that the youth could not react except to watch in total shock, doubting his senses. One moment he was staring at nothingness and the next a foul-smelling aberration loomed over him, blotting out all traces of the shadow world around him. The vile, odious growl that now filled the unencumbered air sounded from far above Nuroc's head, making the monstrosity before him at least as tall as three men.

Willing himself into motion, Nuroc raised his arm so that his puny blade pointed at the source of the beast's disturbing cry. The act was more one of fending off an inevitable attack than assuming the offensive.

Behind him, Myrania whispered, "Here's my sword. Take it and be ready to use it!"

Nuroc felt the hilt press against his hip and he reached for it with his free hand. As Nuroc was shifting the weapon to his sword hand and sheathing the condor dagger, Myrania reached to the ground beside her and plucked up the extinguished torchstick. Its tip was barely visible with the glow of its dying fire, and yet when she hurled it over Nuroc's shoulder toward the attacker, the contact with rushing air reignited the end with another burst of explosive light.

In a split second, the beast before them was revealed in all its horrific detail. It was limbless, with an elongated torso of ringlike segments made of tough hide. The underside was lined with thousands of raised knobs that undulated like the stumps of small fingers. The body extended all the way back into the blackness from which it had come, and rose twenty feet in the air to the grisly head, where the true menace lay. Beneath the lifeless gaze of fist-sized eyes that reflected the torchlight were jaws that widened vertically to reveal no less than five rows of teeth, each one sharp and jagged, stained with decay and trailing shreds of meat that still dripped blood. The head swayed to and fro, like the hooded cobra Nuroc had seen back in Wheshi. All this he and Myrania saw in the time it took for the torchstick to bound off the bristle of spikelike quills that lined the beast's neck.

"Now!" Myrania shouted out, "Strike it between its neck and the first ring of hide!"

Nuroc saw the spot she meant, a narrow band of

soft flesh which formed the pivot upon which the beast moved its head. With the monster reared as it was, however, that vulnerable spot lay far from Nuroc's reach. He cocked his arm to hurl his sword as best he could, but the beast suddenly swung its head back and then forward to strike. Nuroc twisted to one side as the man-sized jaws snapped at the air where he had been only a second before. In the same motion, Nuroc lashed out with the sword, driving it forcefully into the exposed band of tender flesh. The blade sank to the hilt, and Nuroc was jerked off his feet as the beast recoiled from the wounding.

Letting go of the sword, Nuroc was flung to the sand next to Myrania. He recovered and jerked her to the ground as the creature lashed out once more. Pulling out his dagger, he shielded her as they both watched the segmented nightmare pull back and begin its throes of death. A reddish-gray liquid flowed thickly around the imbedded sword as the beast let forth another of its chilling howls, this one louder and more enraged. Writhing madly, the creature drew itself into a mass of coils as it tried to bend its head enough to clamp its jaws around the hilt of the sword, which remained out of reach and still firmly implanted in the neck. The tapered tail snapped in the air and Nuroc pushed Myrania flat against the ground as it swept toward them and struck sharply at his thigh with a force that might have broken bones from another angle. Nuroc groaned at the pain and Myrania held him tightly.

"Are you all right?" she said.

"If that's the worst it can do to us I'll be happy," Nuroc answered. "What is it anyway?"

"An Iatse Crawler. They're only known to dwell on the Tavkyd Isles, and there they never grow larger than a man. This one must have been swept ashore during the cataclysm and grown with the change in diet."

"That's meat hanging from its teeth," Nuroc

grumbled. "Let's get out of here before it adds us to its last meal."

The crawler's frenetic motions had slowed to a point where it lay fully on the ground, forty feet long and as wide as Nuroc, its head facing away from them as its bellowing took on a weaker sound. They rose to their feet and started past the beast. As Myrania was reaching for the still-glowing torch, another crawler filled the night air with its hideous cry, sounding from farther down the defile.

Skin rippling with fear, Nuroc and Myrania looked in the direction of the howling.

"It can't be!" Myrania gasped.

The second crawler was even larger than its dying companion. It slithered through the gash of canyon toward them like a living stream.

"Come on!" Nuroc shouted, taking Myrania by the hand and leading her into the darkness of the tunnel. Behind them, the second crawler pierced the night with another of its vengeful cries.

Twenty-Three

In the vast subterranean chamber that lay directly beneath the obelisk, Augage stood over the narrow shaft that bored down indefinitely into the heart of the earth. Both his arms were stretched out before him in a gesture of supplication. His eyes were closed and the whisperings of the magetongue reverberated off the cold damp walls of the chamber and down the many passages that led away from the obelisk.

The chant was long and difficult, and beads of sweat began to form on the sorcerer's brow from the intensity

191

of his concentration. He knew too well the price of failure. Already the earth was groaning with faint, intermittent tremors. He would have to proceed with caution and not draw on too much of the moon's power at once, for this incantation was but a prelude to the Oath of Summoning. In translating the cryptic symbols atop the highest level of the obelisk, Augage had learned that he was missing a vital element for the chant by which he hoped to imprison Dorban.

Soon a tendril of gaseous fog began to rise from the endless shaft. It seeped out slowly, thick with an acrid smell, and spread out along the floor of the underground chamber. Bones were scattered upon the stone tiles, lying haphazard where Augage had dropped them after carrying them down from the obelisk. The unearthly fog swirled about the bones like crawling serpents. As Augage continued to chant, the fog grew thick and rose to the height of his knees, filling the entire chamber and beginning to spill down the separate tunnels. The tremors sounded a final time, then ceased.

When the chant was finished, figures began to rise from the enchanted mist. Bones had formed into skeletons and the skeletons had been layered with flesh and muscle so that the reincarnated citizens of Cothe soon stood upright in the semblance of their former life. Missing was the gleam of intelligence in their lackluster eyes. They had no thoughts of their own and could act only upon the orders of the man who had raised them.

Augage looked at the handful of men and women, dressed in ragged tatters as the fog drifted eerily around them. He smiled at the sight, exultant at the demonstration of his power.

"Above the ground the armies of Cothe look away from the city in search of their enemy," he gloated to himself. "Little do they realize that they will soon be conquered from within the walls they guard so diligently."

To the mindless souls before him, he said, "Now

comes the time for sorcery to claim dominion over all who live upon the earth. There is but one chant to be consummated, and for that I need the services of one who was not conjured into being by a chant. Go forward, take the catacombs into the city and bring me the first man or woman you can apprehend alive.

"The final oath requires sacrifice!"

The others turned and dragged their stooped forms through the odious haze that permeated the air. Reaching the tunnels, they parted into groups of two and three and walked on until they were gone from Augage's sight. The sorcerer started back up the steps to the obelisk, to begin preparations for the final chant.

As the fog spilled forth into the dank corridors of the dead, it fell upon the crypts where the sorcerers of old lay buried. Through hair-thin cracks the necromantic gas seeped into sealed coffins, and soon lids were pried open from within and gaunt-faced figures in flowing robes stepped clear of their deathly confines to walk once again down the tunnels of darkness, their minds attuned only to the commands of Augage.

Twenty-Four

Nuroc and Myrania edged along the tunnel in darkness, wary of igniting the torchstick and betraying their position to the second crawler. They remained silent, feeling their way, struggling to hold back the nausea they felt at the stench that surrounded them.

When they had followed the tunnel around two sharp bends, they paused to catch their breath. The echoing sound of their footsteps ceased, and they listened for the grating of feelers against the dirt to indicate that the crawler was following them. The way behind them was silent, however.

"I think it's safe to light the staff now," Myrania said. "In this stale air it will burn only slightly, but it will be enough for us to see where we are going."

"Do it, then," Nuroc said. "We have to hurry."

Myrania waved the torchstick until it sputtered to life and lit the way before them. They advanced more quickly, taking in the wretched state of the tunnel. The vile odor that assailed their nostrils came from rotting vegetation, half-eaten sheep and kildwolves, and bestial droppings that lay in shallow puddles. The festering decay had lured into the tunnel a variety of scrambling insects and furry vermin that fled from the light.

"I'd almost prefer the darkness to this," Nuroc said.

"You're limping," Myrania noticed.

"It was the blow from that crawler's tail," Nuroc said. "I'll be all right."

On they walked, following several more bends in the underground passageway before coming to a spot where a large portion of the tunnel wall had collapsed into a vast hollow in the ground. Myrania extended the torch into the opening and both she and Nuroc cringed at the sight of several dozen eggs the size of large melons, resting on a raised hill of sand. The eggs were light green in color, flecked with patches of black. Several had cracked open, and small crawlers the length of Nuroc's arm slithered across the broken shells.

As they hurried away from the orifice, Myrania said, "They must thrive on the decay. It's fortunate they only spawn once every several years. If we manage to make it through our mission, hopefully we can see that their newborn don't grow to become the size and terror of their parents."

"I just hope those two we met back at the entrance are the only ones full-grown," Nuroc said. "I'd hate to think of our chances against them in these cramped quarters."

The farther inland they progressed, the less frequent the signs of inhabitation by the deadly creatures. Even the foulest of the odors began to fade away, replaced by the cleaner scent of thick mosses that covered the tunnel walls that ran beneath the harbor. When they had walked clear of that layered green and felt their feet touch once again the hardened dirt of the tunnel floor, Nuroc knew they were below the city.

The closer they came to the obelisk, the more lavish were the walls of the tunnel. Instead of mere chiseled stone, they began to see clay tiles meticulously fit into place. The craftsmanship had been so painstaking and accomplished that the floodwaters, which had swept Nuroc along this corridor five years ago, had done only the slightest of damage to the walls.

Soon there began to appear alcoves carved out of the walls and lined with mosaic frescoes that surrounded the burial crypts of the sorcerers. Nuroc could not help but marvel at the eerie beauty of the antechambers, most of which had also survived the toll of the floodwaters. Some contained coffins of polished stone that gleamed through even the layered dust, while others contained only the remains of the dead, lying upon stone slabs in their ageless cloaks, with faces waxy from the application of a thin veneer of secret ointment that prevented deterioration of the flesh.

"How is it that worms have not feasted on these corpses?" Nuroc wondered aloud. "They must be old."

"Older than either you or I could trace back our ancestry," Myrania commented. "The sorcerers believed in preserving their bodies beyond death, toward the day when their souls would shower down from the skies and seek out a new life among men."

"But I don't understand why the crypts were unharmed by the floodwaters," Nuroc said. "I was carried through these corridors by a river's force. These bodies were all underwater and should have been wrested from where they lay—"

"You're forgetting the sorcery by which Talmon-Khash saved Cothe from destruction," Myrania told him. "He cast a spell upon the crypts to prevent them from harm, just as he created the endless shaft that swallowed the floodwaters before they could force their way up into the obelisk."

As they walked on, Nuroc said, "All those years I lived amongst the sorcerers without knowing but a fragment of their powers and practices. It seems so— by the eyes of Dorban, look here!"

Nuroc stopped and pointed at the ground before them. They were at yet another junction, and from another of the tunnels, a pair of footprints were visible in the raised dust, trailing off in the direction they were headed.

"Augage," Myrania said, crouching down and holding the torch over the prints. "He hasn't been here long, though. The prints are fresh."

Falling silent, they followed the tracks down the next stretch of tunnel. Halfway to the next bend, the ground about them began to pitch violently. Both Nuroc and Myrania swayed on their feet, trying to maintain their balance. For several seconds more the tunnel rocked and the dull rumble echoed down the horizontal shaft. Loose rock sprinkled down on them from the walls of the cave. Then it stopped, as suddenly as it had begun.

Nuroc turned to Myrania. "Are we too late?"

"No, but we're none too soon, either," Myrania said. "He's just begun, I think. Last time, there were small quakes for some time before the cataclysm struck. Let's move faster."

They plunged on down the tunnel, pausing only long enough to transfer the light of the dying shaft to a tar-dipped torch mounted in the wall of the catacombs. The pitch had hardened, but Myrania was able to soften it enough to take the flame and hold it. The chant she used was one of the least demanding taught to neophytes, and yet the use of it was sufficient to disrupt the tender balance of equilibrium and trigger another minor wrenching of the earth about them.

196

Myrania and Nuroc were thrown toward one another, and each could feel the other's trembling.

"Augage has made it so that none but himself can work chants without tempting further cataclysm," Myrania guessed as the commotion about them subsided. "Even my limited powers are too dangerous to use any more."

"Let's hurry and get close enough to where I can use this on him," Nuroc said, waving the sword before him.

On they forged, winding down the tunnel in urgent strides. As they were coming upon the last series of turns before the obelisk, Nuroc noticed a knee-high river of fog spilling down the tunnel from the bend they were approaching.

"Trapped gas set free by the quaking," Myrania whispered uncertainly, as if she doubted her own words.

Nuroc sniffed the air suspiciously as he followed Myrania into the low-hanging haze. They rounded the bend and abruptly stopped short, seeing a dozen eerie figures hulking toward them, obscured by the odious fog about them.

Nuroc moved in front of Myrania and pointed his sword at those before them. "Another step this way and I'll cut you down like grain at harvest!" His angry defiance masked the skin-crawling fear that settled over him.

The fog-shrouded minions did not so much as pause at Nuroc's warning. They continued toward him and Myrania, their dull eyes wide and uncomprehending. Their motions were stiff and awkward as they slowly raised their hands and made gestures of groping at the air before them.

"They smell of death!" Nuroc snarled. "We can cut our way through them and reach the staircase if we act fast."

Before he could move forward and take the offensive, however, Nuroc felt fingers tighten coldly around his ankle. Looking down with disbelief, he saw a living corpse rise out of the fog and clutch at him with its other hand. Its grip was firm and the touch was like ice, so cold it seemed to burn. Lifeless eyes stared up at him through the sagging folds of bloodless flesh.

Nuroc lashed out with his sword, severing the attacker's arm. The corpseman gave no sound of pain and continued to rise up from the floor, pawing at him with his remaining hand. No blood poured from the severed stump.

Frantic, Nuroc grabbed at the abomination and found that it was only half the weight of a normal man. He jerked the being to its feet and pushed it roughly into the throng of the walking dead before him. They wavered in their approach and Nuroc dodged quickly around them, calling over his shoulder, "This way, Myrania!"

"I can't!" Myrania gasped.

Nuroc looked back and saw that Myrania had been fallen upon from behind by resurrected sorcerers who had lain dead in their crypts only moments before. Myrania tried to shake the attackers away from her, and managed to send a few reeling back with their robes burning from contact with the torch she wielded like a club. But for each zombie she rid herself of, two more beset her. Three of the revived townsfolk fell upon her torch arm and pulled the burning shaft from her hand.

"Go!" Myrania shouted to Nuroc. "Before they get you, too!"

"Never!" Nuroc took his sword in both hands and charged back into the charnel mass he had just broken clear of. The blade cut savagely into bone and unreal flesh, rending limbs free from bodies and causing some of the corpsemen to back away from their assault. Their retreat was only momentary. Once Nuroc was past them and dealing his blade against the others, they waded back through the mist toward him. Soon he, too, was overpowered by the living dead. Chilled fingers clamped across his mouth, silencing his cries and filling him with nausea. Beside him, he saw that Myrania was no long struggling against her captors. He

198

writhed all the harder, but there were too many of them, and he found himself being carried across the cavern floor toward the main underground chamber and the stone staircase.

The ungodly throng broke into two masses. One group started up the stairs, bearing the limp form of Myrania over their heads. The others carried Nuroc toward the round hole in the cavern floor, where the last of the fog was wafting up from the bottomless depths below.

Nuroc finally tore the rotted hand from his mouth and let forth a shout as he felt himself being passed through the mob. He kicked and tugged, but could not break free of the swarming hands that moved him along and pried the sword from his hand. They finally maneuvered him to the edge of the chasm.

"No!" Nuroc howled, wrenching free one hand and swinging madly at the men around him. But his resistance was futile and at last he was shoved over the brink. Into the darkness he tumbled, his own scream thundering back loudly in his ears.

Twenty-Five

More than a hundred once-entombed sorcerers stood in grim formation about the ground floor of the stone tower. Their unfocused eyes were cast in Augage's direction, awaiting further orders. Augage faced them from in front of the rounded white altar, grinning victoriously at the sight of his predecessors. Some of them had been laid to rest centuries before, while others were among the last to be interred before the evacuation of the city prior to the cataclysm. In their lifetimes they had achieved varying levels of power based on their mastery of the chants inscribed on the walls of the obelisk. But for now they were without that power. As Augage spoke to them, his words were all that dwelled in their thoughts. They lived to do his bidding or they would cease to live at all.

"You have served me well so far," Augage said, raising his voice to fill the chamber. "And now you will aid in the final step to power. As I make ready for the Oath of Summoning, you are to take once more to the catacombs. Follow those routes leading beneath the city and palace. Rise up from the tunnels and set fire to the city. Make to the gates and see that they are open to receive the forces of Ghetite as they ride on Cothe. Do this and, by night's end, control of all the continent shall be mine!"

The corpsemen about him turned in unison, filing toward the opening in the floor that led down to the catacombs. One by one they flitted eerily down the stone staircase, their footsteps noiseless on the cold pave. Few of them would survive their brief resurrection. Augage knew that once they poured forth to the surface within the walls of the city, they would fall swiftly beneath the blades of the Aerdans. But they would strike a moment's fear before any soul dared reach for his blade, and there was the chance that the zombies could make good on their orders to open the gates. Even if they failed, the diversion of their presence would draw attention away from the obelisk, where Augage would be well on his way to completion of the forbidden Oath of Summoning.

Once the undead had vacated the obelisk, Augage turned and strode across the floor to the ornate bench filled with the makings for great magic. His hands moved quickly through the phials, bowls, amulets, and flasks, extracting the desired ingredients and carefully adding potions into a shallow clay tray filled with ancient symbols. Augage whispered to himself between the chantings, and worked the pestle, turning the consistency of the mixture on the tray into a thick paste of ochre hue. It was pungent with the aroma of crushed petals, aged blood, and ripe herbs.

When the potion was readied, Augage took the tray back across the room to where Myrania lay across the rounded top of the alabaster altar. She was conscious and straining at the bonds of knotted vines that held her in place. Her arms and legs were stretched out so that she lay spread-eagled on the egg, facing up at the cold, stone gaze of the carved idol of Dorban.

"How fitting that the condor-god be offered the blood of a sorceress," Augage told Myrania. "Particularly one so desirable as yourself. He will be pleased, I am certain. You should feel honored."

"Untie me and I'll show you the meaning of honor!" Myrania taunted. "Or are you afraid a woman can defeat you once you're without the aid of your mindless lackeys!"

Augage chuckled lightly. "Don't bother trying to bait me, child. We've come past the time where I can be bothered with your schemings. I have more important concerns."

The sorcerer set the tray at the base of the altar and then reached into his robes, pulling forth an elaborately carved replica of a condor's claw, made of jaunwood with inlaid talons of carved bone that ended in deadly points. Augage raised the claw in the air, muttering an incantation before he lowered the talons to Myrania's side and gently scraped the exposed flesh. When he pulled the claw away, three deep scratches began to bleed, sending a stream of crimson flowing down the side of the white altar and into the clay tray, where it mingled with the other substances.

Almost instantly, the potion began to give off a luminous green vapor, far less thick than the fog Augage had earlier unleashed. Instead of widening into a layer, the vapor became a thin, undulating tendril that wound around the trickle of blood still falling down the side of the altar. Augage stood back and watched the strange serpentine haze trail up the altar and slowly begin to wrap itself around Myrania, whose eyes bulged with terror at the sight.

"Don't be alarmed," Augage told her gently. "As your blood feeds the vapor, death will come slowly and painlessly. You will drift off as in a dream, even as your life becomes the spark that will give life to the stone idol."

Myrania tried to speak but Augage waved a hand before her face and shook his head and no words would come forth. The vapor continued to surround her. Overhead, outside the obelisk, the last of the moon vanished and total darkness claimed the sky.

Twenty-Six

Far down the endless shaft, Nuroc gasped for breath. His head was throbbing with a fierce pain from the constant blows against the jagged rock-facing of the hole. He could feel himself bleeding from countless wounds and scrapes he'd suffered before realizing how narrow the passage was and stopped his fall by reaching out to opposite walls until he had wedged himself in place. He was now huddled awkwardly in the cramped space, supporting himself by the pressure of his shoulders and legs against the walls of the shaft. Far up, he could discern the faint circle of light marking the surface.

When the pain surging through his limbs eased to the point where he could add more to its burden, he grit his teeth and began the slow climb to the surface. The task seemed insurmountable, as each motion upward required full strain on all parts of his body, which was already weakened from the battering and loss of blood. He would brace himself against the rock-facing with his back and shoulders and carefully raise one foot up the perpendicular grade, then the other. Then, shifting the weight of his upper torso onto his hands and forearms, he pulled himself up a few more inches.

Several feet were gained by this slow, interminable pace before Nuroc gave up watching the space above him. He concentrated his full effort on the climbing, forcing himself to ignore the constant scraping of rough rock against the open wounds on his back. Several times tremors in the shaft shook loose bits of gravel and sent them showering down on him.

When he was within twenty feet of the tunnel's surface, a fierce jolt shook the ground and an entire section of the shaft wall gave way beneath Nuroc's feet. Losing his footing, he began to fall back down toward the consuming black void. Reflexively, his hands groped at the walls and, miraculously, his fingers closed around a pronounced indentation in the wall. Clinging desperately, Nuroc brought his other hand in line and secured a better footing. He tucked his head against his shoulder until the falling debris scattered past him. The sound continued rattling down into the black beyond, but he could not hear anything strike the bottom of the chasm.

When the quake passed, Nuroc found that the shaft's wall was now peppered with deep indentations where rock had broken free. Using the cavities for handholds, Nuroc made better time clearing the last stretch of tunnel before reaching the surface.

He stopped short of emerging from the hole, however, as he saw that the cavern was filled with the drifting forms of the undead. Toward the various branches of the catacombs they went, heading off on their mission to reach the city's interior and rise up to begin the siege of Cothe.

Once he was alone in the chamber, Nuroc rose to solid ground and brushed himself off. Tearing off a loose scrap of his tunic, he wiped a thin rivulet of blood that coursed down his face from a pair of deep

203

cuts on his brow. His light hair was darkened with more blood and the dirt from the shaft. But he had no time to concern himself with wounds. Light poured down the steps leading up to the obelisk. Nuroc headed for the staircase. His hand went to his waist and his fingers grasped the sacred dagger, which had fallen halfway out of its sheath. The touch of the carved hilt gave him a vague feeling of assurance and power.

He stole quietly up the steps, dagger in hand. He was not yet within view of the main floor of the obelisk when still another quake tore at the earth, vibrating the ground so intensely that Nuroc was forced to spring forward onto the floor of the obelisk, lest he fall backward toward the hole that already had once tried to claim him.

As the thunderous din of the earthquake was fading, Nuroc's ears rang with a piercing, inhuman shriek that sounded far above him. Terror-stricken at the sound, Nuroc slowly looked up from the floor, past Augage and the limp form of Myrania on the altar.

The thirty-foot high statue of Dorban was wrapped in a vaporous bond of sorcerous light that dimmed and brightened in shortly interspersed intervals. At first Nuroc thought his senses were playing tricks on him, or that the wavering light was distorting the outline of the idol. But, when a second shriek filled the chamber, Nuroc saw that the sound was coming from the moving beak of the condor-idol.

Dorban lived!

Again the great bird raised its head and voiced a shrill cry toward the summit of the obelisk. It tried to move farther, but the vaporous binds held it in place on the pedestal of carved stone. Dorban was prisoner of Augage.

Nuroc's eyes swept down from the massive head of the condor-god to the altar before it, where Myrania lay with her blood still flowing down the rounded stone and into the sacrificial tray. Augage remained before the altar, his back turned to Nuroc as he stared up at the great being he had succeeded in enslaving.

Although he feared it was too late, Nuroc ran to the cover of the treasure chests and began to fulfill the call of his destiny. Shielded from Augage by the lucent dazzle of gems and jewels, Nuroc took hold of the sacred dagger and began to mutter the chant Myrania had taught him from the scrap of parchment Inkemisa had salvaged as his last act on earth. At the same time, he looked down at his wrist and carefully drew the razor-edged blade across the exposed artery.

Before his eyes, the blood from the wound drained into the blade of the knife, turning it red. When he had finished the chant, Nuroc marveled hopefully at the success of his incantation. It took another cry from the living idol to draw his attention back to the other side of the room, where Augage turned about, his eyes glazed with suspicion.

Nuroc hid behind the chests, but Augage boomed out, "Who dares to disrupt me!"

Nuroc stood up and stepped clear of the treasure, holding the crimson blade before him as he took in Augage's fierce gaze, refusing to look away.

"So," Augage said, recognizing Nuroc. "Another child who would stop the inevitable. You'll share the girl's fate soon enough!"

Augage whispered a single, unintelligible word, and from the tip of his pointed finger there shot forth a jagged shaft of hissing light, much like the bolt of destroying force held within the guardian jewels that lined the winding staircase behind Nuroc.

Nuroc fell back against the assault, his blade held out before him. The light struck the shaft, fading at once into nothingness.

"So," Augage said, unphased, "You've transferred the lifeblood of Talmon-Khash into the dagger. A lot of good it will do you."

Nuroc moved carefully toward Augage. He stole a swift glance to the altar and was fuelled with wrath at the sight of Myrania. "Another death you've claimed from those I love," Nuroc said hatefully as he looked

205

back to Augage. "I only wish I could slay you more than once."

"You are wrong," Augage laughed savagely. "I am immortal now. I will never die!"

Behind the sorcerer, Dorban wailed anew and strained at its unearthly binds. Augage turned his head to observe the rebellious god, and Nuroc sprang into action. It was too far across the room for him to reach Augage before the sorcerer turned back, so instead Nuroc reached to the treasure chest, plucking up a gilded warrutore. Constructed similar to a boomerang, the warrutore was made of a light-yet-sturdy stone that was chiseled along the edges to a razor sharpness that could slice through a man on contact when properly thrown. So dangerous was the warrutore that it was seldom used in conflict, for fear that it might be deflected or miss its target and fly errantly into the ranks of one's allies. Nuroc was familiar with the weapon from sporting meets at the field outside of Wheshi, and he snapped it accurately through the air with a turn of his wrist.

Augage turned as the warrutore flew lethally toward his face. He had no time to react, and yet the sharp-edged weapon burst into splinters as it struck him across the cheek. Instead of severing Augage's head, the shattered warrutore imbedded its many fragments into whatever surface they struck along the walls, be it wood or stone.

"Now you die," Augage said, raising his arm toward Nuroc.

Nuroc tensed, hand clutched tightly about the sacred dagger. Augage stood between him and the altar, where he was supposed to place the condor-knife in hopes of reviving Talmon-Khash. Whatever spell of necromancy Augage was about to unleash, Nuroc knew that it was apt to be of a force that the dagger would be defenseless against. There was only one last, desperate chance he could take, and he had no idea if it had any likelihood of success.

Before Augage could level his pointed finger at

Nuroc, the youth shifted his grip on the sacred dagger, holding it by the tip and letting it fly.

Augage jerked away reflexively, but Nuroc had not been aiming at the sorcerer. Instead, the knife sailed over his head and buried itself to the hilt in the breast of the condor-god.

"Fool!" Augage shouted with anguish, turning away from Nuroc to face the living statue. Nuroc watched on as well, and they were both galvanized with awe at the sight before them.

The bands of vapor wrapped about the condor-god glowed their brightest, then rapidly gathered about the hilt of the ceremonial dagger, with the same stunning speed by which iron filings seek out a magnet. Instead of a single, winding thread of vapor, the bands altered in form, and for an instance Nuroc could see the outline of Talmon-Khash, suspended within the cocoonlike shroud of the vapor, holding onto the condor-hilt. Then the image of the former sorcerer-king distorted, as if he were being sucked into the hilt.

The condor-god let out another cry as the vapor shot out once more in its single, snakelike thread, winding a swift course around the outline of the great bird and then back across the floor to the altar. The vapor trail once again surrounded Myrania before vanishing into the sacrificial tray. Myrania's wound was gone and she began to move.

All this happened in seconds, before Augage could mouth any chant to counter its course. He could only watch on, filling with rage and fury at the setback to his master plan. When he did finally act, it was too late.

"Hold, Dorban!" he shouted up at the idol, raising his arms and extending his fingers. "Be still while I purge you of Talmon-Khash!"

But without the binding vapor, the condor-god was no longer imprisoned at Augage's mercy. It screamed and for the first time flapped its wings. From tip to tip, the great bird's wingspan was almost sixty feet, and as the wings brushed against the tiered platforms lining

207

the walls of the obelisk, railings broke free and plunged to the ground. One of the fallen guardian gems gave off a bolt of its vibrant energy and the volt neutralized the similar shafts crackling outward from Augage's fingertips. Augage recoiled from the exchange, moaning painfully as he looked at the scorched flesh of his hands. Panicked, he raced across the room to the jaunwood bench, seeking out the curative salve. Before he could find it, another flap of Dorban's wings sent the bench crashing to its side. Augage was near the winding staircase that wound up to the upper platforms, and he started hastily up the steps.

Nuroc rushed to the altar, breaking the sacrificial platter and using the jagged pieces to hack at the vines that held Myrania prisoner.

"I was close to death," Myrania said weakly.

"We're still not safe," Nuroc told her once he had all the vines cut clear. He helped Myrania from the altar and they ducked to the ground as the arc of the condor's wing swept over them.

"Talmon-Khash now lives within the condor," Myrania said. "It won't harm us by choice."

"Death by accident is just as final as death by design," Nuroc said. "Let's get clear of those wings before we're splattered across the floor!"

As the condor-god continued to rail from its perch and watch Augage's hurried flight up the winding staircase, Nuroc carried Myrania in his arms across the stone shrapnel littering the floor and down the steps leading to the underground chamber.

"I can manage on my feet," Myrania said once they were below. Nuroc let her down and she picked up the fallen torch, which was still burning in the dirt. Nuroc grabbed up the sword that the corpsemen had taken from him.

"Which way?" Nuroc asked as they faced the outreaching tunnels. "These shafts will be crawling with the beings Augage raised from the dead."

"I think not," Myrania said. "With his powers in

check, I would suspect the life he instilled in the others has left them."

Indeed, as Myrania led the way down one of the shafts running beneath the sorcerer gardens, they came upon the crumbled remains of one of the revived townsmen, lying disheveled in the middle of the tunnel. Farther down, a dozen more of his kind had similarly reverted to the prior state of fleshless bone. There was no trace of the strange fog that had given them their ephemeral second life.

"What happened up there?" Nuroc asked as they moved on, stepping carefully around the strewn bones.

"I think you know," Myrania said. "You gambled that Talmon-Khash could be revived in the idol as well as the altar, and you won, breaking Augage's domination over the condor-god. Whatever happens now, it is unlikely that Augage can escape the fate due him for his blasphemy. We can only hope the retribution is not also at the cost of another cataclysm. Talmon-Khash may live within the god, but I doubt that he can control it. Dorban may seek to punish us all for the sins of Augage."

Rounding the next corner, Myrania halted abruptly. Nuroc came to a stop beside her and they both looked down the long straightaway of the tunnel before them. A familiar stench filled the air as they watched the largest of the Iatse crawlers squirming down the cramped width of the passageway toward them. Its slavering jaws snapped disgustingly before it, crushing the bodies of fallen sorcerers that lay on the ground.

Halfway between the crawler and the point where they stood, Nuroc saw a narrow opening in the wall of the tunnel. Acting on impulse, he took Myrania by the hand and led her down the tunnel.

She resisted at first, crying, "Nuroc, what are you—" but stopped once she saw the opening and followed Nuroc into it. As Nuroc had anticipated, the opening led to an equally narrow staircase that extended to the surface. Up they went, clearing the steps as the crawler below howled its anger at being deprived a taste of their flesh to go with the old bones of the dead sorcerers and townsfolk.

"The torch is almost out," Myrania said as they continued up the last flight of steps.

"It's just as well," Nuroc said. "We'd be wise to emerge in darkness. I have no idea where this staircase leads to."

At the top of the steps, Myrania set down the torch and Nuroc stepped on it with his boots, grinding out the last of the flame. He then turned his attention to the paneled door, pushing against it with his shoulder until it opened outward.

They stumbled out to find themselves standing in the sorcerers' gardens, close to the main gate that connected the realm of the sorcerers to the rest of the city. And they were not alone. The gate was open, and a full force of Aerdan's military was marching through, with Palem, the king's aide, leading the way. Several dozen weapons were immediately pointed their way by the startled soldiers.

"Nuroc!"

Nuroc recognized Tudier's voice and saw that the recruits were among those marching behind Palem.

"So," Palem said seethingly as he walked past the outstretched weapons of his men to Nuroc and Myrania. His eyes were on Nuroc, "Not only are you a deserter, but you appear to be an accomplice of Augage as well, after all."

"No," Nuroc protested. "You don't understand!"

"Silence!" Palem roared. "We've heard the commotion within the obelisk. I thought it might be a diversion perpetrated by the likes of you. Now you've saved us the trouble of . . ."

Palem's voice was drowned out by a disturbance from the obelisk. All eyes turned to the center of the garden. The mighty tower was shaking at its foundation, and soon the pointed peak collapsed, falling inward and bringing a large portion of the wall crashing down after it. Like a castle made of cards subjected to an ill wind, the entire obelisk thundered loudly as its stone walls crumbled in on one another, raising great clouds of dust and sending the waters of the moat splashing violently over its banks.

"I don't believe it!" Myrania said. "The obelisk is supposed to be indestructible!"

"Perhaps it's come up against something even more so," Nuroc suggested. He was proved correct, for there soon rose from the rubble the winged figure of Dorban, carrying between its closed beak the still form of a man in robes.

"Dorban!" several of the soldiers mouthed in awe. By the hundreds the men fell to their knees, humbled by the majestic sight of the great bird flapping its immense wings in the air above the ruins of the obelisk. For several moments the massive condor hovered over the gardens, then it worked its wings harder and rose up into the night, flying off until it blended into the blackness overhead. The soldiers in the gardens, along with the thousands more who roamed the city, all turned their eyes upward, seeing the first sliver of the new moon shine forth amidst the mantle of black night.

"It is a miracle!" one of the recuits shouted out.

"We have been saved!" cried another.

Nuroc turned to Palem and said, "The sorcerer you saw clutched in the claws of Dorban was none other than Augage. He will pose no further threat to us."

"You still expect me to believe you are on the side of Pencroft and Aerda?" Palem said skeptically.

"I don't care what you believe, dog," Nuroc said angrily, stepping clear of Myrania. "I've heard enough of your insults. Step away from the others and we'll let our blades decide whose honor emerges untainted."

Palem paused to deliberate the challenge set before him. Before he could act on his decision, however, there sounded from the distant battlements strident blasts of the war trumpets. Everyone turned his attention to the direction of the ominous sounds.

Palem said, "Augage may have been stopped, but his men now ride toward Cothe." He glared at Nuroc, sheathing his sword. "Here is your chance to prove

211

your loyalty. Join your motley crew of upstarts and fall in behind us as we leave to meet the enemy. And you, woman, get yourself to a safe place before the blood begins to flow."

"My place is at Nuroc's side," Myrania said firmly. "I only ask for a weapon I can use against the Ghetites. I have a score to settle with the followers of Augage."

"Suit yourself," Palem said, handing her his sword, then rejoining his force and snapping his fingers. One of his men handed him another sword and Palem led the group away from the gardens and back toward the city.

Nuroc and Myrania fell into step with Tudier and the other recruits from Thutchers, many of whom cast final glances over their shoulders at the rubble of the fallen obelisk.

"Where have you been?" Tudier complained to Nuroc. "Out cavorting with this winsome wench while we've suffered through the drills of initiation?"

Nuroc winked knowingly at Myrania, then told Tudier, "Let's first tend to the Ghetites, then I'll tell you a story or two and we'll see just who's been cavorting!"